APOCALYPSE

THERESA POCOCK

Immortal Works LLC
1505 Glenrose Drive
Salt Lake City, Utah 84104
Tel: (385) 202-0116

Cover Art by Rebecca Barney
barneydesign.com

ISBN 978-1-953491-32-9 (Paperback)
ASIN B09QZKX95D (Kindle)

*There is a Being that inspired this work. It was my privilege
to merely be the hands.*

CHAPTER 1

S eth did not know if he was strong enough to do what needed doing. The actual act of the thing; lying, drugging, kidnapping. Could he do it? It was necessary, all right. It was life or death. But could he really do it? Fear intruded upon these waves of uncertainty the way a rip tide would drag at a shore-bound man battling sucking sand and crashing whitecaps. His hands balled under his sheets, and he squeezed his eyes shut.

What of Miriam?

What did Miriam know about his deal with the Joneses? If she'd taken his memories, did that mean she knew all? That he was a spy? If she did, she would also know that Lillian was sick. If she knew that, then it had to make a difference, right? She might be able to forgive him. Right?

As if his own voice could echo in his brain, words from earlier in the night rang in his ears; *"I know who the dangerous memory person is. It's Miriam, Miriam Miller."* The memory of his betrayal reverberated in his brain like echoes in a canyon.

Seth flipped the blanket off his hot feet, pinched his eyes closed yet again and covered his face with his hands. But the inside of his eyelids revealed images of Miriam's white-blonde hair, startling violet eyes and perfect peach lips. He tried to focus his mind on something besides her face.

His anger at life, which was always waiting behind a controlled dam of willpower, sprung up instantly to distract him. She betrayed him first. Entering someone's mind and taking their memories was so, so, SO, not cool. He flexed his biceps, pulling his hands off his face in a violent sweeping motion and locking his fingers behind his head. His jaw clenched. The consequence of meddling in his head was this.

Just as he warmed to this mental tirade, his focus skipped, jumped, and landed someplace else as if it were a separate thing. As if it had free will.

His mind's eye saw the stoic face of Talbert Jones, his grandfather. Tally looked like his father and himself, golden brown skin, black irises and white hair cropped short. The way Tally took in a deep breath before beginning a story reminded Seth so much of his father. Tally acted like them, too, gestures and everything. Seth did not know gestures could be inherited, but 'blood will out' as the saying goes. But this betrayal felt more perplexing and frustrating, not quite as hot with rage as the Miriam betrayal was.

Seth admitted he felt a connection to Talbert, or Tally, but he wasn't certain he liked the man. Seth spent at least an hour talking to him. He did not let him off easy when it came to the whole backstory bit. He questioned the crap out of him, and the story he relayed was like some sick real-life drama.

According to Tally, Seth's grandmother, Jade Turnbull, was an ex-marine. A talented officer who had gotten into some trouble because of her temper. She decided to step aside from a government job and was hired on by Wallace Jones, Seth's great grandfather. Jade caught Tally's attention right away. They began a romance. Soon she was pregnant but refused to get rid of the child.

Seth recalled how Tally, his grandfather, with tears glistening in the corners of his eyes, said:

"She was a fighter, so terribly strong that in a fit of rage, she could have killed any man on the compound, even me. But..." a tear tumbled down his cheek, *"...but childbirth! It got the better of her body. She hemorrhaged and bled out in moments. There I was, with an infant I didn't want and no woman."*

Seth turned over on to his side and punched the pillow under his head. Tally told him how his brother and future leader of the Jones clan, Willis, came to him with a plan for the child, a long-game plan; but one that, if it worked out, would yield an immeasurable reward. In his grief and anger, Tally had agreed.

They snuck into Edenia the very night of Ezekiel's birth and left the child on the first doorstep they came to. The hope was that one day, when he grew and left Edenia for sabbatical, he would come back into the fold with all the secrets of Edenia to boot. *"It wasn't until we got home that we kicked ourselves for not going for the tree. That was the only time we got in and got out without something weird happening."* Tally chuckled like giving up his child was his fondest recollection. At the memory of it, Seth punched his pillow one more time for good measure.

Tally was waiting when eighteen-year-old Ezekiel left Edenia. Tally told him everything and asked him to join his *true* family.

"It didn't work out that way. We hoped for a baby Moses but got a Judas," Tally reported. *"We miscalculated. In the end, Ezekiel could never betray his adopted family, nor could he betray the Edenian girl he fell in love with. He abandoned us and swore he would never see us again. I could not believe it. But I knew Jones blood and loyalty could conquer all. It has a power that sings in the veins of every Jones. I felt he would come back.*

"I didn't know it at the time, but my father kept track of Ezekiel, sent him that watch you found, and I like to think it was the termite that ate away at his loyalties to Edenia. A year later, while he was still away from Edenia, his romance ended nastily. So, we approached him again. But he would have none of it. He wanted nothing to do with our family, but he also wanted nothing to do with Edenia. He betrayed us all. Still, we never gave up. We would find him every couple of years and pay him a visit." Tally had laughed at this, and now that Seth was at home and had time to think, his mind brought forward memories of his father coming home at night covered in blood and bruises. He'd said it was the job, but now Seth wondered.

These remembrances of his father pulled at Seth's heart strings, and Seth wondered at the pressure and anxiety his father must have felt at this choice, and how he had stuck to it. From how he chose his job, to how his family lived; all the lies he told, everything, was meant to protect Seth and his sisters from the secrets of Edenia and from their rich and dangerous relatives, the Joneses. The sacrifices he'd made were huge and worthy of respect.

Seth wiped his nose and cheek from the emotional leaking he was doing and wondered who his father was protecting now? How was his father helping Lillian now? In fact, it was almost like he was acting against his protective nature in bringing his sister Lillian here. Why? It was a mystery, one his father promised to tell them in just a couple of days. Seth might never learn the truth since he would be long gone with Lilly by then. There was no way he would lose the opportunity to meet with Lillian's doctor (the man was scheduling months in advance) on a slight chance his father's desperate plan had merit. Lilly could die.

Willis Jones had made a mixed impression on Seth earlier that night. The man was massive, with a full head of shining white hair and an equally white, manicured beard. He stood so straight and thick, so intense and menacing, he completely intimidated Seth in two seconds flat.

Seth shook his head at himself in the dark, wanting to laugh because his feeling of intimidation did not last long. As soon as the man had opened his mouth to speak, Seth forced back a giggle. Willis Jones had a high, airy voice. Seth recalled his words; *"My goodness, are we glad to finally meet you, Seth."*

"Hello, Mr. Jones. Pleasure to meet you, Sir. Sorry for showing up unannounced, but..."

"Sir? What is this 'Sir' nonsense? Call me Uncle Willy." The big man stepped close. Seth felt the true power of Willis' size as he rolled Seth in a huge bear hug.

Seth had attempted to hold his ground but felt even now the tightness of that hug. When Willis had let him go, he'd had to suck in air. Then Willis took Seth by the shoulders and said, *"I hear you have some news."*

Now that it was all over, Seth felt ashamed at how short the struggle was. His gut clenched, but his mind felt compelled to relive the betrayal.

Willis had cleared his throat, waiting.

Once Seth's mouth opened, the floodgates did too. *"Uhm, well, the eyes do indicate which power they have. They call it a Nature. Miriam, my cousin and my friend, has violet eyes and she can take memories. Peter has yellow-brown eyes, and he goes invisible. That's all I know for certain. I do know, though, how they get their powers."*

"Really?" Willis asked with interest.

"It's the river Eden. The water there comes from inside the Garden —which is there, by the way; I stuck my arm into it. I didn't go all the way in because it freaked me out. But my arm disappeared. It's about ten feet past the bridge."

After Seth told the Joneses everything he possibly could tell them about Edenia, Tally had wrapped Seth in a bear of a hug and told him, *"If I can't have my own son as an ally, you'll do. But know you take his place in the most unexpected of ways, and for that I'm proud of you, kid."*

He also shucked his big hand across the back of Jeremiah's head. *"I can't believe Jeremiah tried to trade information for help with Lillian. She is my blood. She is a Jones. You get her to us, and we will take care of everything."*

A plan was made to get Lillian safely to the edge of town the next night. Seth made the mistake of telling Jeremiah that he would be on a date with Miriam the next night. Jeremiah made it very clear that capturing Miriam was the Jones' top priority, and only if he facilitated that capture would he be going to Baltimore with Lillian. Otherwise he could just leave Lillian in Jeremiah's care. Jeremiah told Seth to drug her if he had to and gave him a white powder in a glass vile with a cork lid for the job.

With acid in his throat, Seth looked at the small container. It sat on his windowsill. Seth felt backed into a corner by this part of the deal. To make matters more confining, Tally would be leaving for Argentina the next morning, so he would not even be there when the plan went down. Seth again was on his own. Regardless of Tally's words, Seth had to give Miriam up to the Joneses, or Jeremiah would not help Lillian. He felt it down to his toenails.

Even now, Seth's gut roiled within him. The Joneses were mercenaries. It was written all over their swarthy, militant, gun-carrying, cigar-smoking, F-bomb using faces. He could only trust them so far.

He'd agreed to Jeremiah's terms under duress.

They all swore they would not hurt Miriam. They only wanted her out of the way.

Seth rolled over again, more conflicted than ever. Could he do this?

He had to.

He forced himself to think again of how Miriam had taken his memories. And the dirtiest, most disgusting part of it all was that she did it knowing he was falling for her. There was no way she could not know. She'd probably just used him. He thought about how deceitful and horrendous it all was.

Then he reminded himself that the price tag for not taking the Joneses up on their offer was the death of his sister and banishment here to Edenia, where he would become a mutant like all who stayed here.

With those justifications rolling around in his head, he closed his eyes, feeling his stomach settle, his heart slow, and his tears flow. All were symptoms of the weightiness of this decision. He allowed that necessity to lull him into a fitful sleep.

CHAPTER 2

Peter ached all over. Old Bull had won this battle fair and square. The dreadful horse would be his death.

Still, he would never forget the look in the great bully's eye as Peter used his Nature to pop in and out of existence. The old stallion wannabe was scared out of his wits. Peter smirked in his half sleep, half reverie, wondering fleetingly if Old Bull wanted to wave the figurative white flag.

Perhaps the gig wasn't up quite yet.

Peter floated back into sleep with a grin on his face and plans for retaliation for his injuries whirling around in his head.

He woke again. He did not know how long he had been unconscious. It was dark in the room, making it hard to tell what was happening or where exactly he was. His body was prickling with unpleasant sensations.

His eyes slid closed again, but instead of blacking out to a semi-conscious limbo, his mind went in and out of that other sight; that sight he'd gained from his yellow eyes, from his Nature.

The ribbon of time, timing and choice slithered before him like a great multicolored, never-ending, serpent. He moved closer, his perspective sliding to the side where he saw a great tapestry of colors imaginable and unimaginable, of light and darkness, of music, of thunder, of screams of horror and squeals of joy. This was humanity. Past, present, and threads of future that were all woven to make up the human race. It was glorious, beautiful, the most pleasing and most haunting image his eyes could see, or his brain could comprehend.

One of the threads—one of eight billion—looked...strange. He was not sure why it stood out to him, but it did. That was how this worked the last time as well, and somehow, he knew that was how it would always work. Something else he intuitively knew; he could never make sense of it until he saw it up close, where he would finally comprehend it. This was a place where order and chaos balanced on the edge of a sword.

Moving closer to the troublesome thread, he concentrated.

In the part of the ribbon that represented the near future, the part not yet woven, he watched the thread of his focus veer sharply from its previously charted course, leaving the ghost of its light behind it. It bent far to the left amid the weave, and with the sideways movement, it pulled many threads with it as if by magnetic force. Once the threads moved, all of them itched in his mind with discord.

The weave of time, however, seemed to take the deviation in stride, moving to fold the thread with new threads, but did so in a way Peter knew was not optimal. His heart hurt with the trajectory of the threads, for he knew what it meant. These threads were people, the movement, encounters, and choices. He knew something damning was about to happen.

He zoomed in toward the threads, a sinking in his gut, and saw soon enough why. The troublesome—yet incredibly bright—thread was Seth Johnson's and the brightest thread of them all, the one that had a newly darkened path before it, was one he knew as well as his own.

Miriam.

And with this vision, he knew Miriam was in danger. He felt it to his core. Her path, her future, had been pulled by Seth's into a dark place, far from her parents and her home.

He needed to wake up. He needed to tell someone. But his body remained still, painfully still. His consciousness closed off from the world. He struggled. Angry in the black void, he fought to awaken. But after what felt like forever, with no progress, he held himself still.

Why? The question was all he had left in him. Why would he be told Miriam needed help and then be rendered incapable of helping? An image of his Nature taking him in the cafeteria in front of Lillian, Abigail, and Seth took over his vision. *Timing. This was about timing.*

CHAPTER 3

"I don't know what to tell you, Greg. My dad just said to report for work here." Seth yawned and looked out at the Edenian sunrise. Over the barn to the east, the sky was orange and red. It was truly beautiful, though the cold air smelled strongly of cow. "Do you think I would be out of bed if I wasn't sure I was supposed to work here today? So annoying."

Seth had to learn how to drive a wagon. Today. That was what this part of his plan was about. He needed to have a way to get the girls to the rendezvous point. He had no idea what Lillian's condition would be. She was so sick last night. And he had no idea what Miriam was capable of. Positive she would not go outside of Edenia willingly, Seth patted his pocket with the little vial of drugs he'd gotten from the Joneses. There was no way he could drag a drugged girl and a sick girl a half a mile outside of Edenia. He needed a wagon, thus he needed Greg.

Greg cut the wired bale of straw and spread it on the ground. A cow unceremoniously flopped herself down on the fresh cuttings and began chewing her cud. He moved over to the cart, plucked a basket of apples from the back, and walked toward the driver's seat of the wagon. "It's strange no one told me. Aren't you supposed to be mucking out the barn?" Using a narrow metal bar as a step, Greg climbed fluidly up into the wagon. Setting the basket down and taking the reins, he looked at Seth, waiting for a response.

"I don't know. I have this whole week. Honestly though, I'm stoked to be here with you. I've had enough horse crap to last a lifetime." He paused. "Maybe after what happened with Peter, the barn's off limits or something. By the way, how is he doing? Peter, I mean. Have you heard anything?"

"Oh, he's fine. Looks like it was just a few bumps and bruises" Greg looked away, and that annoyed sense that everyone knew something Seth *should* know, but *didn't*, burbled up anger in his gut. His sisters had told him he was in the barn, but he had no memory of it and that was how he discovered that Miriam was the one Willis and Jeremiah Jones were looking for. How she was the memory girl. The dangerous person. Everyone here sure acted like she was dangerous or strange.

Seth pulled his mind back to the present and calmed himself down. "I'm glad I wasn't there yesterday, though I was supposed to be." He paused for effect, but when Greg did not respond, he went on. "I don't understand why I can't remember why I didn't make it. It's weird..."

Still, Greg's face remained stony. Wow, he was really good. Seth wondered if there were classes here on deceit. But that seemed almost like an oxymoron for these people. "Well, anyhow, this Peter thing got me thinking. I really need to learn more about horses and how to deal with them, since it seems I'm going to be forced to be around them."

"True," Greg added, relieved to join in the conversation. His face turned thoughtful.

"And as far as I can see, driving seems as good a place as any to start. That way, I am far away from feet, mouth, legs—ya know, things that could kill me."

Greg smiled, "They're called hooves. And a bite cannot kill you. But yes, I do see your point. And really there is no harm in it, we all must learn. Hop on up. We can take these apples to the cellar."

Relieved, Seth ambled to the passenger side of the cart.

CHAPTER 4

The logical part of Miriam knew she was not feeling or acting rational. She felt quite out of control. The thought of Seth—his shiny dark hair, his eyes like agates, his openness, his humor, and the connection they shared—clenched her middle, distracted her and sent her mind racing down crazy paths.

She thought about him as she fed the chickens, as she watered the flowers, as she chose her dress, as she scrubbed her teeth, as she braided and then unbraided her hair.

Not even thinking of the combat they were in—and it was a combat, one she had just played the winning hand in—did not distract her fanciful imaginings and budding feelings. She wondered how he would handle it. Would he ask her about his phone? Would he wonder aloud about the hole in his memory?

The anticipation of seeing him for lunch climbed.

And then there was their date...

Her hand went to her quivering belly as she walked to school, alone. She watched for Seth. She did not see him.

As she sat in *History of America*, her feet bounced, and that little thing inside her—the same thing that had told her to make a connection with Seth—whispered to her now; questions, doubts, reality.

Why was he trying to destroy Edenia?

What had the Joneses promised him?

What deal had he made?

Why was there an air of desperation about him? Could she help him?

She had a sneaking suspicion these questions were inspired by a source less mortal than herself, and thus they haunted her.

AT LUNCH, she waited for him under their tree. Finally, when Seth stood next to her, he asked quietly, "Are you excited for our date?"

His mouth was at her ear, his breath tickling the side of her face. She could feel the nearness of his body, the warmth of his breath. He held her hair out of the way so his mouth could be close to her.

Her body did a full shiver at the whispered words.

Hands trembling, heart racing, she answered his question with a nod and attempted to calm herself.

Alone, in the cool September air, practically touching; that magic between them built. She turned to him and he slid his hand from her hair to her shoulder, then down her arm. She shivered again.

He spoke. "I've got something fun planned, but I need your help."

All she could do was nod again.

"Well, not to give anything away, but where could I get a football?"

Instantly, her mind cleared, the magic gone, her heart shuddering to a stop...then starting up again for an entirely different reason. Images of her typical relationship with balls filled her being. She cleared her throat. "Uhm, I don't really do balls." Her cheeks burned. "They tend to fly in a direct course for my head."

He smiled, "Well, awesome. Headers can be brilliant shots. I'll teach you how to make the most of them."

"You don't understand. Balls are physiologically incapable of doing anything else if I am near. I'm cursed."

This time he laughed. Genuinely laughed. He felt the ring of it, too, because when he looked over at her through his lashes, his eyes became tortured despite the smile.

A strong wind came up behind her and threatened to blow her

into Seth's arms. She held her ground, all except her hair, which took on a mind of its own, flying this way and that. It seemed to claw at Seth in feeble pulling motions.

Mystified by the whirling hair, Seth obeyed the pull and stepped closer, his eyes on the blonde tresses. A gust of wind directed at Miriam's back flung all of her hair forward. For a strange and beautiful second, it spread out from the back of her head, perfectly all around her like a fan. Jutting in a glorious arch, it encapsulated her and Seth in the stillness of a moment. One tiny moment. A heartbeat.

Awe showing on his face, Seth's eyes traced the little cocoon of her hair. But it was over as soon as it had begun. The wind settled, and Miriam's hair fell around them. Seth gathered the tresses up and pushed them to her back as she stood in silent wonderment of the moment she'd just had, and the moment that still lingered between them.

He broke the silence. "I don't think you're cursed, Miriam, I just think you're struggling to figure yourself out, or, like, find your place."

Miriam blinked. "What do you mean?"

"Outside, people get to figure themselves out. They don't have to be all serious; raising chickens and growing vegetables and sewing their own clothes. They get to be a teenager, mess around, go to parties and football games. They are allowed to try things, have all sorts of jobs and relationships. You're really secluded here, really sheltered and controlled." He looked out to the town of Edenia, and Miriam saw what was happening to him. He wasn't exactly feeling sorry for her, but he was looking at her like she was a prisoner, and he wanted to break her out. "Your mind probably races a hundred miles an hour asking all sorts of questions, like what does freedom look like, feel like. I wonder...I wonder if I could help you with that. I wonder if at some point you and I could...I don't know...leave here, together. You get your answers, you figure out what it is you are chasing, and I keep you safe from a world that would love to destroy you. Like maybe, just maybe we could save each other."

Miriam's heart leapt into her throat. "What are you say...offering?"

He toed the ground, his cheeks heating. Then he smiled and looked up at her through his lashes. "I don't know, exactly. Maybe nothing, maybe everything." He let silence reverberate between them as the heat in the gaze they shared heightened. Finally, Miriam cleared her throat and looked away. She gathered all her hair together and wrapped it around her wrist before pulling it into a knot. Then she swung it behind her back.

He spoke up again, drawing her eyes to him. "But maybe you don't need something so drastic as escape, maybe..." she could see a glint of mischief in his eye, "...maybe you just need a distraction." This was a challenge.

"I thought that was why I did chores," she shot back and was surprised by the smug flirtation that was in her voice.

He laughed, but it did not take long for him to get serious again. He took a step toward her, as if he were being pushed from behind. "Maybe I could be that distraction." His mouth whispered, and it perhaps was not exactly by choice, for he quickly turned away from her, his cheeks going red.

Miriam soaked it in. She closed her eyes, remembering the sweet feelings he'd had for her yesterday in his taken memories. She knew him. She knew exactly how he felt about her, and it wasn't fake. It wasn't a ploy to get her to run away with him, or to tell him secrets—though she was sure he wanted her secrets as well.

Just as she opened her eyes and mouth to admit that she felt things for him too, Seth asked, "Miriam, do you know what faith is?" The instant their eyes met, she knew she wasn't the only one struggling. He continued in a way that told her he was not saying the words he really wanted to say. "I mean, you must know. You live here, right? It must take a lot of faith to live here. To be separated from everything for no reason other than that is what your parents want. How do you do it?"

His words made her mind whirl. This conversation was like being flung into the air and smashed to the ground repeatedly. She sighed and focused on answering him. "I know what it means to trust in something you can't see, you can only feel," she said carefully. "I know what it feels like to move forward in a direction you are not sure is correct in your head, but you are certain is correct in your heart. That's faith, I think. Why do you ask?"

Seth licked his lips and blinked at her before sniffing and turning away. After a minute, his hands went to his head and slipped into his hair.

She reached for him. "Seth?" Her hand touched the sleeve of his shirt. "Seth, what is it?" He half turned and her glance studied his beautiful face until finally his thoughts led his gaze back to her.

"I'm just trying so hard..."

She waited for him to finish his statement, but all he did was slowly curl in on himself. Each muscle constricting with a myriad of emotions she could not possibly understand or untangle.

"Tell me," she pleaded with him, and this time she took his hand in hers. *He was trying so hard.* Miriam's mind pulled her out of the mist of hormones Seth always triggered inside her. *Seth knows about the phone and now he is stressing about his deal with the Joneses.*

Miriam bit her lip at this thought and carefully let go of Seth's hand. When she looked up, Seth's hand came to her cheek. He licked his lips as his eyes darted down to her mouth. "I care about you Miriam. It is an inexplicable rising ocean of I know not what. I just need you to know that it's there." The words were life to her heart and nothing more than sound to her ears because Seth's face moved inch by slow inch toward her own. His eyes held her captive, the essences between them unable to stop connecting them deeper and more profoundly to one another. *Was this normal?* her mind fleetingly considered, but then it was not just his fingertips touching her. His hand slid across her cheek. His other hand found her face, and their breath mingled. Her heart raced. She flushed and burned. However, her mind thundered her inexperience in this, like a lightning bolt through her body.

"Seth," she whispered. His eyes lifted from her mouth to her eyes. "I've never..."

"...felt like this before. I know, it's so strange and awesome," he finished.

She smiled and literally felt his legs wobble. *Kissed anyone*, was what she was going to say.

"You are so beautiful," he added. That, along with the wind picking up again, startled her into pulling back. She rolled her lips between her teeth, her youthful self-consciousness pulling her out of the moment. "You really mean that?" Speaking the question aloud made her heart jump into her throat as her eyes searched his for the truth.

He looked at her mouth again, then closing his eyes and nodding vigorously, said, "Uhm, yes." and emitted a small nervous smile-laugh.

She bit her lip again, trying to hold back a smile of her own in response to his demeanor. Her gaze left his and traced his face as she whispered, "I find you very handsome as well."

A smile and a quick exhale preceded his words. "I'm relieved." His thumb caressed her cheek bone—one hand had not let go of her face—and his expression turned serious.

Hesitatingly, he spoke, "What would happen if..."

The bell rang.

His hand fell.

Sucking in a breath, and self-conscious of her actions, she turned her eyes away, searching the school yard. When she glanced back at him, his face was down, his hands in his pockets. "So," she forced into the tension-filled silence. "I'll see you tonight?"

"Yep." He shook his head and stepped back from her again, "Uhm, yes."

"Maybe we can finish this...talk, then," she hinted and took her entire bottom lip into her mouth. Her cheeks flushed with embarrassment at her brazen comment.

He pulled his hand through his hair, looking at her from the corners of his eyes. "Oh, yes. I can't wait."

She smiled and turned away from him to move toward the school.

He put his fingertips to his forehead. "Oh, hey, can you bring a ball?"

Miriam groaned. "If I have to."

He smiled and said, "You won't regret it."

WHEN SHE CAME HOME from school, she assumed Peter would be up. He was not, and everyone was nervous about that. Obviously, his injuries were worse than they suspected. He could have died.

To pass the anxious time before her date, Miriam sat in Peter's room. She reached for Peter's hand. Sitting by his side, seeing him crumpled, brought her incredible clarity. In fact, when she was not around Seth, she was always clear on what needed doing.

It was converting clarity into action that was her problem.

Her mind flitted from idea to idea when the door handle moved, and their mother poked her head through. "Miriam, Seth is here to see you."

Within a breath, Miriam's heart was in her throat. "Oh?" she asked.

"Were you expecting him?" her mother asked back.

"Uhm, yes, I guess I was." Miriam stood and found she was on the edge of throwing-up she was so excited.

"Miriam." Her mother interrupted her thoughts. "Hello, there? It is your mother."

Miriam turned to her mother and saw that the woman's arms were folded across her chest, amber irises ablaze, and she could sense the slightest heat in the room.

"Oh good, you are ready to communicate. I have called your name about three times. Where is your head, Miriam?" She did not answer. "So, would you mind telling me why Seth Johnson is standing in our living room under the assumption you are going someplace with him?"

Miriam stood and looked at her mother. "Because we are walking over to the open field." She knew she had to make it sound as benign as possible. "I explained how terrible I am with balls and how all they do is hit me in the head and he said I could learn to use that to my advantage. It is called a header, I think. So, I think he is going to try to teach me how to play football, which I think is soccer, but he thinks he's English or something, so he calls it football?" She knew she was rattling on and on, but she could not help it. This made her nervous. Her mother could put a stop to it here and now.

Her mother relaxed. "Why on earth would you need to know how to play soccer?" This nosy penchant of her mother annoyed Miriam no end.

Feeling half crazed with the need to see Seth she moved away and said, "I do not need to know how to play soccer, Mother. It is just something fun to do, and I get precious little of that. I do not know if you have noticed, but there are no other friends asking to help me overcome one of my fears." Before she knew it, defensiveness turned to anger. "Do you have a problem with me having a bit of fun? Or having a friend?" Miriam's tone was sharp, and she had no clue where her moxie came from. Never in her life had she spoken that way to her mother, and why of all times had her mouth opened now?

Her mother's face did the exact opposite of what she thought it would. It softened.

"Of course not. I am happy you have a friend." She took Miriam by the shoulders and gave her a half smile. "You work hard and are very serious, so I do think a little fun is in order." Her eyebrows scrunched. "I do worry, though. Ezekiel told me that Seth is struggling, and I can see it. So, I just..." She bit both her lips and swallowed hard. "I know things are not how you would like them to be. I know what is in your heart, Miriam." She lowered her voice. "Seth is handsome and interesting and can tell you all about the wonderful, beautiful things you think you are missing out on. I understand these feelings, believe me." Her hands rubbed up and down Miriam's arms. "I just hope that you will use that great big brain of yours and your big heart to help Seth. To be his *friend*. Listen to Seth, find out why he is struggling. Help him if he will let you. You have many natural gifts, Miriam. You can use them to bless those around you."

Then she did something she had not done in nearly two years. She hugged Miriam. Not a small side-hug. A full, tight, loving hug. Tears crowded Miriam's eyelashes, and she hugged her mother back, fiercely.

When her mother pulled back, she smiled again. "Do not pretend you do not think of him those other ways. Believe me, I understand, the Miller men are almost irresistible. But please, Miriam, wait, and think. I have always been able to count on you to think." She raised an eyebrow and in a shocking display of sass added, "You can fall in love with him later." Miriam blushed deeply and her mother laughed. "I was young once. I see what is happening. Part of me is very happy for you and part of me is scared to death because your father and I have not blindly chosen a road for you. It was to help you. Does that mean we have to stay on our current road? With Foster as your intended? No. But please trust us and trust me on this one thing; your cousin cannot be what you want him to be, *right now*. He is not a rock; he is not as steady as the river, *right now*. He has turmoil inside. But give him some time, all right?"

Miriam was grateful for this act of love from her mother, but the words did not have the desired effect. Instead they scraped at the bloody sore that was their mother/daughter relationship. Besides, this was about so much more than just her feelings. Her mother did not understand all that was involved, with the Joneses and everything else.

"I hear you, Mother." Was all she could muster, and she added a small smile. Then she turned and walked toward the living room and Seth's amazing face.

CHAPTER 5

The Miller's couch was just as comfortable as his own—i.e. NOT comfortable. Still, he allowed the hard spindles to push into his back. It made his mind focus on the tasks at hand; escape and possible kidnapping.

What kept distracting him was the strange feeling that he knew exactly where Miriam was. Like he had and arrow in his brain that pointed to her, sort of like the way he could tell Abby and Lilly's voices apart without seeing them. They sounded similar, but he knew which of the two called out for him. Somehow, he just knew. He turned toward the back of the house and felt drawn to a specific part of the house. She was there; he knew it. He could walk directly to her side without calling out to her. It was a weird feeling. He wondered if it was accurate.

It made him think of the soldiers he had hitched a ride to the Joneses compound with last night. The red-haired man said he could point directly to Edenia no matter where he was. Seth's forehead wrinkled with the idea that *he* could point right to Miriam. He was sure it was her. To the men at the compound, there was no distinguishing between the two. But Seth was here. He could.

Seth felt goose bumps raise on his arms as he considered this idea. The soldier from last night seemed obsessed with what was happening to him. What would he do when he figured out it was Miriam causing his compass-like tendencies?

A shiver thundered its way up his back.

He didn't want to think about what would happen if that soldier got ahold of Miriam.

Or about the promise *he* had made to betray Miriam in exchange for freedom and medical care for Lillian.

Or even about the fact that in a few short hours whatever was between him and Miriam would be over forever.

Could he do this?

His body answered his question for him. He felt his head shake seemingly of its own volition. He seemed to lose all sanity when she was around. At lunch it was as if he had never even heard of the Joneses. He saw her, he touched her, and that was it. Nothing else mattered.

The house was full of typical noise, but he heard and felt her when she came. Pulling his face into a smile, he stood. Two heartbeats later, she walked in wearing a pair of blue pants that showed off her long legs and slim waist, and a yellow cotton shirt. Her hair was down and curled on the ends.

His smile was probably 100 watts.

This girl was literally mesmerizing. Her blonde, extra-long, shining hair, her unforgettable violet eyes, her full lips, they all got the boy bits of his brain way too excited. But the way she smiled and spoke sunk him. He wanted to get inside her mind and know everything about the way it worked so he could just smother himself with her.

As that thought completed, it startled him. How could he want that? Didn't he secretly hate her for doing just that to him? Not to mention it sounded psychotic. Mentally he chucked those thoughts into a box, shut the box, and threw it into the blackest corner in his mind.

He moved toward her and held out his arm. "Are you ready?" he asked lightly.

Her eyebrows wrinkled up, "How, exactly, is one to get one's head ready for rapid assault via soccer ball?"

He loved the way she talked; it was all-formal, but it just made everything sound so funny. All she needed was a British accent and she could be a right comedian.

"You wouldn't happen to have a helmet, would you?" He played along.

"That is absolutely a wonderful idea. A helmet?" She thought, tapping a finger against her lips. Then her face brightened, "How about a bowl? Will that do? Though I don't relish the thought of wearing a bowl on my head." She eyed him doubtfully.

She was teasing him, right?

"You wouldn't happen to be a very sensible British woman trapped inside that fetching teenage body, would you?" Now both her eyebrows shot up questioning him. He went on quickly, "I just love the way you put things, you sound like a nanny or something, minus the accent, of course."

"Oh," knocking her head to the side, "Is that what your accent is, British?"

"I have an accent?" He smiled. "I think you're the one with the accent."

She rolled her eyes. "So, you like British accents?"

"Love them. When we lived in London, I totally faked one, well, until I had a real one."

"So, you do have a British accent?" She looked completely confused, her face all bunched and pouty.

Beautiful.

"My accent isn't really anything, I've lived too many places for any one way of speaking to stick."

"Oh, how nice for you." There was a healthy portion of ire in her comment and she turned away from him pretending to pout.

Plastering on a fake smile he offered, "Let's go and I'll tell you all about Great Britain." He leaned in close and whispered. "I'll start with my favorite place, the white cliffs at Dover."

She turned back to him all smiles now, "Oh, I'd love to hear about them. But first what do they smell like?" she asked, completely serious.

Seth laughed out loud. "What kind of question is that?"

Miriam blushed. "Uhm, well, you said that the world outside was stinky, so I figured I should ask first, just so I don't completely romanticize it."

Seth shook his head in utter happiness, a smile as wide as the Nile on his face. "You are something else, you know that?" he said and couldn't help himself, he reached out and slid his fingers down a silky gathering of blonde hair flowing over Miriam's shoulder and down her arm. He repositioned it with the rest of her hair and offered her his arm. "Shall we go?"

She took his arm, and they walked to the door together.

When Miriam saw the horse and buggy, she stopped abruptly and slowly turned to look up at him. The vibes he felt rolling off her made him feel like he was in a horror movie. Her face seemed completely blank, every feature relaxed, as they should be. But, with a father like his, he had practiced detecting the nuances. She was ashen, and despite her apparent lack of expression, he thought he saw alarm.

Unsure, he started slowly. "I know tonight is supposed to be about the real world. Unfortunately I don't have a car lying about, so I thought buggy. Romantic, slow, and out there in the world, if a guy pulled up with a ride like this, the girl would be, like, squealing with excitement." He turned his whole body to her now and realized a foolish part of him wanted her to have fun tonight, but he would not be able to pull that off if she wouldn't even get in the stupid buggy. The other voice in his mind reminded him that if she refused to get in the buggy how would he get the buggy to where it needed to be to meet the Joneses? The two opposing desires felt like they might break his brain. Either way, he had to be convincing.

Miriam was not charmed. Her face was blank, uncertain.

So he poured it on. "Of course, most normal people don't live with horses. But it was the best I could do. And our food is in the back. I made it myself. Please don't chicken out on me." Giving her his best smile, he offered her his arm again.

After several moronic seconds of him standing there with his arm extended, a falsely enthusiastic smile on his face, she answered him. "Unfortunately, I am going to disappoint you."

She looked away from him to the buggy and his heart plummeted, what was he going to do?

But she turned back to him and delivered deadpan, "I do not squeal." Her whole demeanor was serious, but then a tiny little grin lifted one side of her perfect lips. She took a step forward and asked, "How did you get this, and do you even know how to drive it?"

And though he was relieved, he also felt guilty. He cleared his throat. He had to sell it. "Hey, lady, I got connections. My connections have connections."

"I noticed you glossed over the how-are-you-going-to-drive-this, bit."

"Do you really think I would put you in a vehicle I don't know how to drive?"

Miriam only thought for a moment and said with certainty, "Absolutely."

He laughed, and taking her hand pulled her down the steps to the buggy. "I promise, I know exactly what I'm doing...sort of." He cleared his throat again, "Okay, mostly, I hold the long leather things in my hands right or, crap..." He put a flat palm to his forehead. "Miriam, do you think you could drive, I'm completely full of it."

Miriam's face wrinkled as her eyes probed him. He held on for just a moment more, then said, "Just kidding. You should see your face." He laughed. "Greg showed me the basics. It's not that hard." He pulled, but she didn't move. "We're fine, I swear. I won't be chariot racing anytime soon, but I think I can get us to the field."

The distance between them closed as Seth pulled on her hand again. They moved together to the buggy, sweat slicking his palms. As he tried to help her into the buggy, his hand ended up around her waist, her body pressed against his. A bit of awkwardness happened, where Seth examined her, wondering why she was not moving. But she did not move. She waited, her eyes intense, her expression guarded.

He did not know how to reassure her, so he said, "Can I help you into the buggy, my lady?"

She surprised him by asking, "You promise you will take care, and not do anything that will hurt us both?"

In his head he panicked a little. That was a pointed, carefully worded, question, he could tell. Why was she asking this? Her face gave nothing away.

Deciding that all he could do was do his best he said, "Of course. The last thing I want is for you to be hurt." And it was true. He did not want her hurt. If she doubted, he supposed she would use her voodoo on him and he'd forget all of this.

She checked his eyes and must have seen this truth there, because she nodded to herself, took his hand from her hip and turned toward the seat.

This was going to be so hard. He was not sure he could do it. As he walked to the other side of the buggy, he brought Lilly's face to the front of his mind. He had to remember Lilly.

CHAPTER 6

Miriam

Her hands trembled.

Miriam could hardly stand how they—she and Seth—balanced on the edge of...something. One chasm wrought with opposing purposes, the other a treacherous slope of desires. Neither, purposes nor desires, could she begin to understand, except that she could feel them, swirling in her stomach.

He turned onto the main road of Edenia. The bumpy dirt moved underneath them in a way that reminded her of their relationship, tumbling and jolting and rolling by without concern for the details.

Seth urged the horse to pick up speed, which was frightening and exhilarating. This thrill held the same blood rushing, heart throbbing, stomach swirling that being with Seth, in this critical moment, did.

She wondered if Seth knew how things stood here. His deal with the Joneses was over—whatever the reasons or details—Peter had his phone, she had destroyed its power source, and in twenty-four hours Seth would be a Guardian. Did he know he had failed? And of course, there was the question of what was the "why" behind his quest in the first place.

She looked over at the beautiful boy that fluttered her stomach and gave it knots all at the same time; he might know. There were moments she swore she saw rage in his eyes. But there were more moments where she saw affection. There was fear. There was a yearning. There was confusion. She saw it all in him and wondered.

And yet...

For some reason, the thing she cared about most was if his insides were as swirly as hers.

She hoped so.

He certainly was concentrating hard; forehead all wrinkled, nostrils flaring, fists gripped tight as if life depended on them. It was as plain as grass that he was either nervous and anxious over his plans or, like her, nauseously excited and high-strung.

A spike of fear raced up her back, and a thought foreign to her trusting character formed; what was stopping Seth from continuing down this road, with her in the fast-moving buggy, and heading straight into the hands of the Joneses?

Maybe Seth had a contingency plan.

Her mother's words rippled through her thoughts. *'Be careful. Help him. Fall in love later. He's not ready.'* With that thought, her Nature unexpectedly took her. Surprised, she wondered what the Master expected her to do? She considered the three tenets of her Nature. She couldn't take his memory; she'd promised not to do that unless directly asked to by the Master or her father. There was no need to compel him at present, because she didn't know if he was even doing something that could hurt her. What about peace?

Her Nature had not stopped pulling at her, so she turned her head to the opposite side of the buggy so that he would not see her eyes. Then she surreptitiously reached out with the calming part of her Nature and brushed it over him, offering him the peace she had.

Never had she felt calm pulling out of her as she did in that moment. Seth was beyond upset on the inside. He lapped at her Nature as a thirsty dog does water. She felt his trepidation, she felt his anger, she felt his confliction. It surprised her.

There was something strange about it. It almost felt like what happened when she pulled a memory from a Jones; a ghost of feelings, experiences, chemical reactions that all pulled together to form an event that she neatly snipped away from the brain of the Jones. At least that is what she'd thought it was. This felt like a ghost of a ghost, and it left no residue, no pieces of the other persons being, inside her the way that taking memories did.

She thought about the memory she had taken from Seth, how it was like watching a picture of his life from inside his head. It was complete and detailed and full, with all five senses involved. The memories in her secret place floated up in her awareness. They were devoid of the color and emotions she now pulled from Seth. It was if they were black and white and the mass of chemical reality that she felt from him now was vibrant color.

It snapped her understanding of her Nature into a different perspective. This calming that she was doing to him right now was the missing component to the black and white memories that she pulled from the Joneses. There were two components.

She felt her blood race to her cheeks, her mind racing with excited discovery.

When she pulled the memories from the Joneses, she only pulled one component. When she soothed with peace this way, she pulled the other component. Seth's memory was a pulling of both of these components, and that was why it was different.

She wanted to look at him, she wanted to see if her power was making a difference on the outside as it was on the inside but also, she could not give herself away. She closed her eyes and basked in the feelings she received from him. They felt almost like a colorful rainbow of...energy...she coaxed out of him. With the memories, it was like she was pulling, taking, cutting. With this it was like she was inviting, coaxing, and then setting free. She felt it making a difference in the human sitting next to her, but she wanted to see it.

She released her Nature and looked at him. He was still stiff, but his eyebrows were more relaxed.

She spoke, hoping to coax him to relax even more with her words. "So, is this driving thing a bit much, or do you have a death grip on the reins for some other reason?"

Seth considered his hands and smirked as he released the tension. "I don't want to die before I have the pleasure of seeing you get pummeled by a soccer ball."

Looking over at her, he smiled fully, and she saw peace. It transformed his features. Little changes in the tightness of his eyes and his lips, the heaviness to his breathing. Those expressions of stress and anger were gone. His black eyes sparkled at her.

Helping him felt good.

She smiled back, but before she completely lost herself, she ripped her eyes away to say, "I'm sure you'll get your wish. Though for me death might be preferable, so perhaps you should hand those reins over. I'll just do myself a favor and take care of it now. Don't worry, it will be quick."

She did not reach for the reins, but Seth still moved them to the opposite side of his body as he laughed out loud, "Slow down, kamikaze. You are not allowed to die. I want to see you play soccer first. Then, have at it." He laughed.

"What's that?" she asked, pleased at their banter and his strange word.

He looked over at her confused, "A kamikaze, you know."

Miriam didn't know, but that was not what stopped her heart in its racing tracks. For a moment, a small moment, Seth had forgotten where he was. The horse and buggy, their homespun clothes, the Edenian homes sliding by all disappeared. She was just a girl, and he was just a boy. And they were on a date. For one tiny moment.

She savored his confusion, closed her eyes, and reveled in it as Seth explained what a kamikaze was.

When she opened her eyes, all she knew was she wanted that to happen again and again.

ALL TOO SOON, they stopped in the field. Seth helped her down from the buggy, still speaking his feelings about suicide bombers. "I am just offended by it. A while ago, well I guess like thirty-five years ago, several of these whack-jobs attacked the United States. Several airplanes crashed into the Twin Towers, and in a second, thousands were dead. Just like that, no respect for life, not even their own."

"Twin towers?"

"Yeah, they were some financial buildings in the heart of New York City, I guess. I'm not sure exactly what they were. Anyhow, my parents were living in Quebec, which is part of Canada..."

"Yes, Seth, I know where Quebec is. Go on."

"Okay, anyhow my parents can tell you exactly where they were and what they were doing when it happened."

"Why?"

"So, uhm, these two huge buildings, they like, represented, the New York skyline."

"Skyline?"

He laughed, "Yeah all right, so, my dear deprived cousin, since you've never been to a huge metropolis before I will school you on its ways." He picked up a stick and proceeded to draw stuff in the dirt that helped explain the big city to her.

After a while, Miriam felt disconcerted. "Why did no one tell me all this before? It sounds like the seven rings of hell."

His face was serious. "It's way worse."

"Why do people let it be that way?"

"Because, they're, I don't know, afraid, maybe. But that's too generous. I saw evil men in Cairo and in London. They're rich, they like their privileges and power. They like doing what they want. And as my father says, if you don't have a moral compass in your life, you can justify all sorts of ill treatment of your fellow humans. And many people live that way. In their mind, all the, quote, moral laws, that conscientious people—like yourself—see as good, they see as a hindrance to what they want. And when a lot of people in a society feel that way, quote, *bad stuff* becomes good and good stuff becomes bad. Nowadays they have taken it even further, people who personally want to live the morality taught in the Bible, or the Pali Canon, or Dojo-Kun, or Avesta or whatever moral code you accept, are called old fashioned, or worse, a bigot, prejudiced, or a hater."

"Sounds scary."

"It is, in some places more than others. But you're here. You don't have to worry about any of that." He pulled out the soccer ball of doom. "I saw it in your yard, so I grabbed it." Then he did some crazy bouncing thing off his knees and said, "Enough serious talk. Let's have some fun."

No one, not a single person, had told her anything bad about the outside. Or about the outside people. Of course, she'd read history, but that was history. Miriam was confused by the disparity between her perception of the outside and Seth's description.

However, she could not think too much about it. Watching Seth control the ball and do his tricks got her excited and eager.

After a few minutes of awe, the ball bounced off Seth's knee at a weird angle and it hit her right in the face.

"Oh my gosh, I am so sorry." Seth moved to her and started rubbing at her cheek, rather violently. "Rub it out, rub it out. Sorry. I am out of practice, I guess."

"No," she muttered through his rubbing, "...cursed, remember." She took his wrist and stopped his assault. "What are you doing?"

"Rubbing your booboo out."

"My booboo." She eyed him, wondering if he was serious.

"Yes?" His pitch rose as if he were asking her a question.

Miriam could not help it. She covered her mouth and giggled. Seth's cheeks flushed red, but he reached up and stopped her from covering her mouth for some reason. "I love your smile," he whispered, and watched her.

That made the air sizzle. The awkwardness led her to pull the conversation back toward his choice of word. "Booboo."

He smiled and blushed yet again, then he began laughing. "It is a rather childish word, isn't it? Funny, I never thought of it like that before," Seth added, laughing harder.

Maybe it was the stress or the high stakes, but his laughing made her laugh more and her laughing made him laugh harder. It was madness. Tears poured down cheeks, but when she began hiccupping, Seth died. He could not stop, so neither could she.

When they finally calmed down, Seth gave her one more long look then shook his head. "My throat hurts."

"My stomach hurts."

Holding up the ball, he raised his eyebrows. "Too bad. Let's work those stomach muscles some more."

She sighed; this was so not her. "Fine, but I want your expectations to be as low as possible. I will probably hate this and get all bruised."

"Sounds like a day on the streets of Cairo. You wanted to experience the world. Well, the world is full of bumps and bruises. They make you tough." He nodded in the most unsympathetic way she could imagine. And yet, she felt the challenge in the words, and part of her was eager to prove herself.

Seth started in with his show-off maneuvers again and asked, "You ready?"

She took a deep breath. "Yes."

"So, soccer, or football as I like to call it." He scooted next to her and dropped the ball on the ground catching it with his feet so that it did not roll away. "So, the first thing that you need to know is how to place your feet." He turned his feet out like he was going to do a shallow plié.

CHAPTER 7

The vision of Miriam pushing that stupid deflated soccer ball around with her hair flying everywhere and her long legs running and her face completely happy and energized, was...

Sigh.

She was competitive and lithe and athletic and, holy cow, he loved everything that came out of her beautiful mouth.

They took a break. She was flushed and sweaty, with her hair all wild. It was distracting to the maximum.

She walked over to him as she simultaneously ran her fingers through her hair and looked around the green field. By the time she got closer to him she had her hair separated into three sections. It was so dang long that it went all the way down past her waist. When she was satisfied with the lack of knots, she expertly took the two sides and folded them back to the third piece in back. Her hands were moving deftly down, and he realized she was braiding. Soon she was craning her neck forward her arms bent uncomfortably behind her.

In an instant, before he realized what he was saying he asked, "That looks like it hurts. Can I help?" Her eyes met his questioning, as her hands stopped their work. "Yes, I know how to braid," he said in hopes of answering her question. Then to reassure both of them he continued, "I just thought, you have all those people in your house who probably finish that for you because you can't go..." he stopped speaking as Miriam pulled the long tail of hair from her back, to over her shoulder, her fingers moving expertly down the braid.

However, her hands slowed, and without saying a word she held out the golden strands to him. In one deft movement she'd proved she didn't need his help—of course he was such an idiot—*and* demonstrated that she wanted him to step closer to her and touch her.

He felt heat rise to his cheeks as he reached out and took the rather windblown locks. "I didn't realize..."

She stepped closer to him and put a finger up to his lips almost touching them. "Shh," she whispered.

Her hushing him brought on a shiver that started at the base of his spine and shuddered its way to his head, which felt a little light.

It was Miriam that ripped their eyes apart. She looked at his hands in her hair expectantly.

"Oh yeah," he stated with a fumbling lack of class and started braiding.

After a few moments of awkwardness, a glorious silence settled between them; the only sound, his fingers moving through her hair.

As he neared the end of the braid, Miriam whispered, "I'm officially a soccer fan."

Seth relived in his mind how gorgeous she looked running around, kicking that stupid ball. "Good." Seth smiled impishly at her and tickled her nose with the ends of her hair. "That means we can be friends," he said, and handed the braid over.

With the corner of her mouth up in a half smile, she rubbed her nose with one hand and took the braid with the other. As she tied a ribbon around it, she said, "I thought us being friends was inevitable."

He said nothing for a long moment.

She lifted her head to look at him. He hoped his face was unreadable, for her words had struck him to the core. How could he answer? He had to remind himself of Lillian. *This is about my dying sister.*

He said nothing, only moved away feeling more like a robot than a human. "Are you ready for your surprise?" His voice rang so false to himself.

Confused, she closed the distance between them again. "You mean dinner, right? I'm famished."

Seth smiled tightly at her and turned to walk over to the buggy, his mind whirling. He'd successfully locked out reality for sixty minutes, but now it snapped back with full force. It was time to choose; there would be no do-overs.

Seth pulled out all the food he had prepared for their picnic. He organized it meticulously on the platter before he pulled out the small vial Jeremiah had given him. He had to do this. It did not matter that he was falling in love with Miriam and Edenia; this was life or death.

Wasn't it?

Part of his mind reminded him that death was unavoidable. Even his plan was not guaranteed. Plenty of people still died after surgery and treatment. Regardless, Lillian would be weak and vulnerable for a long time afterward. She would need him. That meant if he followed his plan, he *had* to betray Miriam.

Didn't it?

His mind brought forward his mother's and father's face when they asked him and his siblings to trust them. He knew that they truly believed that there was one chance for Lilly to live, and it was here.

Their plan, whatever it was, was another option, right?

There was no question there was magic or power or whatever here, and who was he to say that it could not heal Lilly? It would be so easy to tell himself that his father grew up here, of course he knew exactly what was possible in this place. But why had they not done anything yet? Lilly was worse. Why did they not even tell him it was possible? Why did they not give them hope? They gave him nothing! And then asked for his blind trust.

But could he trust Edenia? Trust his father?

Could he put faith in something he knew nothing about? This was Lilly's life. He opened the vial of drugs.

His brain wavered with images of Miriam. She was good,

regardless of her penchant for digging in people's minds and taking their memories. Could he really drug her, kidnap her, just so that he could be with Lilly and escape this place? He looked at the soup he and Lilly had made, and he had an overwhelming love for his baby sister. Memories of her goodness and kindness flooded his mind. This had been happening a lot since he found out she had a brain tumor.

His mind was torn back to reality as he heard Miriam sigh. He looked around the buggy to find her. She stood looking over the field, fanning herself.

In one moment, he felt overwhelming love for her and overwhelming hate. His heart hammered. She did that to him. He realized it was ridiculous. Never once in his life had he been around someone he felt so completely attracted to. It felt like a cliché, like a fairytale, or something out of a country song. It made no sense to his brain, but it infiltrated him nonetheless. He would never feel this way about anyone else.

In the next moment of daydreaming he saw his possible future. He saw the beginnings of something real with Miriam. If he were to choose that, it would become an epic love. He could see it. He could feel it.

But he also saw the yin and yang of having a love like that. It had a price. The universe had to be in balance. This thought devastated him. What was the choice here? Epic, world changing love with Miriam and what... Lilly's death? Was that really it?

He looked away from Miriam. He looked at the vial again, he raised his hand and it hovered over Miriam's bowl.

His brain tied his insides into knots while his heart ripped his insides to shreds.

His parents plan, Edenia, mutant powers, Miriam and uncertainty with Lillian.

Joneses, betrayal of Miriam, doctors which brought a certain amount of certainty, goodbye Edenia.

If only he could trust his parents and this place. If he knew Lilly would be okay, all of his problems would be solved.

He closed his eyes. As he stood wondering if he could do what he thought he had to, an unknown force, an unrecognizable power entered his mind, silently, quietly. It literally came into him like a quiet peace. It whispered to him to trust and reminded him how wonderful his parents were. How much they cared for him and his sisters. It urged him to trust. He remembered how he'd seen Peter go invisible. There were miracles in this place. He felt like maybe he could. He could trust. Yes. Yes, he thought he could.

There still was the becoming a freak bit. But couldn't he get over the freak issue, for a love of epic proportions? He wasn't sure. Maybe.

The hand holding the vial dropped to his side. He wouldn't do it. It was crazy. Kidnapping. Drugging. No, he wouldn't. This was right, he was choosing the right thing. He reached into the basket to find a place to hide the vial when he saw a slip of paper lying at the bottom. With his free hand he pulled it out.

You can do it Seth. Think of Lillian.

You are her only hope.

Mom and Dad are crazy; if you don't do this, Lilly will die.

Can you live with that? I know you can't.

I know this is hard, but do it.

Do it for Lilly. Do it for me.

I can feel her life mingled with mine, Seth. If we lose her, it will kill me too.

Be strong and think of your family. We need you. You are our only hope.

Love, Abby

Seth breathed deeply and crumpled the note. All feelings of peace vanished. What an idiot he was! He couldn't chance this. He couldn't trust magic to save his sister. Why had he even entertained the idea? Risking the life of a sister for a stranger, putting faith in something that made no sense at all, putting faith in his parents who'd lied to him over and over again.

Anger flooded through his veins. This was life or death. This was not about faith.

Without another thought, he dumped the liquid into Miriam's soup. He might be willing to lose an arm for Miriam but, Abby was right, he couldn't lose two sisters for her.

CHAPTER 8

Miriam

It was getting close to dusk. The warmth of the sun melted behind the landscape of trees and hills. The apple-flavored breeze cooled her sweaty face. She raised her eyes to the sky and closed them. She smiled with the memories of playing soccer with Seth.

Yes, the ball hit her in the head several times, but Seth taught her how to take it and give it back some of its own. She liked it. It took the victim sensation out of ball games and made her feel more like the boss.

Between the booboo comment, the hair braiding, and the thrill of the exercise, Miriam did not know if she had been so happy or laughed so much in her entire life. Nothing felt abnormal or tainted with Edenia weirdness. It felt awesome.

She laid out on a blanket Seth had set up for dinner. This was the very oak she had hidden under when she had followed him that first day. They were only a few feet away from the border of Edenia and the shack, but it did not bother Miriam a bit.

He took quite a while rummaging around in the back of the buggy.

"Seth! Did you get captured by pirates? Eaten by snakes? Abducted by aliens? I'm starving."

"Soccer is a workout, right? I am really glad you had fun," he responded to her enthusiasm. Emerging from the back of the buggy, he gripped a platter with all sorts of stuff on it. "I think you really got the header move down."

She snickered, and when he sat down next to her, she touched his arm. "Thank you." Her gaze pushed into his. "I think I've been afraid of balls my entire life, and I know it seems silly, but it feels really good to have a bit of my own life back."

He smiled and tilted his head, staring at her.

"What?" she asked and looked at the towel-covered platter he carried.

"You just..." he stammered, and she looked back up at him, but he did not go on.

She raised her eyebrows, "I just..." Her head bobbed in encouragement.

"Nothing. Never mind." Shaking his head slightly, he unveiled the platter. Two bowls of soup, cut fruit and ice cream in saucers. He handed her the ice cream. "So, dessert first."

Miriam squealed with glee. "Really?"

"Yes. It's the only way to do it. And I thought you didn't squeal."

"I don't."

Seth laughed. "I beg to differ, my lady. That right there was a squeal."

"No, no, no."

Seth knelt and raised his hands to the sky. "I am victorious!" he shouted.

Now Miriam laughed and pulled at his arm. They settled down, and she took a spoonful of the soft, white, indulgence and hummed with bliss. After a few more bites she asked, "How did you do this?"

"A gentleman never reveals his secrets."

She noticed the redness of his hands. "You churned it by hand, yourself, just now, in the back of the buggy?"

He glanced at his blistered palms and shrugged his shoulders.

"And the ice?"

"That's my secret."

Miriam smiled. "Wow. Thank you so much. This is such a treat." She touched his hand again and ran a gentle finger over the sore spots. Then, without thinking, she brought it to her lips and kissed the worst welt between his thumb and first finger. As soon as she realized what she had done, she dropped his hand and turned away.

After a few seconds he tenderly said, "I think I like your way of taking care of booboo's far better than mine." She laughed and shyly turned back to look at him. He touched her cheek with a fingertip. "Red looks better on you, too."

His hand fell, and he looked away.

Scooping up some ice cream, she remained silent.

"You know, around here, courting is essentially sitting on someone's porch or in your intended's front room and talking or taking a walk. Basically, it is a lot of talking. I think I prefer this way." He turned to her with something she did not understand in his eyes. She got to the point. "Again, just, thank you so much. This date has been so invigorating. But I think you've ruined me." She looked down at the empty bowl in her lap and her voice became hard, "I don't think any of the boys on my parent's potential-husband-list would go through the trouble you have, and I know Foster won't."

A myriad of emotions passed over Seth's face. None she really understood, but in the end, he said, "Well, you are pretty devoid of civilization here. Everything takes ten times longer to prepare. I suppose it's not reasonable to expect them to take the time."

"Why did you? Take the time."

Seth looked at her and then down, his face hardening a little. "I wanted this to be special...and because we had a deal, remember?"

Miriam swallowed and looked him in the eyes, "Yes. Speaking of which, I assume you have finished your business? You said you would be done by now." Putting out her hand in a moment of Peter-like trickery she added, "Can I see the phone? I would be happy to get it to my father."

Seth examined her closely. And she must have done a great job at holding her expression because soon he looked confused. "I don't have it on me." His words faltered.

Miriam sighed. "Well, okay, but please remember to get it to my father. It is really important that you set aside the things of the world and embrace life here, Seth. You'll be much happier."

His eyes narrowed, "That seems a little hypocritical coming from you, doesn't it?"

His words shocked her. But he was right. He hit on her biggest guilt and her fondest dream. Not wanting to fight with him, she lowered her eyes and responded, "Yes, in a way, I guess you're right."

"Come on, Miriam. Embracing? I'm right? You are so hypocritical, even now with your humble down-turned chin."

Miriam admitted to herself that she was not used to this type of communication. In fact, his openness in calling her out on her so-called hypocrisy made her want to run away. No, made her *need* to run away. Setting her bowl aside, she got to her feet. She moved five steps away before she stopped, uncertain of what to do. Despite her embarrassment, she did not want to leave. She wanted to talk about this with him. She glanced at him. He stared at her, a challenge hanging in the air. So, she paced and organized her thoughts. A moment later, she turned to him, eyes and words ablaze with indignation. "I can't set aside the outside, Seth, because you can't set aside something you've never had, or even experienced. It's a hope or a dream, not an actual breaking of rules."

He rose, too. He leaned toward her as he threw his words at her. "Rules are more about heart than action. So is embracing, Miriam. What does your heart want? A life here, or at least one adventure out there? And pardon me for throwing your words back at you but, *decide and let the other thing go.* Because you are not a victim. You are free to choose." He pointed to the border.

She wanted to scream at him; *As long as I have you, I* don't *WANT the outside anymore!* She turned away from him. How could she tell him he made a difference? She felt tears come to her eyes.

Then Seth was at her side, turning her toward him. He looked angry, though she couldn't understand why. He was the one pressuring her to change the world that existed between them with some kind of declaration.

"What do you want?" he asked in a no-nonsense tone. Miriam

heard the desperation in his voice. Like somehow what she wanted made a difference in the pattern of the future between them.

Maybe it did. Was he asking her to tell him how she felt about him?

He pulled on her shoulder more and finally saw that she was crying. His face softened. Leaving her shoulder in his grasp she turned away from him again.

"Miriam. Miriam, I'm sorry." But his voice didn't sound sorry, it sounded disappointed. The words were hollow and flat in cadence. If only she knew what this all meant.

He took her hand. She faced him.

"I just took out my own questions and frustrations on you. I'm sorry." He pulled her back to the blanket and sat down pulling her hand for her to sit too. "Here, let's have our soup." When she complied, he said, "I might be hangry."

She sniffed. "What's hangry?"

"Angry because you're hungry." He lifted one side of his mouth for her.

She wiped at her nose and said, "That's a pretty clever play on words."

"And so accurate. I'm sorry," he repeated, and this time the words rang true to her ears. He picked up a bowl and a spoon and handed it to her. "Now, no making fun. I made this myself."

Miriam smiled again, "A great manly feat."

"Yes, it was, and for that comment I expect you to eat every last bite. I was going to let you off the hook if it was gross. I actually packed sandwiches, too, but now you've wounded me."

Miriam examined the lumpy liquid, "What is it?" she asked in as kind a way as possible.

His voice tinged with offense, he announced, "It's soup."

"I had gathered that. What kind?"

"Vegetable?" he said uncertainly.

"Interesting. I see why we had dessert first. It was to lull me into a false sense of confidence. Why does mine have all the black flakes in it?"

"I don't really like pepper. So, yours has pepper and mine doesn't."

"Looks like you assumed I love pepper," she commented.

"Well," he answered sheepishly, "I thought it might help it taste better."

"I'm in for it then," she whispered out the side of her mouth.

"A bit, yeah," he answered apologetically.

Not wanting to seem ungrateful for all his hard work, she took up her spoon and ate. It was extremely peppery and lumpy—not in a good way—but she'd had worse. She did notice a strong aftertaste. It was extremely bitter, a sort of chalky ickiness she had never tasted before. She chased it down with some water and took a hurried second bite.

Seth watched her eat, his face unhappy.

She paused, "What is it?"

He looked to be about to tell her something, then he touched his shirt pocket and his face-hardened. "Nothing. How is it?"

She was hoping if she kept her mouth full, he would not ask her. Swallowing, she nodded. "Not bad, not bad." She spooned in another bite so she would not need to continue.

He ate, too, and silence fell over the gorgeous twilight. Miriam attempted to focus on how perfect the evening was and ignore her abused tongue. They sat in companionable silence for some time munching on fruit and watching the clouds.

She thought about the questions Seth had yelled at her, and how he said they were *his* questions. What *he* was trying to work through. So, was Seth truly wondering if he wanted to stay here or leave? Was that what the Joneses had promised him? A place to go? Was it his own life he was trying to save? Regardless, he was trying to figure out what he wanted. Maybe she could talk to him, help him with that choice.

She swallowed the bite of apple in her mouth, wiped her face, and said, "Thank you so much, Seth. I just feel like a weight has lifted off me, like..." She felt nervous, but decided to be brave again. "...like as long as I can come to you, as a friend, and get my *outside* fix maybe I can move on. I know you were hangry, but your words struck home. I just want you to know that." She leaned over and touched his arm. "Really, and if I can ever help you, I mean, if you have things you need to work through, things you feel uncertain about, I hope you will talk to me. I really want to be there for you. This can be a hard place to start over in. I'm certain about that. And I want you to know, I owe you one. Big time. I don't know if I've ever had this much fun." She smiled and squeezed his arm.

Seth pulled his arm free and shoved at his bowl, "Don't say that," he muttered.

Miriam paused at his reaction, then carefully asked, "Why not? It *has* been." She did not understand the crinkle in his brow. Why was he so upset?

She saw him gather himself to speak, once, twice but nothing came out. His face was red now. What was wrong with him?

Hoping to distract him, she said, "It's getting late, and I still have so many questions I want to ask you. Do you mind?"

A huge breath exploded out of him and he wiped his hands down his face. When he looked back at her, he had regained his composure. "Shoot."

"Okay, I want to know...oh my gosh, everything. Uhm, how does it feel to drive a car?"

His eyes flicked to hers, then to the blanket. "That's it? That's your big question? Why a car?"

"Well, no one gets to drive on sabbatical. So, I just wonder about it. It seemed like a strange sort of utter freedom." She looked at him. "Is it?"

He smiled, but it did not touch his eyes. "I guess it depends on what you're driving. My buddy Conrad, well his girlfriend, Fifi—I kid you not, that was her name, rich people think they can name their kids anything—anyhow Fifi had this Mercedes-Benz SLR McLaren, it was so sweet. She didn't ever really let me drive it except around an empty parking lot, but that was the best bit of driving I've ever done. Conrad got to drive it all the time. The perks of having a loaded girlfriend."

For some reason, during this entire speech he wouldn't look at her. He kept his eyes on the ground or the sky.

Wanting to bring him back to her, she asked, "Have you ever had a girlfriend?"

His eyes glanced at her. "Of course." But he looked away again.

Miriam glanced down at her hands; she honestly wished his answer were 'no'. But who was she kidding? She re-imagined him while he was playing soccer with her, his hair and legs and smile. Of course girls flocked to him. She had to move on, "Was she loaded?" She made herself laugh using the weird word.

He smiled too but didn't look at her. "A few of them were."

She tried again. "Were any of them...special?"

Leaning over, he grabbed the soccer ball from the grass and rolled it around between his palms. "Like, have I ever been in love?" He looked at her after the question was out.

"Sure." She could handle him liking other girls, but for some reason the thought of him loving someone made her feel faint. Come to think of it, she felt faint in general. Kind of tingly.

He laughed through his nose, a smile barely touching his lips, "No." Her brain snapped back to Seth, and after a moment, Miriam's breathing started to feel a little heavy. But she ignored it and paid attention. "There was this girl named Mandi, she lived in Angel at Islington, which is a Borough in London..." When he talked about London his accent changed, it was subtle, but it was there. She wondered if this was what a British accent sounded like, if so, she could see the appeal. "I was thirteen, so was she, and we just ran into each other over and over again. Mum and Dad said I was too young to date, so we hung out at old record shops and walked the Thames, stopping at patisseries. She loved football—soccer—like, loved it, and I played. She would come to watch. It was all very quaint for a first romance, I guess. I liked her a lot. Anyhow, she was the first girl I kissed, and I think things could have gone somewhere, but we moved to Cairo."

Wanting to keep him talking she asked the first question that came to mind. "What do you mean things could have gone somewhere? Would you have married her?"

He really did laugh out loud this time. "There are quite a few steps between kissing someone and marriage." He looked at her with eyebrows furrowed and mouth smirking, then he added, "at least on the outside there is."

Now that she had his attention, she did not pull her eyes away from his, though her cheeks warmed. She hated her ignorance. But she was confused, because always before, Seth was kind about her innocence. Since they ate dinner, his attitude had changed. It was sharp now.

Hoping to draw out the Seth she had before, she asked, "What steps?" Her eyes remained on his, though he was a bit fuzzy. Like the outside of him was blurred. She blinked a few times but tried to keep her focus on him.

He shook his head. "You don't know a thing about relationships, do you?" He waited and looked at Miriam. She remained calm and took in his face; it had changed in the last half an hour. "But aren't you supposed to be getting betrothed or whatever? How can you promise yourself to someone when you don't know the first thing about love?" He cut off, then went on. "You know, in the real world, people your age figure out what love is about first-hand. They mess around for the first time, and fall in love with the totally wrong person and..."

Miriam's stomach swirled as his words surrounded the two of them like a hot breeze. Their eyes locked. Something about the topic and where it took Seth's face both warmed her and frightened her.

He looked hurt, and oh so angry. Like he did in the lunchroom that first day. She reached out, her Nature coming upon her out of instinct. She pushed the tiniest bit of calm into him.

He didn't notice the power, but he did notice her eyes. All of a sudden, he stiffened, "Why are your eyes, like, shuddering?"

She blinked and pulled her Nature into herself. Looking up at him she wrinkled her forehead, "What do you mean?"

"You know exactly what I mean." He stood up and walked to the tree trunk, shaking his head and kicking at a root.

Was it finally time to have the elephant in the room conversation? The Natures conversation? Why hadn't he brought it up before now? He saw Peter. He saw him. But he said nothing. That was really strange. It was like he was pretending Peter's Nature hadn't taken him in front of everyone. Like he was pretending his sisters had not told him what Peter revealed to them, that he too would have a Nature soon.

She moved to stand, wanting to be ready for this battle. However, as she began to move, she felt extremely dizzy. Bending over, she balanced herself against the ground. She'd never felt this way. After a few seconds, she thought perhaps she could stand without floating away.

When she did, she saw Seth watching her. When their eyes met, he moved toward her in a way that made her instinctively move back. After only a few steps, the huge tree behind her pressed into the small of her back and she leaned on one of its great armlike branches.

She was trapped.

But no, because all her dreams were coming true. Seth's warm hands went up her arms as he moved into her space. They folded around her, one falling down until it was stopped by the tree behind her and the other combing up her neck and into the tender hairs at the back of her head. With a sleepy sensation coming on strong and her gut feeling weak and queasy, she did not have the strength to stop him even if she had wanted to. So, both his arms and hands tightened around her, his body pressed to hers.

The hand in her hair clenched a tender wad and slowly, fairly gently, but still urgently, pulled back, forcing her chin up. Without her fighting, it did not hurt, but it felt dominating, almost angry.

His eyes forced her to melt on the inside as he pinned her emotions, her heart, her mind to him with the intensity in his look. A potent cocktail of emotions and hormones swirled within her, and not knowing why, she desired him to pull harder, to press her tighter.

Slowly he lowered his face so that the soft, panting, breaths escaping his nostrils sent goosebumps racing down her skin. His lips hovered two inches above hers, but he paid them no mind. His eyes were locked steadfastly on hers; the world was there between them, and yet there was nothing at all between them.

His lips curled back in a snarl. "Why did you do it?"

The trance was broken. Confused, she tried to back away from his face, but his fingers now hurt in her hair. What was he talking about? More confused than ever, Miriam thought hard, trying to clear the haze in her brain.

Again he asked, "Why, Miriam?" He sounded hurt now. "You have no idea what I have to do now, how much what you did could cost us."

Fear spiked down Miriam spine. She attempted to let her Nature take her, but she couldn't find it. It was like there was a fog over her sensitivities. Like she somehow was not herself. What was happening?

Then Seth was talking again, and this time through clenched teeth. "I hate myself for this. I will always hate myself for it."

He loosened his grip on her hair and moved his face back a few inches. Then he glanced at her lips and bit his own lips between his teeth. He let go of her entirely and took two steps back from her. It wasn't until he moved that she realized how much his arms had supported her weight and how the butterflies in her stomach were not butterflies, but nausea.

"Something in here," he continued and beat at his chest, "is forcing me to love you. I want you and I love you and I hate you and I despise you, all in the same heartbeat." His hands went to his head, "I feel like I'm going crazy. I'm so angry. This will haunt me, I know. But you have to understand it is life or death." He turned in a half circle as he pulled at his hair. "Why did you do it? If you hadn't done it, I never would have known it was you and this would not be happening. But I know it's you, and now my hand is forced."

Miriam's knees buckled under her. Seth caught her before she could go down. He lowered her to the ground and put his lips next to her ear. "Don't worry, it won't hurt you. It's just a drug that will put you to sleep." Then he gently kissed her cheek once, soft, mournfully. Then his lips met her cheek again, but harder this time, hard enough she could feel his teeth. Then he stood and walked away. Eyes bleary, mind cloudy, she couldn't put a thought together except to wonder what could be happening to her.

She couldn't fight the need to sleep any longer. As she drifted, one thought broke through the fog. There could be only one reason Seth so openly told her his feelings; he didn't expect it to matter, the way a deathbed confession didn't matter.

CHAPTER 9

Seth

Lilly, pale and limp, sagged against Seth making him push the stupid horse to move faster. Their plan was not to meet until ten when the sun was good and down. This had all moved faster than he would have liked, so Seth decided to take the horse and buggy to the compound.

Within ten more minutes, he took a left onto a paved drive. A massive, well-lit gate stood before him. A camera rotated his way. They must have recognized him, for the huge metal gate opened.

He nudged the horse forward, but before he'd gone more than a hundred yards, he heard the rumble of motors heading his way. Not knowing what to expect, he guided the horse to the side of the road and pulled up on the reins.

Only a moment later, three incredibly posh cars surrounded him. Out of two jumped armed military types. Their guns did not point at Seth, but he felt the weight of their presence. Out of the third car hopped a chauffeur type, who instantly pulled the back door open. Jeremiah and Willis got out looking polished. "Good to see you so soon, Seth. I trust all went well?"

Seth nodded and hopped down from the buggy.

Willis' companions all gathered around him, and their collective forward movement told Seth they wanted to see Miriam. He went with them to the back of the buggy. "She looks half dead. How much did you give her?"

That wrenched Seth's heart. "That's not her, that's my sister, Lillian. As you can see, we can't wait any longer to get her medical attention." He motioned them toward the back of the buggy and pulled up the coverlet.

Even in the darkness Miriam's glorious hair shone like captured moonlight.

"This is the memory thief? There is only one of them and it's this little girl? You're certain?" Willis asked.

Seth couldn't speak. He only nodded.

Just like that, the armed men put their hands on her. They easily picked her up and carried her to one of the vehicles. Jeremiah got in with Miriam, and before Seth could process it all, she was nothing but red taillights.

He took a few futile steps toward the leaving car, then turned to Willis.

"They aren't going to hurt her, are they?"

"That's not really any of your concern now, is it?" the man stated seriously, then considered. "Of course we aren't going to hurt her. We just need her out of the way." He rushed on. "Seth, you have done more than I can tell you. I never could have expected this. Thank you." He put his hand on Seth's shoulder. "Do you have any other news for me?"

"Like what, sir?"

He used his knuckles on his jaw again, "Well this might be a strange question, you said she used her memory power on you."

"Yes. She did."

"Have you felt a..." He paused knotting his eyebrows, "like a weird pull toward Edenia?"

Seth concentrated on that other sense. His eyes followed the little back-of-the-brain tickle. It was pulling him toward Miriam, not toward Edenia. Did he want Willis to know that? He decided quickly that it would not matter, if the soldiers he'd met before had the same ailment he had they would tell Willis. "Yes and no, now the pull is coming from that way," he answered and pointed toward the direction Miriam went. "It comes from her."

Lillian moaned, "Seth."

"I'm coming. Hold on." Seth turned back to Willis expectantly.

"Ok, well, good. That answers another question for me." The man clapped his hands together in absolute glee. He rubbed them vigorously and said, "This is quite sufficient. Again, thank you, my boy. This info is priceless to me. Now, I am nothing if not a man of my word." He reached into his pocket and pulled out a credit card. "As per our agreement," he handed the card to Seth. "This has no limit. Put anything and everything you could ever want on it. Medical bills, food, lodging, a car, I really don't care. I will pay any and every bill for the next month. That should give you enough time to get settled and get your sister settled. After one month, we will pay for any and all medical bills only."

Seth looked down at the card overwhelmed with awe and gratitude. "Are you sure? Brain cancer...it can be expensive...and I didn't find out where the tree is."

"Hush now." The man said and put the card in Seth's hand as he grasped his shoulder. "We Joneses care for our own. Lillian is one of us. I'm so sorry I have to see her this way. Anyhow, when the time is right, I have a plan that will get me what I want from the Edenians. In the meantime, we can keep the status quo going. Who knows, we may get lucky now that she..." He thumbed over his shoulder toward Miriam, "...is out of the way." He squeezed Seth's shoulder. "I am satisfied, Seth. Believe me."

"Okay. I'm really glad." It seemed clear Willis just wanted Miriam out of Edenia, not dead or anything. Though it did bother him in a peripheral way that he spoke of her like an object instead of a person.

Seth looked down at the credit card. This would take care of all his problems. He couldn't believe his luck. "Thank you," he added.

The man laughed, "No, no, Seth, thank you. My boy, words cannot express." He shook Seth's hand again. "Well, it looks to me as if you have more important things to do than to shoot the breeze with me." He pointed to Lillian as he backed toward his car. "We'll see you around, kid."

Seth waved completely stunned at how easy this all was. But then he thought, "Willis, sir, sorry, uhm can I borrow a computer or something? I need to arrange plane tickets and bus tickets and…"

Willis paused, then walked to his car. The driver got out and opened the door. "I'll do even better, leave the horse here, hop in with me, and I'll have James drop me at the compound, then he can take you to my personal air strip. We'll get you to the hospital of your choice before the nights over."

Unbidden tears flooded Seth's eyes. "Thank you. Thank you so much, Mr. Jones."

"I said call me Uncle Willy." The man sat in his car and motioned the driver over to Seth. "And it's my pleasure."

The driver came over and picked up Lillian as if she weighed two pounds and carried her to the car. She'd gone freakishly still, and Seth couldn't think about anything other than her well-being. Before the night was over, they would be in Baltimore seeing Doctor Lillehei.

For the first time since he'd found out about Lillian's condition, he felt relief.

CHAPTER 10

Miriam

When something sharp bit into Miriam's arm, the fog lifted. She heard a moan and realized her own mouth had made it. Never before had it been this hard to wake up. What was wrong with her? Her mind was buzzing from one thought to another and she couldn't latch on to any one subject. Though the dialog in her head seemed normal, the fluidity or control was not there. She almost felt like she was pretending to be asleep because her mind was awake, but she just couldn't control anything else.

Voices came next. At first, they were just deep and warbled together with no individual words, but then, slowly, she began to recognize a word here and there.

"stable"

"power"

"safe"

Then there was whispering.

"a weird sensation"

"know her"

"her eyes"

"can't kill"

"we do"

Then as if her ears finally tuned in to the sound around her, full sentences developed and understanding came with them.

"We both went in and came out without remembering anything."

"And we both feel it?"

"Yes, I can't leave this room without wanting to come back."

"Boaz, we can't tell them."

"I know. They might kill us if they know."

"You don't think it's just because..." She felt something touch her face. "...she is so beautiful?"

"I don't really think she's beautiful. I just can't stop looking at her."

"Are we weak?"

"No, I think we are under her spell."

There was a pause.

"I just thought of something." The whispered voice went even quieter. "What if everyone is this way?"

"We need to buy some time and watch."

"Yes. Who comes most often?"

"I'll look into the records if you take care of this on your end."

The sound of a drawer opening and closing and then a sharp pain in her shoulder.

"Copy," was the last word she heard.

CHAPTER 11

Peter sat up in bed, finally loosed from his state of forced solitude. Without thinking, he jumped to his feet and fumbled for the light. A moan came from the corner as he flipped the switch and Eve covered her eyes. "Peter," she complained, "What in the name of all..."

"Miriam!" he said as he pulled on his pants.

Eve finally blinked away the sleep and said, "You're up!" Getting up herself, she walked to his side as he buttoned up his shirt. Brushing his hands to the side, she lifted his shirt and examined his previously injured chest. "Well it's about time."

"Can I go?" Peter huffed.

"Yes, of course, and you're welcome," Eve said in an annoyed way.

Eve had probably not left his side over the last several hours. Turning away from the door he looked at her. "Thanks Eve. You... are...just, awesome." She smiled, and he swung the door open and took the two steps to Miriam's room. The moment he stepped into the hall, his gut clenched. Uncharacteristically, the door was ajar and all the lights were on throughout the house. Peter, followed by Eve, who must have also felt the strangeness, went toward the living room.

He stopped when he heard hushed voices.

"We know nothing about that boy?" His mother's voice spoke.

"He is Ezekiel's son."

"They probably are just having trouble with the buggy."

"What is taking Garren so long?"

He entered the room, and they looked at him. "Peter, are you up?" His mother's eyes went to Eve.

"Mama." Peter interrupted Eve's reply. "Miriam's in big trouble. We have to save her."

The blood drained from his mother's face. "What on earth..."

"Seth. He has a deal with the Joneses. They want Miriam, and so he took her. Seth took her to the Joneses."

"No," Peter's mother cried. "No, no, no," she repeated, pacing the floor of the Miller family living room.

Peter's father turned toward a window. The movement faced him away from Peter and his declaration that Miriam was kidnapped by the Joneses. Hirum Miller, leader of the Edenia, hugged his elbows and stared. His face became whiter with each passing moment.

Suddenly Peter's shoulders were in his mother's grip. Her normally blazing eyes frightened. "Peter Jonathan Miller, tell me every detail of what you know."

Peter stiffened his arms. This was time wasted, and he wasn't sure where to start his story. "Mama, Miriam is convinced..." Peter began, but Garren, Peter's elder brother, raced in through the door. He had Ezekiel in tow, and the imbalance caused him to nearly run smack into their mother. Luanne Miller stumbled backward a few steps and exclaimed, "Garren Christopher Miller, how many times have I told you, water Natures are not allowed to race into this house."

After ascertaining his mother was not hurt by the almost-collision, Peter took the opportunity of Garren's distraction to back a few more paces away from her. For some reason he felt unprepared to explain how he knew what he knew; he'd watched how Edenians had treated Miriam for her unusual ability the last three years and wanted none of it.

Garren didn't acknowledge his mother's comment. He was in his business mode and went straight over to their father. "I did not find them," Garren announced, even less concerned that he might be interrupting an important conversation. "But I brought him," Peter's brother added with a haughty look at Ezekiel Johnson.

The beeline Ezekiel made for Peter's mother seemed unconscious. But it made Peter think of a photo he'd found a few days ago. A young woman and man caught in an embrace, the young man kissing the woman's cheek tenderly. Peter looked at this older version of that once young man and narrowed his eyes.

It was evident that Ezekiel still loved Peter's mother, and if a thirteen-year-old could see it, then Peter's father was sure to. He couldn't imagine how that could go down well. Peter's father and Ezekiel were childhood best friends, and then brothers through adoption. But the majority of Peter's family did not know that 'Uncle Zeke' wasn't related by blood to the Miller family because Hirum Miller, Peter's father, had claimed him as blood. Though he only did this after he'd returned to Edenia six days ago. Before that, Hirum never mentioned his long lost 'brother'. Ezekiel was a name used only in hushed conversations, and only among the older generation, because Ezekiel was Edenia's one and only deserter.

Needless to say, no one liked to talk about that. Peter only knew of this little juicy piece of info due to his many eavesdropping escapades.

He wondered if the master called 'Uncle Zeke' back to Eden just to throw life into some sort of crazy alternate universe. Because that was what life was like now. For the first time in the history of Edenia, the Joneses had infiltrated Edenia, they were attacking often, and now they had Miriam, the one person with her strange Nature that could stop the Joneses very advanced ability to gain access to the garden. It was a time to try a Guardian's soul, that was for sure, and Peter was absolutely thrilled to be a part of it.

Thankfully, his mother did not respond to Zeke. She did not even look at him. She went so far in her not noticing him that she pushed right past him and stood before Peter. Her eyebrow rose as her hands went to her hips. Her laser focus trained on him. Again.

Peter cleared his throat and went on as if Garren never

interrupted. "Miriam and I found out that the Joneses used the Johnson's return to Edenia to infiltrate us. Seth was their pawn. He had a cellular phone, and it was not destroyed by the wind interference. He used it to make plans with the Joneses. Miriam heard him do it. I confiscated the phone." Eve, who'd followed him into the living room pulled the cellular phone from her pocket and handed it to his mother who gave it a terrified look and handed it off to Garren. "So..." Peter narrowed his eyes at Eve, letting her know they were going to have a conversation about her digging through his pockets. "Seth must have flipped out, or something. He probably found out who Miriam was, or more what her Nature is, and took her to the Joneses."

Stunned silence reined for a full heartbeat, but was interrupted with Zeke adding, "Lillian's gone too, and I think I know what this is about." He shared a look with Peter's mother.

The stunned, silent faces turned to Zeke, and Peter's father cleared his throat and impatiently said, "Speak man."

Zeke took a deep breath and looked at both of Peter's parents in turn. Then his eyes turned heavenward as he spoke these words, "Two months ago Lillian got diagnosed with a brain cancer called DIPG, diffuse intrinsic pontine gliomas. At first, we thought 'Oh, brain tumors, it's 2033, we can deal with that.' but no, DIPG is different. It's a fatal childhood illness. In fact, Lillian is rather old to be presenting with it. Still, it is one hundred percent fatal." He shook his head, his eyes on the floor. "There are barely any treatments for it, either. It's diagnosis...then funeral." Peter had never seen a more defeated man.

Hirum interrupted, his face still turned toward the window. "That was when you made up your mind to follow the summons and come here."

"Yes. We didn't tell the kids that was why we were coming here. In fact, we didn't even tell them the tumors were fatal. We said that there was an American doctor in Baltimore, Doctor Lillehei, who was doing some great things with combining medicines and diet for

DIPG patients, which is the truth. But we did not have to come here for that help. Doctor Lillehei was happy to share his regimen over the phone with my doctor and we have had Lillian on it for five weeks, now. It has improved her quality of life. But..."

As Peter processed the thought of Lillian with brain tumors, he felt confused. Edenians didn't get illnesses like that, so he didn't really understand.

Zeke continued. "This," he waved his hands down at the homespun he wore, "was not entirely about Lillian though. I *was* summoned. For a year I've been running into summoners. However, Lillian's diagnosis a few months ago was the biggest motivating factor in me considering that summons." Zeke looked at Peter's mother, and there was pain in his face and sadness in his eyes. "But I also am privy, as we have discussed, Hirum, to a view of the circumstances we find ourselves in as a global community, and that also affected my decision." Zeke cleared his throat and lowered his eyes and voice. "I know from history what comes next in this political atmosphere. We lived through the beginnings of it in Cairo. People get scared, they get violent. Marauders, rioters, mobs equal a breakdown of all services and attacks on authority, everyone becoming a law unto themselves. There is no place for my family in a circumstance like that... I just couldn't do nothing."

"You knew that living here in Edenia would heal her, or did you only *x* that it would?" his mother asked Zeke.

"I knew. And that was the only thing that could induce me to put my family through the change this place will force on us. I hoped the children would understand."

"Well, they can always just leave after they get what they want," Peter's mother spat in her scary, quiet voice.

His heart became less hammer-like as pieces of several puzzles fell into place.

Peter saw Seth's motivation in taking Lillian to a doctor because he didn't know or believe that Edenia could help her. He thought his parents had abandoned her. No wonder he had a chip on his shoulder the size of Baltimore. If only he'd known that one little detail, all would be different.

He understood how one choice could change the shape of many things because of the ribbon of time that now lived in his head.

Eating and drinking here must really be the magic some thought it was. So, his friend wasn't going to die as long as she got back to Edenia in time. He took a deep breath and quietly asked his mother, "It is true, then. Our food keeps us healthy, long-lived, and gives us our Natures?"

His mother nodded. "In a roundabout way, yes. More directly, it is the river Eden, which feeds this town. But it is a great secret. Can you imagine what would happen if the Joneses knew?"

That sent Peter's mind galloping off to how he'd told Abby and Lilly that exact information. "Oh, no." Peter whispered to himself.

Luckily, Garren had interjected a question that covered up his words. "Is that why you are so stingy with the food?"

"Yes. We can't give too much away. If it lasts more than a week..."

Esther was standing next to him, though he hadn't noticed her until she smugly said, "I tried to tell you that, Peter." Her face changed as she turned to her mother. "But I think someone else has figured this out, too, mother. I did not want to disturb Papa right now, but I just came from the orchard sentinel and caught at least twenty black-clad men stealing apples and pears."

"What did you do?" his mother asked, her full attention on Esther.

"I did not engage, of course. What could I do against so many? But I did ask the fruit to rot and wither away before the intruders made it back over the fence. It was the only thing I could think of."

"I know you hate to waste the Master's goodness, Esther, but you did the right thing."

Peter knew what this little intrusion meant. Seth had already told the Joneses, and they were on it like honey on bread.

"If the reports are correct, it is not the Joneses that are stealing. It is those forgotten members of society that are starving," his father added.

It was time for Peter to fess up. "It is both, father."

They all looked at him.

"I told Abby and Lilly that I wasn't sure about the food and water bit. Seth is with the Joneses, and I am sure he used that information to leverage whatever help he needs for Lillian." At this, the tension in the room finally bubbled over into excited conversations as everyone attempted to talk over each other.

A breeze filled the room and pulled breath and words out of each speaker's throat. It wasn't a very nice thing to do, but it certainly stopped the contention. Peter looked at his father's trembling irises, which vibrated and swirled as if the pattern of the wind were within them.

Watching his father use his Nature sent a need for action through him.

Peter had not been talking, so his breath was not gone. In the quiet, while everyone else wet their lips and sucked in stolen air, he took the opportunity to speak up. "We are wasting time. Lillian needs to get back here if Edenia is to help her. Miriam is in trouble. She is being hurt. We have to find them both, and we do not have time for argument."

The calm in his mother's voice rattled him. "How do you know she is being hurt, Peter?"

"I..." He paused. "I just know. Okay?"

His father's eyes turned to him alight with something; hope perhaps? Hope for what though? "Yes, Peter, but how?" The resonate, patient voice of his father asked. "Did the Master speak to you Peter, or did you see someone hurt her? Seth perhaps?"

Wanting to draw the attention away from himself he yelled, "Why are you not jumping up and running to help your daughter? Let's go!"

"Peter Johnathan Miller!"

His father held up a hand to silence his mother. "I am not

concerned quite yet, because I know the Joneses. I have been battling them for years. They do not hurt us. Besides, we need to consider this. Getting us to leave Edenia to save a child that they are probably not hurting is an effective way to get us out of the way." His father walked over to him and placed a hand on his shoulder. "Now, answer the question, Peter. How do you know what you know?"

Peter sighed and rolled his eyes as he picked the least revealing thing he could say to satisfy. "It must be the Joneses because I don't think Seth would hurt her. I think they..."

"They what?" There was a slow menace to his father's voice now.

"Can we just not talk about this? Let's just go to the Joneses." Peter felt squirmy, and he shifted his weight. "We are wasting time."

"No, we will talk about this now, young man. Speak up." He paused for a moment, but Peter did not respond, so he added, "Now, Peter." And his voice had that unnatural bite to it that meant he was using his Nature to tighten the words around Peter's ears, another not-so-nice thing to do.

Still, Peter jumped, and rattled out the truth of the matter out of habit. "I'm almost positive Seth would not hurt Miriam, even though the Joneses wanted him to look for her specifically, though he didn't know it was her he was looking for, of course. Miriam was freaked out about the whole thing, but she couldn't tell anyone but me." He realized he was rambling when he heard a surprised and frustrated exhale from his father and saw looks of fear on sibling faces, so he finished. "I just don't think he would do it because...because, I think he loves her," he spat out, and then added in a mutter, "as disgusting and questionable as that might seem." His tone betrayed his feelings.

His mother touched him carefully. "Peter, I need you to be very clear. What do you mean the Joneses wanted Miriam specifically?"

Peter thought, confused. "I've said it twice, how can I be any clearer? The Joneses know that someone has been taking their memories, and they tasked Seth with figuring out who it was."

The blood drained from his mother's face.

It was Zeke's turn to be shocked. "She can take memories?"

His pa answered, "Oh, she can do so much more than that, Zeke. They see what we do all the time. There's so many of them. The biggest fear is that they will decide they don't care about the tree any longer and just sell the information to the world."

"That would be highly problematic," Zeke added.

"And with all the attacks this new leader—Willis Jones—levels, we barely have time to live, let alone think of new ways to combat their attacks. We need new strategies, which was why Garren went to Korea to study combat strategies and fighting for his sabbatical. Further, there are fewer wind Natures than ever before, and with the plethora of electronic devices at Willis' disposal, we cannot keep up with every angle. I fear we are losing this war for the first time since the Native Grandfathers were slaughtered."

"I don't think the real war has even begun for you. The Joneses are a trifle to what will come next, what will come out of the world and to the gates of Edenia," his uncle commented ominously.

Peter was shocked. He'd never heard any of this talk, not even with all of his listening in on private conversations. How could they be losing the war? And the end? The end of what? Like, life?

"I told you things were happening," his father added. Zeke nodded to him and there was a look of concern in his eye. Peter wondered what it was for.

Peter's thoughts were interrupted by his father's voice.

"How could Seth even be in a position for Willis to know about him? Put the pieces together for me Zeke, because I don't feel like I know what's happening here anymore."

Zeke ran a hand down his jaw and shook his head.

"I told the kids my family was all dead," he replied in a hurry. "So, there was never any reason to talk about you, Edenia, or any of this."

Silence reigned, then mother finally whispered, "That does tie it all up nice and tight."

"Yes, it did, until Seth found something I'd kept from here." Zeke looked at Peter's father guiltily, then rushed on. "It was the pocket watch. I didn't even know what was happening, we were so busy with terrorists and Iranian suicide bombers, and the Egyptian government turning on us...but then my military liaison came to me with questions about some phone records. Why in the name of heaven they were concerned about a few phone calls when there were women and children dying in the streets, I have no idea, but they said it was because the guy was from the watch list. This man had called the house. With spies everywhere, and the mission of peaceful negotiations between the US and Egypt in the works, the Secretary of State—if you can even call her that anymore—determined I needed a little interrogation to determine my viability."

Peter's mother sucked in a breath. "Did they hurt you?"

He ignored her. "It was later found out that it was all Seth's doing. My superiors decided it was necessary for me to have a conversation with my son. So, I questioned him about it, and soon the truth came out. Seth posted the watch on a website called Lost-to-Found where an American recognized it and contacted him. It was Willis Jones' son, Jeremiah. Come to find out, the Joneses get their funds from some rather shady dealings. Jeremiah trades arms and drugs with some pretty bad dudes out of Mexico on a regular basis."

"You are kidding."

"Nope."

"How in the world is Edenia even on the to-do list of a man like that?" Garren asked.

"From what I gathered, immortality is more of a pet project for the latest generation of Joneses. A hobby. But Willis isn't a stupid man. He sees what is happening in the world. I am certain he wants immortality more than even his ancestors did."

"What did Jeremiah tell Seth?"

"The truth, as far as I can tell." At this point Zeke went quiet. He looked uncomfortable.

"So what did Seth do when he found out about the watch?" Hirum asked.

Zeke sighed. Peter would swear it was a sigh of relief. "Well, he didn't get the answers he wanted from me, let me put it that way, and since then, the trust between us has been strained."

"As it should be. What were you thinking, Ezekiel? Lying to your family. That is below you," Peter's mother chided.

"Come Luanne, let us not judge Zeke. How could he tell them?" Peter's father touched Ezekiel's shoulder, "Please, go on."

"Well, then, everything happened, the tumors in Lilly's brain, everyone getting nuclear weapons, and the micro-nuclear weapons, the USA pulling all the diplomats out of the Middle East, more summons, chaos in America. I just thought coming here was an answer to all of that."

"In one fell-swoop all your problems could be solved," Luanne whispered.

"The government was forcing you to come back to the US, so where else would you go but home?" Hirum added. "Might as well see your family for the first time in thirty years."

Luanne listened with a raised eyebrow. "And Seth would have all the answers he wanted..."

"...and be physically surrounded by his roots, which the poor boy has always longed for," Zeke said, looking at the floor thoughtfully.

"And you would get the summons off your back."

"But most importantly, there was the possibility that if the kids could accept Edenia, Lillian would be healed."

Zeke continued, "It seemed like a win-win."

Peter listened to all this and thought how perfect it was. So perfect, in fact, he started laughing. The adults all turned to him, so he said, "I'm afraid you got played, Zeke."

The silence that followed quickly turned into chuckles.

"I suppose I did," Zeke admitted, "and I deserved it."

Hirum added. "The Master has been at this game far longer and he has an unfair advantage, so don't take it too hard, brother."

That started more laughing.

When things settled down, Peter's mother looked over at Zeke and sighed. "I see the wrinkle in your brow and the dejected tilt to your mouth, Zeke. Let me guess, being here has made things worse." Peter's mother then looked pointedly between his father and Zeke before adding, "Secrets, big ones, often tend to do that."

Peter was interested in the look Zeke and his mother shared. However, his father stepped in with some analysis. "So, let me guess, the call from the Joneses allowed them to find you, our one and only defector."

"Exactly."

"From there, they must have kept track of you, and when you came back, they came up with a plan to get to Seth."

"Ironic, isn't it?" He looked again between Peter's parents, and Peter felt like a whole secret conversation was being had.

"But when did they have a chance to get to him?"

"Not that it really matters, but the only time I can think of was when we were at this restaurant not thirty miles from Edenia. Cairo doesn't have restaurants anymore. Not for six months, at least. So, everyone was excited. Anyhow, we were sitting there, and Seth needed to go clean up, something he'd done a dozen times on our way across the states. But he was gone for like fifteen minutes, and when he came back, he was different. Cold, angrier, more determined. I wondered about it at the time, but then we all got our food. Later, after we were done eating, we had to wait for the rain to stop, and so we just hung around in this gas station. Jenna found Seth talking intensely to a stranger. Her description was telling; military muscles and camo pants. I tried to ask him about it, but Seth was really ticked with me, he wouldn't talk, and he's not a child. I can't make him talk to me. So, unless they were on the boat with us, those are the only times it makes sense for him to get recruited."

Everyone stood around considering Zeke's story for some reason, but ten minutes had passed since he woke up, and they were not mobilizing to go get Miriam. He wanted to inspire haste, so Peter took charge. "Well. I feel like this topic has run its course. Shouldn't we be looking for Miriam now? She literally is being tortured. I know it," Peter interrupted.

"Your father says they won't hurt her, Peter." His mother said.

"Unless you have more information you would like to share, son?" his father probed.

They all waited as Peter considered sharing a secret he himself did not understand. However, he was beginning to understand that this was a major problem. He had no way to explain what he saw, how he felt, or what he knew, except he knew what he knew. It might end up that he himself would need to rescue Miriam. Realizing there was really nothing to share but his feelings, Peter kept quiet.

After only two seconds, Garren interrupted, "I have a question Uncle Zeke. How many times does one get summoned? I thought it only happened once."

Zeke looked at Garren and shook his head. Then looking down at the floor he asked, "You don't remember a thing? Not even a tickle in the back of your mind?"

Everyone in the room looked at Garren, and then back to Zeke. This threw Peter's focus off, and he wondered out loud, "What in the heck are you talking about?"

The sentiment was echoed in the faces of all present.

It was Father that caught on first. "Was one of them Garren, then?" And now the stares bounced between the trio, father, Zeke, and Garren. Everyone wondering at the mystifying partial conversation.

Finally, Zeke put everyone out of their misery. "When I saw you, Garren, I swear I thought the clock turned back thirty years. You look so much like your father..." Zeke took a deep breath and glanced at Peter's mother before turning back to Garren. "I was in Korea, negotiating a...well that's classified. Anyhow, I walked into a market, and you were on me in an instant. A weird hazy look in your eye. I was startled and called you 'Hirum' before you touched me and began the words of the summons. That was exactly one year ago from yesterday."

Peter was less impressed that the Master used Garren to deliver a summons than he was with Zeke's ignoring it for an entire year. "It took you almost a year to obey the summons?" Peter asked.

His father commented, "But I thought the summons only went out a few months ago." That also was an interesting question. Supposedly, his father always knew when a summons went out.

Of course, Peter's question was ignored and Zeke answered his fathers.

"A few months ago, Jenna and I were sitting in our car in Cairo bawling like two babies because we just found out that Lillian was going to be dead within a month or two. That her tumors could not be removed because they were in her brain stem." Zeke walked over to Peter's father and looked straight into his eyes and said, "Right then, in the middle of our grief, a Guardian knocked on the window of our car and spoke the words of the summons. That is when this idea was born, and I vowed then and there, in my heart, that if Edenia could save Lillian, I would come back here and do my part.

"I'm ashamed to say that after that, I doubted. I told Jenna all she needed to know because it happened right in front of her, and she was confused and sad, and it was a mess. But I did not go.

"Then the dreams began. Things at work were code red, and I worked around the clock with no time for my doubts or belief to take hold. But every moment of sleep was plagued with dreams. Then Iran launched its first successful nuclear bomb, and I knew that was it. It was the apocalypse." Zeke turned from Peter's father and knuckled his forehead, his voice breaking with emotion, "It was like, He knew... God or Allah or the Master or whatever you want to call Him, He understood with perfect clarity my struggles. He knew how I was in shock, and grieving and doubting myself; how I was afraid to tell my family how their being a part of me would affect their futures. But with that one fact on my side, 'the world ending,' I could say, 'It's not safe. We have to go to America.' It was perfect, because I didn't have to go into any more detail. Just: let's get out of here, everybody's going to blow everyone else up."

His shoulders crumpled, and a hand went to his mouth. Tears

slid down his cheeks. "That mercy of taking it out of my hands, taking me at my word that I would go, but making it so easy for me to do so, tipped the balance for me. I know I haven't been acting like I'm all in, but that is my pride." He looked between Peter's mother and father before going on. "I am all in. I will do my part, no matter what that part costs me."

Peter finally thought he understood why his father let this conversation go on when things needed to be done, besides not believing the Joneses were hurting Miriam. Zeke needed to prove that he was not with his son and the Joneses. Up to this point his actions could have been interpreted for either side.

Hirum Miller embraced his adopted brother, and the love that was in his father's face spoke volumes about how personally important this conversion story was.

Soon, the whole family gathered around Zeke giving him hugs and words of support except Peter and his mother.

His mother spoke up. "So, what I see is a boy confused about whom to trust, then ripped out of his home because a terrible war has started. So he's scared for his life, scared for his sister's life, and left with no information. Then he is forcibly brought here to a strange environment, and sees that, sure, he might be safe now, but what of his sister? Am I right so far?"

"We did try to talk to them about it," Zeke explained. "Seth understood the first night that something was going on. I ended up admitting our Guardianship over the garden but only because he asked me point blank. Now, I wonder if he was prepped in some way. He is a smart boy, but the story here is so far-fetched, no one could just come up with it."

Ezekiel's words attached him to the garden as a Guardian, and it felt weird how gratifying that was.

"Yes, that is strange," Peter's father offered.

From his mother, "How did it end?"

"We made a deal with them; if they would just try to fit in for one week, we would tell them everything."

"And they all agreed?"

Zeke was shaking his head before the question was out of mama's mouth. "No, Seth did not. He was very rebellious about the whole thing."

"So, now we have a smart, savvy boy locked in 'prison' for a week, with a dying sister, and parents who are, as far as he knows, delusional and not doing anything to save his sister. Furthermore, these crazy parents won't tell him anything about why they are doing what they are doing." His mother paused in her motherly way, with glazed eyes and tilted head, her mind certainly making necessary connections.

Finally she added quietly, "But this brave boy was presented with a way out." Her eyebrows rose, and she sucked in a breath. "At first, he probably dismissed the Joneses information. He might have thought they were nuts. But once he got here, he soon realized it would be his only chance to save Lilly."

Everyone in the room understood that Peter's mother was adept at understanding motives. It was one reason she was mad a lot. Because, in her words: *nine times out of ten the reason behind incorrect action sparks from selfishness or stupidity.* He could tell by her tone she did not think Seth's action selfish or stupid. They listened as she finished Seth's saga.

"So he is presented with a way out. The choice is easy, all he must do is betray the secrets of a people he has no loyalty to. But what did he get in return? That is what we need to focus on because it will probably tell us where he is."

Peter was surprised they didn't all say together: *Seth is getting medical care for his sister,* and was about to say it himself, but someone clomped up the porch steps and spoke through the screen door to them all.

"What is going on here?" It was Jenna. She didn't bother to knock on Butch—the screen door—she just let herself in. She was followed by a petulant Abigail. "Zeke, you've been gone forever. Do you know where our children are? I'm feeling uneasy." Zeke held out a hand to her. She pushed herself into his side as he wrapped her in a protective hug.

His mother went to the woman. "Seth has taken Miriam and Lillian outside of Edenia. That is what we know for a fact. We are trying to uncover the rest."

Jenna put her hand over her mouth. "But why?"

"He is taking her to the doctor."

Jenna's forehead wrinkled. "In Baltimore?"

"Yes."

"Oh my goodness," she whispered and her face went pale.

"He took her pills, mother. She will be fine. Once Doctor Lillehei cuts her tumors out, all will be well," Abigail said and smiled smugly.

Both of Abigail's parents looked at her, their eyes and faces shocked and angry.

"I would hate to think you had anything to do with this, Abigail," Jenna stated as Zeke yelled, "Abigail Johnson, you knew about this?"

Abby yelled right back, "Of course. You think I was just going to sit and watch you let Lilly die?"

Zeke's intense jaw muscles begin to clench. "Tell me the details of this arrangement instantly, Abby."

"Lillian could die!" Jenna squeaked and balled her hand in Zeke's shirt.

His mother stepped in. "Abby, listen to me. There are things your parents did not tell you about. Serious things concerning your sister. If we do not get her back to Edenia, she *will* die. You must tell us what the Joneses promised Seth."

The blood drained from Abby's face, but she complied. "Any and all medical bills paid and travel for Lillian and Seth, in exchange for Miriam. That's what he got. With Jeremiah's phone, Seth rescheduled with Doctor Lillehei, the appointment is set for tomorrow morning. So that is where they are."

"Oh, my," Peter heard his mother exclaim, and her eyes found Zeke's.

Peter walked to her and touched her arm. "What we need to know is where Miriam is."

Abby slowly nodded her head. "Seth took her. He drugged her, and I helped him put her in a cart so he could take her to the Joneses. He had to. It was the only way."

Zeke stepped away from his wife and towered over his daughter, face red. "It was NOT the only way! I was taking care of it! This might ruin everything. Lillian may die! Do you get that? Do you understand what you have done?"

Tears filled Abigail's eyes. Then one of her famous gushes came out, "Lillian was getting worse, and Seth and I were really freaked out, but then we figured out that Miriam was the one that Jeremiah was looking for. We just did it. Lillian was dying!" She began crying in earnest. "She's out there without me. She could die? How could she die, Daddy? Tell me what's going on." She ran to her mother, burying her face in her chest.

After a few moments of silent anger from all sides, the room exploded into action, everyone looking to his father for direction. "Perhaps we can get them back before they get on a plane."

"And Miriam?"

"Of course, we will get your sister. She will be unharmed, trust me. But Lillian...we do not want her out there dying without her family at her side."

"If she eats anything not from Edenia..." His mother added with an ominous look.

Hirum Miller used his wind Nature to call the essential people to him. With one whispered word from his father, the whole town could converge to begin a rescue mission for Lillian. Miriam was nothing but an afterthought. That bothered Peter, forcing him to make plans of his own.

CHAPTER 12

It was late, but Seth was almost hyper in his exhaustion—there was too much to consider now that he had Lilly's life in his hands —and he needed to conserve his brainpower.

The Joneses private jet was incredible, though. He remembered the last time he'd flown. It was three years ago, when they moved from London to Cairo. With the world going down, he never imagined he'd get to fly again.

Miriam would love this. He looked out the window at the black landscape speckled with lights, knowing instinctually which way he had come from. A piece of him stayed behind with Miriam. He gripped the amazingly soft leather of the armrest and forced himself to focus.

Should he take Lillian right to the hospital? Her appointment was at eight the next morning—though, according to the stewardess that might not matter, the hospitals were being overrun—but Lillian looked too horrid. She was losing the battle inside her again. She looked close to death. While in Edenia she seemed like she was in a stalemate most of the time. There were even some moments that seemed almost normal. Like, as if the real Lilly was with them, and not this tired creature she'd been in the week's prior to Edenia. Now, she looked like a zombie that hadn't lost any flesh or limbs yet. Her skin as pale as a sheet. Her eyes blood-shot. Her hands trembling. Okay, maybe, not a zombie, more like a druggie in rehab.

Seth pulled out the totally decked out iPhone XX from Mr. Willis Jones and checked the time again. Eleven on the nose. He clicked the awesome new device off, and thought of all the ways Willis Jones had proved to be as good as his word. He prayed he would be good to his word regarding Miriam.

CHAPTER 13

Miriam's consciousness jumped into her with the feel of lips to her ear. "...don't know what you've done to me you little witch, but I'll kill you before I let you control me..."

She heard a screeching drawer again, and Miriam felt blood struggling to pump through her veins as her fear ratcheted up. A scream welled up in her throat, ready to burst forth.

Then a door banged open. "Frank, what in the hell do you think you're doing?"

Miriam heard grunts and metal hitting the floor.

Then as if lightning struck her, mind and body connected. She sat up, her eyes blinking at the lights and the stark, metallic surroundings.

Glass hit the floor, and Miriam's eyes went to the men struggling on the cement. The one on the bottom of the wrestling duo had a sharp silver object, a scalpel perhaps, which he was attempting to shove into the other man's face. But the man on top was bigger and stronger. He slammed the bottom man's wrist to the floor again and again. Cracking it against the concrete until finally the silver object clattered across the floor. The moment it was gone, the larger man punched the other man soundly in the jaw; once, twice, and a third time. The other man stopped struggling.

The big man was bald, and his chest was as round as a rain barrel. He stood, his head seeming almost to touch the ceiling. Righting an upended metal cart, he picked up the scalpel and placed it carefully inside the squeaky drawer. Then he turned toward Miriam.

The moment their eyes met, she knew the man. He had entered

Edenia on a horse, he'd worn a gas mask, and he threw small green cans that smoked as he rode. It took several men and all the Natures combined to take him down. Ultimately, if he had not hit his head on a rock while falling off his horse, who knows how far he would have penetrated Edenia. Still, in the end, he'd seen too much, and Miriam was called upon to use her Nature.

This man's eyes assessed her now. "Are you hurt?"

Pressing her back against the wall she shook her head. "No, I am not." She looked down at the unconscious man. "Will he be all right?"

The big man laughed, "Wow. You know, Frank here, he was going to pluck out your eyes and then slit your throat."

Miriam felt the blood drain from her face. "How...how do you know this?"

"It's his MO," the great brute said, unblinking.

Miriam's wrists were loosely but securely tied to the metal frame of the bed she sat on. She pulled at the soft, silvery cords that held her, and all the events of the night before flitted through her mind.

Seth.

She yanked at the cords again.

Seth betrayed her.

She pulled at her manacles hard enough it hurt. Seth said goodbye and took her to her death. That's what this was—pre-death. Her eyes stung.

"That's fly rope," the other person in the room said. "You'll never get it off unless you cut it." His deep voice rumbled through the cement and cinder block room.

"Why am I tied up?" There was panic in her voice, and her limbs trembled.

"You don't remember?" The huge man took a step toward her but stopped and laughed, "Oh yeah, that's right. That boy, Seth, he drugged you. He's the one who brought you to us."

He hadn't answered her question, so she tried again. "How long have I been here?"

The big man checked his watch. "About three hours." He looked at her again. Not in a scary way; more of a curious way. Still, it made her uncomfortable. After a few moments, she looked away. That is when he approached her, free of hesitation. Soon, he stood right next to her and looked into her eyes.

"Do you know why?"

She shrunk back as far as the wall would let her. "Why what?" she asked, vague and apprehensive.

He whispered. "Why I," he shuffled back and forth, "I don't want to scare you, but..." he looked away. When his eyes came back, he whispered, "Why I feel connected, for lack of a better word, to you?" He used his big Frisbee-sized hand to motion toward her.

Surprise pumped Miriam's blood through her limbs again and she eyed the big man fearfully. "Connected?" she whispered back, confused.

"I'm not going to hurt you, I swear," he said in an even deeper whisper. "It's like, it's the end of the world out there but in here, it's all about you. I want to help you. I need to help you, and I don't understand why. Well, I had a dream. It made me think...uhm, I think you're some kind of angel calling to me... I don't know, that was just what I dreamed. Are you? An angel, I mean."

Two men in black with guns at the ready rushed through the door. They assessed everything in the room in a moment. "Gerald, what happened here?"

The big man, Gerald, turned around and stood at attention. "Sir, that idiot Frank had a scalpel to the girl's neck. So I took him down. I have assessed her, and I believe her to be frightened but unharmed."

The armed blond man kicked Frank's foot out of the way as he walked by, and Frank moaned. "Get him out of here, Gerald. And good work."

Gerald did as he was told, but before he left the room, he winked at Miriam. What in the world was she to do with that? Why would he wink at her? Was he telling her that he would still help her?

One of the men produced a knife and sliced through her bands.

Her adrenaline-saturated mind woke enough that it caught up with her circumstances. She was in the Jones compound. Seth had not chosen her. He had betrayed her, and drugged her, and delivered her to her enemies. And her enemies wanted her dead.

At least some of them did.

CHAPTER 14

Uncle Jai arrived first. However, he looked more confused than concerned, which bugged Peter. Uncle Jai's face was easy to read, and Peter knew him well. He could tell something wasn't right. Then Jai had a whispered conversation with Peter's father, in which his papa's eyebrows rose to an unusual height. This intrigued Peter further.

But it wasn't until his father rushed from the meeting he'd just called that Peter knew he needed to know what was going on.

Butch had no more slammed shut than Peter was out the side door. It was just enough time to see his papa and Uncle Jai racing toward the Eden Road. Pulling his Nature to him, he ran as fast as he could after them.

They headed toward the edge of town, and when he finally caught up to them on silent running feet, he saw what was so interesting. A stranger on an Appaloosa waited under a streetlamp near the town entrance. His horse pranced, agitated. When the man saw Papa and Uncle Jai, he hopped off the creature and walked toward them.

His papa slowed and then stopped a few feet away. "Hello, I'm the leader here. What is it you want?"

The man stopped. He was clean shaven, with short hair. He wore an off-white button-up shirt and slacks with boots. "Hello Mr. Hirum Miller. I am happy to meet you."

Papa and Jai looked at one another. They were probably wondering the same thing Peter was. Who was this man? Was he a go-between for the Joneses? Were the Joneses going to ransom Miriam?

"My son-in-law tells me you are from the tent city north of us. How is it you know my name?" With these words Peter realized just how off base he was.

The man smiled with perfectly straight and white teeth. So white, in fact, that they seemed to glow. "I know your name, Mr. Miller, because the Lord God Almighty has revealed it to me."

This statement shut everyone up for what felt like a long awkward period.

Finally, his pa cleared his throat and asked. "If you are sent here on the Lord's errand, I think I would know about it." As always, his papa used frank words, but his manner was so nice no one could take offense.

The man took another step forward and answered, "Pardon my saying so, but you have your mission and I have mine."

His pa thought for only a moment. "All right. What do you need with me?"

"I am here to tell you, before you go to rescue your daughter, to check the news."

"How do you..." Jai began to ask but Papa put a hand on Uncle Jai's chest.

"Well. Okay. Thank you. I wouldn't have thought to do that." When the man didn't say anything else, he only stood there staring at Papa and Jai. Papa asked, "Was there anything else...sorry, what was your name?"

"The name's Noah. No, there's nothing else. It's just not every day you get to come face to face with one of the Lord's Cherubim. I must admit, I am a bit in awe."

Once again, the men exchanged looks, while Peter felt confused. They themselves were not the Cherubim. They were the Guardians.

"How do you know that?" was his Papa's quite alarming response.

Know what? Peter thought. That this was the Garden of Eden or that they were Cherubim?

After the little revelation concerning the food and water, he was uncertain.

The man just looked at them, shaking his head in wonderment. With a sigh, he turned and walked back to his mount. "You're welcome, and I look forward to meeting you again," he said over his shoulder, then he mounted and galloped off without looking back.

"That was... I actually don't know what to say about that." Uncle Jai breathed in his Indian accent.

"Yes, well, I have an itch to follow his council, and right now. Jai, will you gather Wallace, Jeremy, and Brian? We will meet at Brian's house in ten minutes to see what in the world is so important that an outsider needed to draw our attention to it. Then I need you to find who all is responsible for maintaining interference tonight and tell them to cut it off in ten minutes or so. I have the schedule in my top desk drawer, but I think its Pepper, Marc, Ronda, and Phil tonight. Tell them when they see me in the quad, they know to turn it back on."

Jai nodded and was off as he blurred into a man of speed.

Quickly, Peter followed behind his father as he moved toward Uncle Brian's house.

CHAPTER 15

So far, it had just been questions. They wouldn't hurt her. Joneses captured Edenians hundreds of times, but in her lifetime, none had ever been harmed. Well, at least not that Miriam knew of. Of course, someone had attempted to kill her, but it seemed that man was rogue.

She'd been strapped to a chair this time, when the man who claimed to be Willis Jones re-entered the room. His stark white hair gleamed in the florescent lighting in contrast to his warm brown skin. He'd been the one to ask her many questions not ten minutes ago. Of course, she hadn't answered him.

What could she say, *Oh, yes, why not, Mr. Willis, I will just tell you exactly where the tree is, and how to get into the garden. No problem. I'd be happy to tell you everything you don't know about our Natures because, as you know, I have a Nature of my own, and yes, it's the one you hate so desperately.*

Still, he was a large man, and she was drugged, tied up, and in a dungeon filled with scary implements. The idea that perhaps he could hurt her with those implements forced her hands to tremble in their freshly replaced bindings.

Willis was followed by a small, sickly looking man with deep-set, hooded eyes and mousy brown hair. This man went over to the wall of aforementioned tools and pulled a cannister with a spout off the wall. Miriam watched him, and it made her voice quake that much more when she finally spoke. "What are you doing? Who is this?"

"This is Les," the intimidating Mr. Jones replied in his unusual, high-pitched voice. "He knows how to make people talk. It's his job."

At first Willis Jones' distinguished handsomeness threw her off, but now, as he watched her, she could see the wild, viciousness glinting in his eyes. Her gut again clenched in fear.

Still, she'd rebuffed his attempts to get information from her before.

"I won't tell you anything. You might as well let me go." She hated how shaky her voice sounded.

They ignored her as Les held up a shiny metal object, it was sharp and curved in a strange way. Miriam did not recognize it. She did not want to know what it did.

"Why don't you explain, in simple terms, what you're doing, Les. Just in case our Miriam here is unfamiliar with some of these terrifying objects."

Smiling and holding up the instrument to the light Les said, "I don't know Willis, it might be helpful for her to imagine this entering her skin and digging around in some atypical fashion and...areas." He purred the last word with a menacing smile.

Miriam couldn't help herself. She pushed herself back into the seat as far as she could and turned her face away from the men and their object.

"I see you are right." Willis said with a laugh.

"Why? Why are you doing this?" Miriam asked. She couldn't stop her voice from trembling.

This question woke something in Willis Jones.

He roared at her.

"Why?" Crossing the room, he bent and put his face a foot away from Miriam's. "How old do you think I am, Miriam?" he said with scary calmness.

The combination of this anger and this question made no sense to her, so she looked over at him. When their eyes met, she not only saw but also felt the anger there.

"How old do you think I am?" he asked again, slowly emphasizing the word old.

She had no idea. His hand slapped the armrest of her chair. "How old do you think I am?" he yelled in her face.

"I don't know," she sputtered. "Fifty?"

"Fifty-five, actually. For fifty-five years I've been obsessed with Eden. My entire family has spent their lives obsessed with Eden. Every ounce of my mind and money has been obsessed with Eden, and where has it gotten me and my family?"

In a moment of bravery, she looked him in the eyes and told him what she thought. "It's gotten you to the exact place you wanted."

Willis Jones leaned away from her, questions knotting his perfectly arched eyebrows. Yet he remained silent, so Miriam took the queue.

"Josiah G. Jones started this because he wanted wealth. He wanted to sell immortality to the world and make a killing. And well, look around you..." she chinned the modern and completely technological torture chamber. "Goal reached. You have more money than God. So why aren't you happy, or satisfied at least?"

Finally, something clicked in Willis' mind because he began laughing in a strange, high-pitched, hysterical way. "You," he still laughed, "You think this is about money?"

Miriam thought, and then answered, "I think it is only about something else because you have all the money you could ever want."

That settled him down. His face became angry, and she couldn't imagine how many years of unsatisfied conquest had put that anger there. He leaned in again. "I don't give a damn about the money. I want the tree."

Miriam's anger rose, she felt tendrils of her Nature swirl within her head and heart but it would not develop into a tangible force. Helpless to do what needed doing, she did all she could.

"You are so stupid. Do you not remember your history? Do you not remember every one of your relatives that have gone for the tree has died? My family has used every breath of our lives, every talent we possess to save you from yourself. Because understand one thing Willis Jones, you will never go near the tree. Never. If somehow you came up with a way to get past my family..." Miriam closed her eyes knowing that she very easily could be baited into saying too much.

Willis smiled, "Oh, don't stop there, my dear." When Miriam stayed silent, Willis sighed. "Oh, well, I didn't think this was going to be that easy." He stared at her, giving her one last chance. Stroking her cheek with the back of his finger, he whispered. "All that knowledge, in that pretty head of yours, will be mine soon enough." He leaned back and motioned the other man forward. "Les?"

Willis wasn't really going to let Les hurt her, was he? They'd tied Edenians up and questioned them, they even denied them food for a few days, but they'd never hurt them, really. This mantra ran over and over in her mind. It was about the chase. Her father told her that. If the Joneses really wanted to, they probably could hurt the Edenians badly, though he wasn't sure how. But he believed it would never come to that, because to them, it was all a game. Something to obsess over. Something to spend their ample gold on. That was why they never really hurt those they captured. According to her father. But perhaps it was more about who was in charge. Perhaps Willis was different from his father.

Les still had the silver instrument in his hand as he walked toward her. Maybe Willis was sick of the game, Miriam thought, as she watched Les pull a lighter out of his pocket and mash the grinders down. Holding the flame to the instrument, Les began to talk.

"Have you ever been burned, Miriam?" His muted green eyes raked over her like she was a piece of trash before returning to the flame and metal. He didn't wait for her to respond to his rhetorical question. "Of course you have. Who hasn't been burned?" He laughed a little to himself and the lighter went out. The end of the thin metal piece was red and smoldering. Dropping the lighter back in his pocket he came closer to her and pulled a switchblade from somewhere. "Hum, where should we start?" He flipped it open. The shiny edge pointing at her. His eyes and the end of his blade went up and down her body.

With a lean forward and a flick of his knife, the top three buttons of her tight blouse were gone, and the sound of them clattering to the floor coincided with her shirt spreading.

Miriam couldn't feel anything, couldn't think, this feeling of dread and fear was too overpowering. She couldn't react. Before a thought could enter or exit, Les leaned over her. He moved too fast. His face a foot away. The glowing metal an inch from her eye. Heat so hot the smell of burning eyelashes filled her nostrils.

But Les was speaking, "This is really simple. You answer my questions and you won't get hurt. You don't answer, you do." He moved the heat down her face to her neck and finally to her chest. "For starters we could see how the name Jones branded on this exquisite skin of yours would look."

"Les," Willis called from the corner. The man's head turned toward his boss. "Let's get on with it. I think she is sufficiently cowed. Look at her, she's wet herself."

Miriam was separated from her body. She couldn't feel anything, had she wet herself?

Finally, her mind was back with her. *Holy Master, what is happening? Please be with me and save me from this.* The prayer went out of her consciousness and to the ears of the Master. But before anything else could process, a question was asked.

"Can you take memories?"

Miriam couldn't turn away, she blinked, and her head nodded without her mind's consent.

Les smiled. "Good. Now, are you able to take memories right now?"

This time it was a little easier to answer. She shook her head the slightest bit.

"Okay." Out of the corner of her eye she saw Willis move closer.

"Is the Garden of Eden in Edenia?"

She hesitated.

Les raised an eyebrow at her.

Still she kept quiet.

Les raised a finger dramatically and touched her jawbone with it.

Then moved the finger down her neck, parting her gaping blouse a bit more as he went. He didn't stop moving downward until he reached the ridge between her breast and collarbone. She shifted her chest as much as possible, unable to stand the man's finger so near her most private parts.

Provoked, she admitted through clenched teeth, "You know it is."

His finger stopped. Holding her blouse open so her collar bone and upper chest were exposed, he asked, "Is the Tree of Life within?"

She couldn't shift anymore, and the man's hand pushed on her chest, so she didn't pause this time, to her shame. "Yes, yes. Of course it is."

She saw Willis now hovering over them. He breathed hard; his eyes wild.

"Okay, Miriam, I only have two more questions for you, and this will all be over." He repositioned himself waving the small branding iron in front of her face. "Is the Garden of Eden past the river, in the small grouping of trees at the exact center of your town?"

Miriam blinked. Didn't they know that already? Part of her mind was shocked. But she couldn't think. The heat of the brand came so close to her eye it was painful.

She wanted to answer him quickly. With asking easy questions first, he'd trained her to do that. But she held her tongue. How could she answer? Miriam thought back to her endowment day; the walk through the garden wood, the leading rod appearing before her, and then suddenly, the light.

She glanced at Les and hardened herself. She could not, would not give him what he wanted.

"Don't do it, Miriam. Don't stop now. I know you want to be a good girl. A helpful girl. I know you don't want this." He lightly brushed the tip of the hot metal against her lip. It sizzled and stung, and she screamed.

"Come on, Miriam. It's so easy. Just tell me what I need to know. It's one word. One syllable. Yes or no. You don't even have to say it. Just move your head. You can do it."

Miriam sucked in a breath and ground her teeth. Les must have noticed her resolve because the enticing voice stopped.

"You've already betrayed your people. What would they think if they knew how much you've already said? You'd be considered a traitor."

She bit her cheek.

"They would hate you and cast you out."

Nothing from Miriam. She would not allow these words to affect her. His words were meant to hurt her, to tempt her, to manipulate her. She would not allow it.

"Plus, I know you don't want to be scarred for life. Even if they took you back for not telling us, do you want to live among them with the name Jones branded on your chest? Because that is what is going to happen next. I am going to push this iron into your skin and hold it there until your skin sizzles and cooks and dies. Until there is a valley so deep in your chest, that when the muscle and skin heal it will shape the name JONES forever. Every single sluffing of new skin will be a testament to and a reminder of the pain you will have endured here. A testament of your cowardice. You will never forget. It will never leave you."

Tears flowed freely down Miriam's face. The picture he painted was poignant. Still, she had made a covenant. Could she break that covenant? Could she forgive herself? Would the Master forgive her? She knew he would, but what would that make her? The scars would not stay with her forever, Edenians did not scar. But the terror of this day might stay with her, and if she betrayed the Master or her promises to him, that would most definitely scar her. NO! Her eyes hardened and her teeth clenched. She would not say another word.

"So, it's to be the hard way." The man lowered the metal to her skin, and her mind really woke up.

Pain so intense squealed down every nerve and exited out of her mouth in the form of a scream reaching into the eternities.

CHAPTER 16

Willis kept on giving. When they arrived at the Rochester airport, a car waited for them. As they drove through the large city, Seth asked the driver why there were so few cars. It was only midnight.

The driver, a black man of middle age, remarked, "People are scared. There have been a lot of shootings, robberies, and that sort, so there is a curfew imposed. But don't you worry. Mr. Jones knows how to make those things go away." He smiled a toothy grin.

"But you're not scared."

He laughed. "Now that's not exactly true, but I've got mouths to feed. I know Mr. Jones. He pays good, so, I drive."

Seth was more disturbed by this than he wanted to admit.

"Well, the hospital is there." The driver thumbed to his left. "There are several hotels here, all empty. Travel is a thing of the past, I think." When they pulled into a nice-looking hotel, the driver spoke before ushering them inside. "I give you this one tip; be careful. People will shoot you as easy as looking at you in this neighborhood."

Seth adjusted Lillian in his arms. "I lived in Cairo for four years. I think I'll be alright. Thank you, though."

Before going into the hotel, Seth asked her if she wanted to go straight to the hospital.

"No. If they work the way they did in London, I will just sit there waiting in an uncomfortable seat or bed forever, and I just want to sleep." She'd also added in that annoyingly logical way of hers, "Besides, who wants to see an on-call oncologist? If SCRUBS is an authority at all, you don't want on-call doctors."

"I don't know if we should get our hopes up, Lilly. There might not be an on-call anything."

With her looking like Death's bride (in rehab), his gut told him to get her to the medical professionals ASAP, but she pointed toward the hotel and said, "Comfy bed."

And he had to admit, he too was exhausted and could use some sleep before facing the next day. He moved toward the check-in desk. At least at the hotel they could both spend a few hours sleeping without all the bright lights and interruptions.

CHAPTER 17

Peter hid in the same spot as last time, so he couldn't see the computer screen when his father exclaimed, "Oh my, powers of heaven help us." The council members present made similar exclamations.

An unfamiliar voice filled the small basement.

"Nearly 30,000 members of The Restored Church of Jesus Christ, from all over the world, with backpacks on their backs and hiking boots on their feet, are leaving their homes to hike across country, determined to make a new home in the heart of Missouri. They claim they are following the direction of the Bible and God's prophets to gather in preparation for the second coming of Jesus Christ. This migration, which started on all four coasts of North and South America, began four months ago. It has grown as the 'Saints' (as they call themselves) have picked up like-minded Christians along their way. The Saints intend on arriving in Missouri by the end of this week, where they say Jesus Christ will show himself.

"Many cities and neighborhoods have felt the strain of such a large group entering their towns. Though the group is respectful, they tend to deplete the supplies in grocery stores and disturb wildlife habitats with their large camp sites.

"There has also been an increase in travelers to Missouri by bus, car, motorhome, and airplane..."

When the voice stopped, Jai asked. "Are we going to have 30,000 people traipsing through Edenia in less than a week? Is that what he wanted us to be warned of?"

"It must be, but look at this."

Another voice began to speak.

"*There is utter chaos in the Holy Land this morning. This woman lost her home and her family when Iran deployed two devastating hydrogen bombs just two hours ago. Though she was not killed by the blast, it is certain that those bombs will be what take her life. Exposure has led to acute radiation poisoning.*

"*It has been two hours since the detonation that killed and continues to kill hundreds of thousands of Israeli civilians. As we reported earlier, the bombs were not dropped, but were meticulously placed and detonated in the most densely populated areas of Tel Aviv, eviscerating much of the city and devastating the rest. However, now that the dust has settled, radiation poisoning will be running rampant through the survivors.*

"*As you can see, my crew and myself have to wear these specialized hazmat suits to protect ourselves from the devastating effects of radiation exposure that fills the very air here in the Holy Land. Unfortunately, the everyday Israeli is not so lucky to have that protection.*

"*Despite the fires and earthquakes across the US, and the floods and extreme weather that have been plaguing Europe, relief efforts have been made for our allies in the East. Potassium iodine tablets or radiation pills have been coming in droves, but these will not help most of the people here. However, food, water, clothes, blankets, and medical supplies are scheduled to arrive within the next few hours. They will be distributed by the Red Cross, which is still hobbling along despite the recent scandals inside World Vision; but interestingly enough, the partner most visible here today is The Restored Church.*

"*The Restored Church has been under much scrutiny since it asked its members to leave their homes and gather to specified areas they are calling 'tent cities' over two years ago. Despite that, the RC is still offering aid to the Israelis and they are doing so in a big way.*"

The voice cut off and Peter tried to digest what was being said. However, a new voice started up right away. This time it was his Papa's as he read aloud.

"After the detonation of two atomic bombs, destroying most of the Holy Land, damaging the recently rebuilt temple, and killing hundreds of thousands of Israelis civilians, Iran has proven that all wartime rules of engagement are on the table. Though Iran has not shown its next card, our experts say that the longtime goal of invading Israel and taking back the Holy Land makes that action, nearly inevitable.

"Russia seems willing to make the next move. Correspondence between Russia and the White House has ceased, and experts say Russia quite probably is feeling pressure to put its own power on display. The possibility of that display not affecting us here in the United States is low. Russia and the US have a turbulent history, and with China at our financial gate, forcing the dollar into extinction, the US is vulnerable where we have always been the strongest, our economy. The Secretary of State had this to say about it. *'Russia will press their advantage, to be sure. That is if Syria, Lebanon, or Venezuela don't get to us first...'* This is a pretty candid remark from the normally tight-lipped cabinet member, and it seems to be having an effect. NYPD Commissioner Anderson said this only a week ago, and I quote, 'People all over this town are battening down the hatches. Pretty soon you won't be able to find a loaf of bread or bottled water anywhere. And don't assume you can drive your way out of this. The traffic will get terrible. Make other plans,' he recommends, and then adds a sobering, 'There's just something in the air this time. People can feel it.'"

Hirum's voice spluttered out only to start up again a moment later.

"Though the election is nearing its peak, the President and her administration are attempting to overturn the presidential term limits stipulated in the twenty-second amendment, stating a change in Commander-in-Chief at this volatile time will make America completely vulnerable. She has gone so far as to say she will use her emergency authority, as presidents have done in the past when viruses have attacked US citizens.

"Over the last seven years her abuse of the executive order has led her to believe that we as Americans will disregard all aspects of the Constitution. The twenty-second amendment..." His voice petered off again.

Peter didn't really understand the implication of what his father read, but he could tell by the reaction of the council members that it was serious.

For several seconds Peter felt a strange panic.

Suddenly it didn't matter that he had Edenia rigged; that he knew many of her secrets and that he ruled his own little kingdom here. He wasn't at the top of a game that mattered in the grand scheme of the world. Peter understood that there were many things in the outside he did not understand, and he felt small and scared and he wanted to go sit with his Papa.

"Wallace, I'm frightened." His father's voice trembled. "I believe the end is here, and I don't believe I'm ready."

"Who is?" Wallace answered in an equally humble voice. "The point is not to be so frightened that we can't act for the good of our people."

"I don't believe we will need to do much. If I hadn't gotten onto this ridiculous contraption, I wouldn't have a clue the world was falling apart. We haven't felt the effects at all."

Martin's voice chimed in, "Except the general sense of unease we've all had."

"And the increase in dangerous weather. I've diverted at least six tornadoes in the last month. I feel like I only do that six times a decade typically," his papa said.

"Yes, I thought the unease was just a result of Zeke coming back," Martin said.

"I'm sure that had something to do with it, Martin. But something else struck me, and it may make sense of a few recent happenings. It's interesting that the first report talked about The Restored Church. Hirum, what if one of The Church's tent cities is located outside of Edenia?" Wallace asked.

"I haven't told you all, only because I didn't think it important, but there is a tent city just two miles up the North Road," Papa said sheepishly.

"What?" Martin exclaimed.

Wallace's frustration was clear. "Why would you keep that to yourself?"

"Well, I know the extra visitors we've had are not from the tent cities. I've spoken to them. They are what I am calling tornado refugees. The weather has precipitated an influx of homeless people. That is why I don't have Miriam take care of them if I can help it, and I always send them away with food and supplies."

"You do, do you?" Wallace asked.

"Yes, that would explain a lot," Martin conceded.

"But why not tell us about the refugees or the tent city?" Wallace asked, raising his voice.

"I guess I didn't want to worry about it. It's just easier if our families assume every invader is a Jones. It's safer that way. The only other person who knows is Luanne. And the tent city people have their own means of living. They are very self-sufficient. Plus, they don't bother us. They have never come here as far as I can tell, and they cause no trouble. I send some of the refuges there when I can. I think they take care of them."

"A job we cannot do unless we want an incursion of unconverted Guardians," Wallace said.

"That is a good point, Hirum. How do you know you haven't given enough food to the same people that they will be taken by a Nature?"

"I suppose I left that in the hands of the Master."

There was silence as everyone pondered their own private concerns.

"Do you think the Joneses know about them?" William asked in his quiet way.

"I don't know how he couldn't," His pa answered.

"Willis is obsessed and getting desperate. This Seth business tells me that," Wallace concluded.

"Desperate people are blind," William whispered.

"And now that we're reading what is happening in the world, that explains the height of his desperation as well."

"He's afraid he's going to die," His papa stated flatly.

"Well, gentlemen, what are we going to do with this information?" Wallace asked as if the conversation needed to come to a conclusion.

It was his papa who answered after five heartbeats of silence. "It is a great concern, but for tonight, nothing. Not a thing, because I think the point to this information was the need to get my daughter back. Willis is desperate and desperate people are dangerous. Who knows what he is doing to Miriam?"

A voice yelled down into the cellar. "Hirum, they're back. Nathan, Jacob, Kaydra, Yolk, Weston, and the others. All of them, they have returned from sabbatical."

The Elders made sounds of shock. They hurried to shut off the computer and leave.

Peter waited until they were all long gone before he moved from his hiding spot, his mind whirling with the information he'd just heard. However, the only thing that stuck was getting Miriam away from the Joneses. If it was truly the end of the world, Willis would be desperate.

Peter didn't have time to wait for his father's plans. He would go after Miriam himself.

CHAPTER 18

"We thought you might like to see Les' handiwork."

The words were there, but they didn't sink into Miriam's foggy brain until a mirror was shoved in front of her. Her eyes felt blurry, and focusing seemed impossible. She heard someone moaning, but she felt too sleepy to care. Turning her head away from the bright light in front of her, she let her muscles relax and felt herself drift.

However, before she left all sensory disturbances behind, she heard, "Get Karl in here. He gave her too much this time. Doesn't he realize the time pressure we are under?"

The words fuzzed in and out of her ears like a bee buzzing, and then she heard nothing.

CHAPTER 19

Someone had left the barn lights on. *Irresponsible!* Peter thought as he moved into the barnyard. He spotted movement out of the corner of his eye as someone moved from the shadows and into the light cast by the barn. It was Josie, Miriam's used-to-be best friend. She had her hands over her mouth, her face full of shock.

The expression unnerved Peter. "What is it, Josie?" he called.

She shook her blonde head violently and gave a muffled cry.

Peter moved to her side. "Josie, speak. What is happening?" He took her by the shoulders and pulled her to face him.

She gazed down at him with grey, tear-filled eyes and shook her head again, but the action mixed with her expression looked like shame instead of sorrow.

Peter didn't have time for a weeping girl. "Spit it out, Josie, I have to go rescue someone."

This seemed to get her attention, and she opened her mouth, "I don't know what to say, how to explain. I feel like an absolute freak."

"We all feel like freaks. Speak!"

Cowed, Josie started speaking, "Ever since Miriam's Nature took her in my kitchen...I have been able to feel her." She covered her face and turned away and muttered between her hands, "Peter, she is not in Edenia any longer. She is far away." She raised her hand from her face to point toward the Edenia exit. "She's there."

"You know where she is?" Peter asked, excited.

"Yes and no. I can feel where she is, yes, like the general direction, but I can't tell you where that place is exactly."

"Well, I'm going to go get her. You've got to come with me."

She shook her head before he even finished. "No, I can't. I can't let anyone know. It's shameful."

Peter looked at her like she was crazy, "What's shameful?"

"Never mind. I have to go." And with that she took off running.

Peter shook his head, uncertain what that was all about, and continued walking. When Peter rounded the corner into the barn, he was surprised to find a weeping Abigail. She looked up at his hasty entrance and turned away from him. He was absolutely mad at her. He would totally punch her in the face if she were a boy his age and size, but as it was, he just ignored her.

Pulling his satchel from his special hiding spot, he checked to make sure he'd reorganized it. Shoelaces, check. Rope, check. Flashlight, check. Bandages, check. Knife, tape, glue, check. He had no idea if he'd need these things, but it was better to have them than not. He went on. Magnifying glass, tin can stuffed with socks, paper clips, thumb tacks, screw driver, check. Two shriveled apples. Well, that wouldn't do, he was a growing boy and needed vittles to sustain him.

Turning, he began for the door with plans to sneak food from his mother's kitchen, but a loud sob and a squeaked word from Abby's direction stopped him. "Sorry." Sorrow overwhelmed Abigail's voice.

Peter turned to her with the words, *you should be* in his mouth, but when he saw her stricken face, his anger softened. He didn't have time to even consider a response because Abby was off on one of her tangents.

"I never, in normal life, would do what we did. It's just...she's my twin. I've spent every moment of my existence with her. It's impossible to imagine her dying. I can't live with myself if she is dead. And you didn't see her, Peter. She was at death's door. If Seth didn't get her to the doctors within hours of them leaving here...I'm sure she's dead already. She has to be. Peter, she was so weak when they left. And Dad brings us here to this ridiculous place. No doctors, no treatments. We had to do something, and then Seth had this way out, and we knew it was the only way. I know you care for her. I know you don't want her to die. Please say you understand why I did what I did and say you can forgive me." She pled with her eyes, as the tears overflowed.

Peter didn't forgive her, though. He understood, but he didn't forgive her. The thought of Miriam being tortured because of her betrayal forced anger into rage.

Coldly, he glared at Abby. "You know what is so sad, Abigail?" He laughed bitterly to himself. "What is so very sad is that your father is right. The only thing that can save Lilly is this." He shuffled through his sack and pulled out one of the old apples and threw it at her feet.

She bent down to pick it up. Sniffing, and with a question on her face asked, "What? What do you mean?"

"What I mean is if you would have waited until the seventh day, today, your precious Lillian would be alive and well and cancer free."

Abby's eyes widened. "What? What are you saying, Peter?"

Peter was really annoyed now. "Listen to me. Your ridiculous plan has only done harm to your sister. She would have been healed at this moment but for you." Peter spat out the last part hoping in a small part of his heart that it would hurt her, the way he was hurt. Then he turned and walked out of the barn.

However, the instant he walked away he felt sorry that he'd done it. The anger burned away, and he realized he didn't want her to feel as bad as he did. Slowing his pace, he considered turning back to apologize but just when he decided not to—he was in a hurry—he was plunged into darkness as the barn lights went out.

Running steps sounded behind him. He turned and stood in the moonlight until Abby reached his side. Her eyes showed hope. He hadn't hurt her.

Great. He guessed that meant he didn't need to apologize.

"What now?" he asked in a gruff voice.

"What?" she said, with all the tears scrubbed from her eyes. "I think you are the most wonderful boy in all the world, Peter Miller."

And before he could do anything about it, she leaned in and kissed him on the side of the mouth.

An unfamiliar warmth spread through Peter's body. His eyebrows raised, and the moment slowed. A girl's lips had just touched him for the first time ever. (Dorothea's baby kisses didn't count.) His skin tingled, and he felt some pretty awkward sensations running up and down his body.

"What, what was that for?" Peter stuttered.

"That is for giving me hope that Lilly can live."

Peter sobered. "Abby, no..." His words were stopped when she put a finger to his lips. This again made him tingle.

"They only left a few hours ago. It takes hours to arrange travel, especially these days, and Seth had to talk Willis and Jeremiah into taking Miriam instead of giving them the information they wanted. I think it entirely possible that they are all still at the Joneses. If we can get there in time, we might be able to stop them from leaving." She pointed at his satchel. "I'm assuming that is where you and your sneaky self were heading." She smiled and raised an eyebrow at him as she folded her arms.

This girl was impressive, and crazy selfish. Still, in that moment, he almost loved her. She was his equal on so many levels. He just felt an overwhelming desire to run his fingers through her black hair and...

He slapped his own face, turned and rushed away from her. She was the reason Miriam was being tortured, her and her family.

She called after him in a confused voice, "Peter? Peter where are you going?" She started muttering. "Just when I think we are getting along, you go and make me think you're a lunatic." Then louder to him, she asked, "Why do you slap yourself in the face?"

He didn't answer, just kept walking. He had work to do.

But she stopped him with, "Peter, I'm coming with you."

He turned then, and she almost ran into him. He pushed her back, careful to only touch her shoulders. "Oh, no you're not."

She pushed his hands away, "Oh, yes I am."

"No, you're not."

"Yes, I am."

"No..."

"Yes," she interrupted, but went on, "How are you going to get past all the security and the video cameras and the guards? You probably don't even know what those things look like. Do you? Do you have video cameras here in Edenia?"

Peter hadn't thought of that, but it still didn't matter. He pointed to himself, "Me, invisible. You, not so much." In his mind that was all he needed to say so he turned and began walking again.

She was on him in a moment. "But you don't know how buildings on the outside work. You don't understand how they are laid out and how to get in and out of them."

"I assume they have doors?"

"Yes, but what if they have a keypad?"

He paused, "What's a keypad?"

"You see, you need me." Peter considered. While he did so, Abby wasted no time in convincing him more. "Plus, who do you think they will believe? Me or you? If I go in and tell Lilly that this place will heal her, she will know I am telling the truth. If you go in and tell her that, she will just think you are trying to get her to come back here and get Miriam back."

That was a valid point. "Yes, well, if getting her and Seth back were my objective, I could see how you would be useful, but I have no intention of bringing Seth back here. I am going for Miriam and if Lillian wants to come too, I will not deny her."

Abby pulled on his sleeve so hard that he had to stop or be knocked off his feet. "Peter Miller, how dare you? What ever happened to forgive and forget?"

Peter yanked his shirt out of Abby's hand and said, "I find it so interesting how people with no moral compass at all, always insist on being treated fairly. You can kidnap my sister and give her to her enemies where she will be tortured for information, but me, I can't even talk about how I have no intention of bringing your brother back here without being a hypocrite."

Abby wrinkled her forehead at him, her eyes darting away. She was not stupid, but she said something that surprised him. "Do you really think they will torture her? We were convinced they would just keep her out of the way."

Peter rolled his eyes and shook his head then he turned. "Of course, they will hurt her. Haven't you noticed it's the end of the world? Everyone is going to want immor..." it was at that point that he realized he should shut up. "I am a Guardian, and Miriam, who is another Guardian, needs my help."

Abby looked at him, confused, and then she laughed. "You, you're a Guardian?" She put hand quotations around the word. "A Guardian of what? The Garden of Eden? Come on, give me a break."

Peter wanted to stop to answer her chagrin, but he didn't. He just spoke over his shoulder. "So, when this being Eden can heal your sister, you're all like, Peter you're the most wonderful boy in the world. But when I tell you I'm a Guardian—and you have seen me do my job, by the way, I seem to recall some bloody knuckles—all of a sudden it's a joke." He rolled his eyes, and since she was following him still, he called his Nature to him and felt the invisibility cover him like a warm mud bath.

"You have a poi..." Abby began then interrupted herself with, "Hey, that's not fair."

She could not see him or hear him, so he felt bold. Leaning in close to her, pulled back his Nature from his lips and he whispered, "All's fair in love and war."

He heard her mutter back. "Which are you claiming this is, love or war?"

As he left Abby behind and moved to his house to get supplies, he thought about that question. Did he love Miriam? He guessed he did. She was his sister. Did he love Lillian or Abigail? No, he did not. He liked them. He felt like they were kindred spirits. Was he at war with the Joneses? Yes and no. What they had was not really a war, not anymore. Not like ones he'd read about. Still, he felt like he was at war.

Now that he had grabbed a few apples and bread from his house, he thought of what Guardianship meant in this scenario. It meant protecting. He yelled inside his mind; *Hold on Miriam. I'm coming.* His thoughts continued to plague him as he silently raced back toward the stables.

CHAPTER 20

Seth hadn't realized he'd fallen asleep, but he awoke to the sound of the TV in the middle of the night. Before he opened his eyes, Seth recalled a dream with startling clarity, or perhaps it was a thought he'd just had as he was waking up.

He saw a guy on a white horse toppling backward and crashing to the ground. The young man was not familiar to him, but Seth seemed to know every feature of his face. Something else that was strange was Seth felt absolutely certain that the guy would do this, like in real life, and that Seth was supposed to help him. It was a strange feeling.

He turned to see Lillian curled up in a ball with a look of pure terror on her face. When Seth sat up, Lilly asked him without looking over at him, "Do you think Dad knew Iran was going to nuke Israel?"

Seth blinked away the sleepiness, feeling shocked. "What?" He rolled out of his bed and moved to hers. Taking the controller, he hit the volume.

The reporter looked frightened, as smoke, fire, and running people lit up the scene behind him. Seth listened to the man describe the events of the bombing raid on Israel, how hundreds were dead and the brand-new Jewish temple was damaged, but not destroyed.

Seth's gut wrenched. "I don't know. It's not like Dad to run from a fight," Seth answered by rote, but immediately realized his mistake. That way of thinking was out of date, untrue, even on the verge of brainwashed.

Lilly looked about as if she'd lost something. "I'm watching this and it feels, like scary, the beginning of something big, like everything has been building and building, and now someone just threw the switch, and we need to run for cover."

Seth admitted to himself that he felt the same way. The news made it look like the whole world was lit up. Every country taking sides, bombs going off everywhere, and thousands of civilians dying.

"Seth, what's going on here? Is the world really going to blow itself up?"

Seth shook his head, "I don't know." He continued to listen to the news report. The longer it went on, the more frightened Seth became. China was threatening to invade the whole world and Russia was right at China's back. This Israeli bomb completely set the Middle East on fire. All of Europe called for war. The newsman described how peace, at this point, was impossible. However, he emphasized that though there had been suicide bombers and shootings, no country had formally declared war on the US yet.

A very real sense of terror raced over Seth's body. That could not last for long. In the last few years, the US had cut off aid to almost every country in order to pay the piper, China. But they'd made a lot of people angry in the process. The only things keeping everyone from coming after the US was their own internal issues, and a recently beefed-up US military. His dad was part of that.

If someone attacked the US, though, Seth was sure the global non-aggression toward the USA would collapse, and there would be a power surge for American resources.

Seth couldn't help but consider how all this would affect Lillian's treatment. He knew it would last weeks, perhaps months, to get her better, and she would be practically helpless after brain surgery.

She proved her thoughts were in the same vein when she said, "I'm so glad we are here instead of there. Do you think this is going to affect America?"

Just then the news anchor added this comment, "How the president reacts will greatly affect America's future."

In Seth's mind these words rang over and over. A sense of

desperate urgency prickled his skin. He had to get Lillian taken care of first thing in the morning.

CHAPTER 21

Peter

So, going invisible wasn't enough to keep Abigail from tailing him. Once at the stables, he let go of his Nature only to find that she was right behind him. She proceeded to make such a nuisance of herself he finally gave in and talked to her. "Bug off. I am in a hurry."

The moment he acknowledged her, she stepped out of his way and let him finish saddling the horse. "I know you don't want me to, but I'm coming with you."

Peter stopped his work and looked at her. The look lingered, and Peter couldn't help but think of the kiss. His eyes involuntarily moved to her mouth. She smiled knowingly. Peter shook his head and turned away from her.

After a few moments of quiet rustling leather against leather, Peter softly commented, "You know we are not really cousins, right? Not by blood, anyway." His mind was going a million miles per hour with a hundred things to say. Why had this been the thing he came out with?

She moved to his periphery and touched Marigold's flank. She was a gentle mare, so she tolerated Abby's touch patiently. He glanced at her quickly and away again, his hands moving mechanically through his task.

Her voice was also quiet when she spoke. "What do you mean?"

"You're smart, you figure it out," he said brusquely and footed the stirrup. In one smooth motion he pulled himself into the saddle and steadied Marigold, who danced forward.

Abby stepped away from the animal and looked up at him. "Please don't leave me here," she pleaded.

There was only a small chance of her being useful, still if that chance arose without her being there, it would ruin all his plans. Perhaps they could come to an agreement.

He put out his hand to her, but when she reached for it, he pulled it slightly back and said, "On one condition."

She folded her arms and raised an eyebrow.

He assumed that meant she was listening. "You have to do as I say."

Now both eyebrows were up, and she scoffed. "Do as you say? I don't think so."

Peter stared her down, waiting. She didn't back off, so he shrugged. "That's fine." And he put his heels into Marigolds side. The mare moved forward only two steps before Abby was grabbing his pant leg.

"Okay, okay." He pulled on the reins and looked down at her. "But at least qualify the condition a little more."

"It's simple. Do as I say."

"Well, if you say, *kiss me again*, am I contractually obligated to obey? Or what if you say *clean up the horse's poop*, what then?"

Peter considered this and decided he really liked the way this girl's mind worked. He watched her for a few moments and saw vulnerability in her eyes, in her shaking hands, in her nervous stillness. This was not something he expected from Abby. She was so tough and hot-headed.

Wanting really badly to give her a hard time, he joked. "I don't know. Like I said we aren't cousins, so I suppose I could in good conscience oblige you, if kissing is what you're after."

Her eyes went wide, and she looked at his lips. After a moment of considering him, she answered, "I do really miss kissing." Her voice sounded dreamy, and she took a seemingly involuntary step toward him.

She must have noticed his surprised blushing or his nervous blinking, because she stopped and looked away before turning back and brazenly asking, "You're allowed to kiss here?" Her eyes seemed to smolder, and she took another step forward. She was right below him, her head tilted way back, her face shining up at him.

There were so many things he wanted to say, to do, but his mouth went dry and his head became light and empty.

Marigold sneezed and walked forward away from Abby. It broke whatever trance he was in. Peter shook himself and realized he'd dropped the reins. He cleared his throat as he gathered them back up and stated, "That was a joke. What I mean is; when I say stay, you stay; when I say be quiet, you pretend you're dead you're so quiet, and when I say go, or run or whatever, you do that first and ask questions later."

Abby nodded demurely. "Is that all? Are you sure?"

He looked away from her. "Yes, it's what I said, isn't it?"

"Okay."

He assumed she was agreeing with him, so with reins in one hand, he again reached for her with the other hand. When he looked at her though, Abby had the smuggest smile on her face and her eyes danced with triumph.

He'd been bested, and at a game he started.

Admiration for this girl using his hand to propel herself into the saddle behind him, skyrocketed, and he was certain the ride to the Jones would be unbearably distracting.

CHAPTER 22

Miriam

The smell of charred flesh sickened her stomach and befouled her mouth, but somehow also lurched her into a more conscious state. The moment Miriam's brain changed from a slug in her skull to a semi-functioning organ, she felt her chest burn with pain. Though, somehow, it didn't hurt quite so much this time. It still stung enough to make her whimper like a child.

"Welcome back," came the voice.

Back? Miriam questioned herself. She blinked at the excess water in her eyes and was confused at why her mind felt slippery. One sensation she didn't wonder at was the shiver the voice and the words 'welcome back' invoked. Her whole body contracted in fear. Every muscle. Including those in her chest. She instantly felt the consequence of this reaction. A raw cry of pain tore from her mouth. Her hands forced into claws and attempted to reach protectively toward her décolletage, but her fettered wrists stopped her.

Once again, her thoughts and reasoning slid around in her skull. In her agony she wondered if she would pass out. She hoped. But the moment lingered, and the pain did not cease with encroaching blackness. Consciousness remained, and she suffered.

CHAPTER 23

Peter

It was at least three in the morning, maybe past that. Peter remained quiet, basking in the way Abby gripped his middle. They'd started out at a trot and she'd wrapped her arms all the way around him. But that was too jarring, so they'd galloped, which made her hold on even tighter.

Marigold didn't get enough exercise and could only keep that pace up for a little while. By the time Peter and Abby saw the lights of the compound from a distance, Marigold was walking, and Abby only held onto the back of his shirt. He even enjoyed that, though.

Perhaps it was the lights, or maybe the pace, but regardless, something broke the spell of their connection and Abby spoke up. "I hope that they couldn't leave. I hope the Joneses demanded answers, questioning them all night, not allowing them sleep or whatever men like him do, even torturing Seth, just anything, but not let them leave."

Peter thought of the dark place with the ribbon of time in it. As he waited, not able to awaken, he watched Miriam's thread. He saw in his mind how it bent and twisted terribly in her future. It looked like a blade of grass someone curled by running a knife down the length. All the threads in Miriam's future would have to make room for all the twists and damage done to her thread. They would have to weave around her pain if they wanted to be near her.

Finally, he answered Abby. "I don't think you understand what you're saying, Abby."

He felt her body stiffen. "Of course I do. I would rather them torture Seth than have him so far away there is nothing any of us can do."

"Well, I gotta hand it to you, at least you know where your line is drawn."

"What is that supposed to mean?"

Taking her tone into account, Peter figured it was better to just drop it. "Never mind."

"No, I want to know what you mean."

"Can we just drop it? Look, we have more important things to consider right now. Like, I need you to tell me what all that camera-this and security-that you were talking about before is all about."

"Hmm, I need you to tell me something and you need me to tell you something. Interesting. It seems we are at an impasse." She let that hang in the air.

Man, this girl was a force to be reckoned with. He was not about to tell her about his Nature; he hadn't even told his family about it. It just seemed creepy and weird, and frankly, something that should be happening to Miriam, not him.

So, they sat in silence. Marigold plodded along, and Peter tried to ignore Abby. He thought about the trees and the water and the ground and the road and the owls and the woods and the lights ahead. But all of that took him only a few seconds, and he was back thinking about her hands brushing his back. So, he forced himself to remember that this was all her and her sibling's fault. Finally, he felt some relief as anger bubbled up.

With that clarity of thought, he imagined what he was going to do when he got to the Joneses. He came up with the same plan he'd formed in Edenia; let his Nature take him and then follow his gut. Simple.

His mind wandered.

His daydreams of being kissed were interrupted by a frustrated Abby. "Oh fine. I'll tell you what you need to know."

Peter grinned. One point for him; tied game.

Marigold continued toward the Jones compound as he thought and listened attentively as Abigail described some pretty amazing technology.

CHAPTER 24

Earlier, after the second branding/questioning/screaming session, they'd unbound her again, and she'd dared to touch the tender, flaming skin right below her collarbones. The moment her fingers bumbled over the concave shapes burnt into her, agony both mental and physical struck her. Panicking, she immediately dipped her chin to see if she could look at herself but the motion tightened the epidermal layer and contracted the muscles across her chest. That movement caused immediate unconsciousness.

Perhaps she'd try it again. Unconsciousness sounded wonderful right now; no pain.

What they were doing was working. She was giving in. She wanted to die, to be out of her body, to never experience this pain again.

I can't take much more of this. I might do anything they want to make this stop. How can I trust myself? Help, please. Her plea went up to the heavens, she was sure. She focused on that thought.

CHAPTER 25

Peter

Peter tied Marigold to a tree in the woods on the north side of the Jones compound. He and Abby walked from there. They used his flashlight because the sunrise had not fully penetrated the woods.

After trekking through some dense forest, they came to the outskirts of the compound. A sturdy, well-maintained chain-link fence surrounded the property, with large box lights every so often.

Abby looked around. "This doesn't seem like an electrified fence, and there isn't barbed wire at the top, so at least that's not an issue."

"Not that either of those things would bother me while I'm in Guardian mode."

She ignored him, "Also, I don't see any cameras in the trees. Still, you never know, they could be there." She paused and looked to him.

"I'm invisible. Why do I care about cameras?"

She rolled her eyes. "You're a snob, you know that?"

"Bitter? Jealous? I understand, I would be too." He shrugged.

She punched him in the arm and glared. "So what, do we just climb over and walk in? What's your plan from there?"

Peter didn't answer, he just pulled his Nature to him, but he did it slowly.

"Hey, what..." Abby started when he went invisible.

Peter cut in before his Nature completely took him and quickly said, "I am going to go have a look around, and you are going to stay here like a good little girl. I'll be back." Before he finished this speech, he'd stepped from the trees and began climbing the fence. He ignored her protestations.

After Abby's spiel about security cameras, keypads, entry alarms, retinal scanning, and the like, Peter was no longer certain he could get into the compound by himself. Nevertheless, he still would have a look around to see what guards there were before involving Abby.

The technology she'd detailed seemed otherworldly. Certainly at some point in his education in Edenia, these things would be taught, but for now they blew his mind. It also caused an appreciation for the work the wind Natures handled day in and day out. It was because of them that electronics didn't work in Edenia. According to Abby, electronics were the number one tool for outsiders.

Peter made his way silently through the manicured grass on the other side of the fence toward the first of several cinder-block buildings. Circling around the first, he came to the door, and his heart sank. It had a keypad. It looked just as Abby described. Peter glanced around and saw the little round glass orb that had to be a security camera. Again, it looked just like she said it would. Knowing he couldn't be seen, Peter pulled on the handle and surprisingly the door came open.

Smiling, he stepped inside and understood why it was unlocked. The building was one big room full of junk, boxes and old tools. A canoe that had seen better days lay on its side. A disassembled showerhead lay coiled on the lid of a box. Right in front of him was the bottom half of a shovel, with a roll of duct tape clinging to the broken end. *What idiot thought he could duct tape a shovel?* Peter wondered.

He turned, left the building, and headed for the next one. This one was long and narrow. It was locked when he tried the handle, but there were plenty of windows. Unfortunately, they were high, and there wasn't anything to step up on. Desperate to see what was inside, Peter grabbed onto a window ledge and pulled himself up. His feet scraped silently at the building trying to gain purchase, and finally he managed.

Inside, he saw rows and rows of bed frames. Metal ones with mattresses, some of them looked lived in; most did not. Letting himself down slowly he made the decision that Miriam would probably not be in any of these buildings. The rest were smaller utility structures. She would probably be at the main house. He wanted at least to check that out before he brought Abby into the picture.

He could see the house. It was big and bright, and up a hill on the other side of a wall of trees. This was only one hundred yards away from the furthest gray structure.

Peter made for the house, walking purposefully through the lushly manicured grass.

He couldn't help but admire the setting the Joneses had here. It was a charming spot. And he loved all the grass. They had grass in Edenia, but it was more natural; blotchy and thick bladed, not soft and even like this.

As he rounded the last medium-sized gray building, he nearly walked straight into a man lighting a cigarette. Peter stumbled backward silently, thanks to his Nature.

The rather large man's face lit in a freaky way as the flicker from his lighter scattered the shadows of the structure he leaned against.

Turning with his lit vice in hand, the man peered around the corner Peter just rounded. His shoulder came within inches of Peter's head. Moving away from the smelly man, Peter searched for what the smoker was looking at. It was a rather small structure behind the current one.

Just then, the door to that building opened, and another burly man with short blond hair stepped into the dawn. He held the door open, and several men followed single file. They seemed to be rising as they came. Going on tip-toe, Peter saw that beyond the door were steps leading down. Once six men exited the door, the first man leaned in to switch the stairway and security lights off. Now almost a dozen large soldier types were coming at him. Peter backed against the building and stood still. The smoker called quietly, "Is that it?"

The man in front answered, "Think so. How many are here already?"

"Ten."

"Is Gerald?"

"Yup. He's waitin' inside."

All the men passed Peter, and the smoker opened the door and waited as they all went into the larger shed.

What was going on here? Peter wondered, and his rascally nature took over. Pulling in behind the last man in line Peter slipped into the building on his shirt tails.

A big man with a bald head and markings up and down his arms stood surrounded by gardening tools and some machinery Peter did not recognize, but still found interesting. He weaved his way around the men and tools looking for an out-of-the-way place to observe from. Stepping to a corner, the bald man spoke.

"Who's missing?"

Just as he said this the door opened again and four more men entered the small shed. It was now packed to the brim.

"This isn't everyone," someone chimed in. "Frank went in, too."

"Frank is different from us; we all know that. So, let's just leave him out for now." The bald man paused until everyone was settled. "First, we all know why we're here."

Someone called from near Peter. "Yeah, we do, I ain't a whole man no more."

"Exactly, Marco." The bald man agreed. "And I bet that feeling got a whole lot stranger today. It did for me, at least."

What was *this?* Peter wondered as a chill went up his back. The little invisible hairs rising on his arms and a feeling of purpose pumped his blood with the idea that all the eavesdropping he'd done before now was to prepare him for this one time.

"Yeah, why am I feeling that tug in my skull pull me to the basement now?"

"Me too. Yesterday I felt damn-near drawn toward Edenia, now that itch in the back of my mind migrated to the basement of this compound. What is that about, Gerald?" And all the men grumble an assent to this news.

"How many of you have felt that tug toward Edenia change?" Gerald raised his hand indicating he wanted the rest to do the same.

They all did.

"How many of you feel it stronger than you ever recall feeling it before?"

All hands rose.

"What's going on, man?" someone called out.

Gerald smiled. "Men, we gotta have a real blunt conversation, and we gotta have it now. We are soldiers, and we have orders. Mr. Jones has put us to strict loyalty tests and kept us competitively organized to keep us loyal to them and not to each other, but here we have a common purpose, a common problem. I don't see Willis with some invisible force in his head and hours of his life missing from his mind."

They grunted in agreement.

"I don't see Tally or Jeremiah leading raids in Edenia and engaging with the phantoms and coming out half a man."

The grunts of agreement got heartier. The bald guy had them. Peter smiled.

"So, before I tell you something important, we need to do a little trust exercise." Boots shifted on the dirt floor.

"So, let's get some things out in the open. I would like to know about the mission you lost yourself to."

No one volunteered anything, and the silence went on for several difficult moments. He continued, "When Mr. Jones hired me ten years ago, I thought he was an eccentric old man after the impossible, just because he had money and time to blow. He told me that a small group of backward people had a meteorite land in the center of their town. His machinery told him it might be made of a new kind of metal, and he wanted me and my team to retrieve it. He told me that the people living in the town were simple but that they worshiped the metal like it was their God, so they would trick us and try to stop us, but they would not hurt us if we would not hurt them. I, of course, thought he was crazy and stupid, but it seemed like an easy enough job. Take some metal from a bunch of bumpkins. No problem." Everyone laughed, and Peter heard the frustration of many failed attempts in the laughter. "But it was a problem. A problem we all talk about on the regular. Right?"

"Right," a few men said.

"Well, last year, I became a Phantom Hunter, and I got told the truth. Now I'm going to tell it to you with trust you'll have my six. If you don't wanna know, leave now." More boots shuffled but not a man left. "The mission of the Phantom Hunters is to seek the biblical tree of life, which resides in the middle of Edenia for its fruit, which, if eaten, gives the eater immortality."

Silence reigned in the room. Not a boot moved.

Gerald, the genius he was, let it settle for a full ten seconds before he went on. "Who here was told this Tree of Life origin story?" These were good soldiers, holding their ground and not responding.

"Come on, men. I've let the cat out of the bag. It doesn't matter anymore. How about this? Those who did not know this story raise your hand."

Those boys had no problem letting Gerald know the truth of the situation. No wonder they were not in the upper echelons of this organization. Only an idiot would fall for that trick.

Gerald did not linger. "Let's hear your origin stories. Who was told the meteorite story?" A dozen hands went up. Gerald did some quick deduction in his head. Deduction that impressed Peter. "Ben, Sam, Trent, you're what's left, what story did they tell you?" All three men looked embarrassed and didn't answer. "Come on. Spill it out, soldier."

"Aliens."

"He said they were aliens," two of the three said together.

Peter felt a rush of validation and he almost laughed out loud. Several men chuckled, but Gerald kept a straight face. "Let me guess, you believed in aliens before becoming employed?"

They all three nodded their heads.

One said, "My dad worked at Area 51."

Everyone silenced for a minute at this, several eyes going wide. Peter wondered what that meant.

"Gerald, what does this have to do with the price of rice?" the smoker asked.

"It has to do with us all understanding each other. I just gotta know one more thing. On my first mission into Edenia I did not know what to expect. I had a wacky old Ether Jones saying crazy stuff, and the moment we get inside all our equipment wigs out, our guns though still in holsters, melt on the inside and won't fire. And then there were the trees and plants around us. They act completely unnaturally. Tripping us, slapping us, binding our feet together, and a dozen other oddities. Does this sound familiar to anyone else?"

Men started calling things out.

"Gun's becoming so hot you can't touch them."

"Radios that were in perfect condition not working inside of Edenia."

"Wind blowing so much dirt in your face you can't breathe or see."

"Vines and tree limbs becoming a wall-like barrier right in front of you."

"Walking into an invisible wall."

"Or getting punched in the face by an invisible wall." The men laughed.

Peter smiled too.

Gerald went on, "Invisible. That's right. It's like the place is possessed; we can never get in. We come out banged up. And all there are is phantoms, right? No people are ever seen."

There was silence.

"Well that's wrong. People live in Edenia. A whole lot of them. And they are something you would see on an X-Men episode."

There was a lot of grumbling at this.

Some guy with a bunch of tattoos on his neck said, "He's telling the truth. They showed me some video footage of the people."

"Me too," several others added.

Several men shook their heads.

Another man spoke, "Of the fifteen missions I've been on since being hired two years ago, I have never seen a single human in Edenia. Only possessed plant life. Of course, I've been on two missions that I don't remember at all."

"I've seen blurs. Like I feel like I know someone has been there. I've felt them pull me or push me but I don't see them, only a blur."

"I've seen blurs, too. Like out of the corner of my eye. Images I'm certain are human, but then it's gone."

Everyone agreed on this point.

Someone else said, "I've seen blurs or shadows of people. I've felt people, but I think we are missing the point here, men. That bein', I went in and came back with no memories. I didn't sign up to…"

Someone interrupted him, he moved to stand next to Gerald. He had dark hair and fierce eyes. "People live there. They are regular people just like us except they have powers. They are what are controlling the plants and stuff. Willis regularly kidnaps them to ask them about their abilities. I have been in on several interrogations. It's always the same thing. What are their powers? How do they have powers? Where is the garden? Where is the tree? Is it still in this plane of reality?"

After this man's speech everyone became quiet. Peter thought how proud he was of his people. Those that were questioned by the Joneses when they left for sabbatical had not revealed anything of value; until him, him and his big mouth about the water.

Gerald broke in. "And here is where it gets good, boys." He looked at his watch. "We have already been gone for fifteen minutes. I say we only have about ten more before people start to wonder where all the staff is, so listen up. The reason all our brains went crazy today is that the young girl from Edenia that did this to us, she moved from Edenia to our basement."

That shut down everything.

After a count of ten, the smoker dude asked, "You're talking about that teenager? Do you really think she somehow did this to us?"

There wasn't anger in the man's question, only confusion. "People can't do stuff like that."

"Aliens can," one of the alien guys muttered.

The dark-haired man standing with Gerald said, "The people that live there have powers. I'm telling you."

"Okay let's just stay focused. But I am telling you right now that little girl is why I am here," Gerald stated strongly. "She is why I have risked my job and my honor as a man who keeps his oaths. She is the key. I knew the second I was in the same room with her. I'm telling you, she has the answers, and I think she might be willing to share them."

The same man from the previous question said, "I only saw her for a brief moment, but I felt...attracted, though that isn't exactly the right word because it wasn't like, sexual, I felt drawn to her. I didn't understand it, but I had to keep myself from seeking her out. Literally, like I've found myself walking toward her unconsciously, at least 5 times since she got here."

"Well, I'm not as strong as you, Nate." Gerald said, "I felt the same thing, and I sought her out. I'm glad I did, because I found Frank in there screaming at her, calling her a witch. He had a scalpel and was about to *Frank* her."

The men only displayed their discomfort by shuffling their feet. Peter felt a swelling of gratitude for the big bald man. He'd saved Miriam from death. At this thought, a plan formed in Peter's mind. He felt goose bumps fly up his arms. He knew this conversation was exactly the reason he felt so compelled to take the actions he'd taken so far this night.

"That man is sick."

"He loves to hurt people."

"He needs to be in jail."

There were murmurs of agreement, The room full of men nodded and looked at each other with commiseration.

"They are torturing the girl, boys." The dark-haired man said. "And if she has answers to why we feel this way..."

"We," Gerald continued, "need to get her out of the basement."

Peter felt the mood of these soldiers change.

Gerald must have felt it, too, because he added "This is what I propose…"

Peter's heart leapt, and his mind went a million miles an hour as he listened to the men talk.

As he finished up, Gerald said, "I will tell you now that Willis Jones believes that little innocent girl in there, the one who can take memories, is his biggest foe, and now he has her in the testing room. Willis is desperate. None of us are stupid. He doesn't care about the life of that child, but I do. I don't care what Willis wants. I don't care if it's the end of the world…"

Someone interrupted Gerald speech. "I was on the monitors before I came here and was listening to an AM station. I guess Yellowstone has become one big volcanic vent. The big one is going to explode, they say, within 24 hours. People are racing to get out."

Someone else added, "I called my brother today to tell him I forgive him. Why? I haven't talked to him in ten years. Because the world is on fire, and with this new virus…"

Another man said, "I hear that, too, and they are saying how so much seismic movement might affect the tectonic plates on the west coast. Washington alone has five active volcanoes. We could be talking about a major domino effect here."

Gerald butted back in. "Yes, yes, we have been talking about this for days, and it brings me to my point; Willis is desperate."

The dark-haired man inserted himself once again, "Willis thinks he's going to find the Tree of Life in the middle of that town. He thinks he is going to eat the fruit of it and become immortal, and he's in a hurry now."

"He's been after immortality his whole life and now would be a really good time to be immortal, don't you think?"

There were murmurs all through the room.

"Now, I am not exactly in that camp. I don't believe that we can eat the fruit of some tree and never die. But I have felt the impossible happen, seen the impossible, so there is *something* there. And honestly, I feel a little desperate myself, but in a different way. Three years ago, I went in there and came out with a day of memories stolen. But it is more than that. Something has changed with in me. I'm not the same, and I have to find out why. Since I saw that girl Willis has, I've known I can rectify that. I don't know how, but I just know she will help me understand."

"I feel that, too," someone else added quietly. "It's like an itch on my back. One I can't get to, but it's driving me crazy."

A young man probably Garren's age stepped forward and turned. The moment Peter saw him, he recognized him from just a few days ago. He was the parachuter that landed in the field while Peter was pranking Garren.

The young man spoke. "Since that day a week ago, when I landed in Edenia, I feel a fracture in myself. Besides feeling like I need to go see Miriam—that's her name by the way—I've thought of nothing but her in the ten hours since I saw Seth turn her over to Willis. I feel like I want to abandon my life and goals. Like everything that has happened to me previously has prepared me for this. Like this is why I've been a wanderer. Now I have a purpose other than myself. Save Miriam from Willis. Get her back to Edenia."

Several men cleared their throats and looked away, and there was silence for a moment. Peter was stunned by these testimonies. He wondered what the Master was working at here, because it definitely had a supernal feel to it all. The mood shift in the room was tangible. The men nodded their heads and took breaths of acceptance. It was a thing to behold.

These men all felt the way this man described. They were all adversely affected by Miriam's Nature. He was so glad she'd never taken any of his memories.

It was bad enough the one time she did use her Nature on him. Speaking of which, in that one conversation, Miriam had changed from one of Peter's worst enemies to his ally. How had she done that?

Gerald spoke up again. "Thank you, Remy, for your addition. I think you described perfectly what I've been trying to say. I feel like I've been lost for three years. Now, I have the chance to do something about it. So, soldiers, I have made plans to get that little girl out of Willis' hands. And once she is free, I plan on following her to the ends of the earth to get answers. I need all of your help, though. Who is with me?"

Peter watched in astonishment not only at all the raised hands but at the turn of conversation. Before Peter could even make a full decision, before he knew what he would say, he let go of his Nature and began pushing his way to the front of the room. This was exactly why he was here. These men would help him get Miriam back, and he planned to use them to the last man.

Several of the men exclaimed disgruntledly as Peter moved past them. They all turned toward his progression, confusion on their faces. Peter smiled at them, and when he reached Gerald, he held out his hand.

"Hello Mr. Gerald, I am Peter Miller and I am here to make a believer out of you all."

A confused Gerald touched his hand to Peter's, probably out of habit. However, the moment they touched Peter, he pulled his Nature to him and went invisible.

The men in the room gasped.

Gerald exclaimed, "What the..." and he tried to pull his hand away, but Peter would not let him go. His hands of stone kept Gerald pinned.

After he felt the point was made, he let his Nature and Gerald's hand go.

"Just in case you are confused," Peter added, feeling the high of surprising the heck out of this room full of brawny soldiers, "the girl you are referring to, Miriam, is my sister, and my family and I are coming to get her back. My father, our leader, is angry, and he will not be leaving Edenia with love in his heart. That said, I have listened to your conversation, I believe you to be worthy and able, and thus would like to offer you a deal."

The men had listened to this speech attentively, or so it seemed.

When Peter finished, though, all he got were a thousand questions asked at once. The most popular one—that he could discern—was 'how did you do that?'

Peter raised his hands and Gerald yelled to everyone. "Shut the fu…" he looked down at Peter and amended his wording, "…frick up, ladies." Once the men quieted down, Gerald asked, "You truly have gifts or abilities? Like…like, superheroes."

"Way better than superheroes," Peter quipped.

"I can't believe this."

"Can you do it again?" Someone from the back called out.

Peter smiled, of course he could, and so he did.

But doubt began to form in his mind. Where had his fierce desire to keep Edenia's secrets gone? Where had his mind gone? He was going to be in so much trouble. He let his Nature go again to much jaw dropping, and Peter looked at the men, desperately hoping that he'd made the right choice.

Still, there were words that needed saying. "You are not supposed to know about this. Guardians expend a great amount of energy hiding our powers with all those frustrating occurrences you mentioned a few minutes back."

"We know. We would come home from a ssion completely confused and annoyed. Such an easy thing, but we barely would get inside the borders."

"And we couldn't say exactly why. It always was a million little things going wrong. All this time, you all were the ones doing it?"

"And Mr. Jones never seemed angry about it. He just wanted us to try again."

"Yes. Well, my father is coming here, and he will certainly do his worst if we don't get Miriam out." They didn't seem scared at all by this statement, so Peter chose a different route. "Also, you are right about one thing. The only person who can tell you what happened to you is Miriam."

Gerald stepped closer to him. "You can't tell us?"

Peter felt intimidated by the man, but he didn't back down. "Hah, tell you about what Miriam can do? None of *us* even knows what she does. She is our secret weapon."

"She's not so secret anymore."

"No," Peter said. He wanted to punch Seth right in the face. "Not anymore."

"Well, young man. I don't know about the rest of these men, but I am willing to talk about a deal. I want Miriam released, but mostly because I want answers. If you can guarantee me that, I will help you."

Surprisingly, there was a murmur of agreement throughout the shed. "Fantastic," Peter said with a smile.

CHAPTER 26

Seth

The alarm yanked him awake. He moved quickly to Lillian's side after shutting it off. She was breathing, pale, but breathing. He let out his breath.

Pulling on his pants and a shirt over his head, he whispered, "Lillian, time to wake up."

She rolled and moaned, and once he knew she would be able to move today, Seth's mind bumbled over what he saw last night on the TV. His only tool was Willis' money and clout. Thank God for that. He would have to press for the best, the most efficient, of every treatment available to save Lillian and get her to safety before the world went to hell in a handbasket. He had to.

Without a thought for breakfast, he went to Lilly's side. "Let's go."

She didn't resist him, and after packing up their few things they left the room without switching off the TV.

AFTER HAVING SPENT seven days in Edenia, it seemed the world had blown up. Literally. All the people in the waiting room seemed just as shell shocked as him. The news blaring from the TV made it sound like all the survival nuts were heading for the hills, but the smart ones were already gone. Still, the question they kept asking was, "Is this the end? Did the crap just hit the fan?"

Both were provocative questions to Seth's way of thinking, and ones he knew he would be considering very seriously with his family, if they were in Cairo still. But they weren't in Cairo. His father had gotten them out in the nick of time. That fact stirred even more provocative questions in Seth's mind.

Seth looked at the oncology waiting room filled to the brim with cancer-stricken people waiting for treatment. He hoped all the paperwork was done, and that they could just walk in. He would have to tell the staff here that his parents were dead and that he was Lillian's guardian now. He worried that would affect things but hoped it would work out. So many things could go wrong. He'd seen how quickly things could get out of hand. The world was literally being blown up. There were literal viruses and plagues, wars and bombs, and natural disasters like tornadoes, hurricanes and the Yellowstone volcano was about to blow. Seth looked at Lillian and clenched his fists, bit the inside of his cheek, and sucked in a terrified breath.

What he would give for a magic wand.

Not for the first time, Seth considered that he might have made a huge mistake taking Lillian away from the safety of Edenia. Not for the first time, Seth thought of the sincerity on his father's face and the plea for trust in his mother's voice. In his mind, he saw his family together in Edenia, where some miracle healed Lillian. He saw that road and wished for it, wished he'd been brave enough to choose it, to believe that it was possible, to have faith. Looking down at his hands, he longed to be a different person. He wished he had strength and certainty.

Lilly trusted him.

She hadn't moved a muscle in the last twenty minutes. She must either be in real pain, or feel the true relief he felt at being here. The last few weeks were a nightmare that was now coming to an end. Neither of them had escaped unscathed though.

Besides the obvious hardships, Seth now found it hard to be in the world in some pretty specific ways. Like the time in Edenia changed his view of real life, like he was seeing everything with different eyes.

The room looked strange, almost fake; colorless, white walls and black chairs, all blah and institutional. It felt nearly alien. Then there were the people; all fake smiles and blank eyes, and shallow expressions and countenances. It made Seth want to dig his own eyes out.

How had seven days changed him so much?

Then there was the news making everyone uptight. Even the receptionist left her desk and moved over to the small TV in the children's waiting room, in order to catch a tidbit or two before hurrying back to her duties. Also, most of the waiting patients were gathered around the screen like uncertain sheep.

Seth could hear the muted sound of TV station anchors. After the midnight news in the hotel, Seth felt curious, but also frightened. He was man enough to admit it. War scared him, but it seemed inevitable. Still as he sat there, not thinking of Edenia or Miriam, his attention turned again and again to the stream of media information.

He looked at Lillian. Her attention was also captured by what sounded like a replay of the bombs this morning.

But everyone turned when a nurse appeared and called a name. The named patient and her husband slowly exited the children's room in dramatic conversation.

"Why in the world would I? I'm not doing it, George. I don't want to be tied down in a hospital bed practically dead if that virus reaches the US like they said it will."

"Now, Marty," was all the old man got in.

"No. Twenty-four hours from now all the practically dead people in the chemo ward are going to be completely dead, and not from cancer. I refuse to be one of them." The old lady made a turn and headed toward the exit.

The man stopped, "Marty, it's just a conspiracy. The government is just trying to scare us into staying here in the States."

"I saw those dead bodies, George. Those bodies were not fake." She continued walking but turned and spoke loudly addressing everyone in the room. "This is it. I testify Jesus is coming. Get yourself right with God." Her husband hurried forward shushing her. But he was too slow. She'd said her piece and turned for the exit again. Once there, she looked over her shoulder at the old man. "Are you coming?"

The poor man sighed and sniffed, then shuffled toward his wife.

Seth caught Lillian's glance. Her eyebrows were knitted with concern.

"Do you want to go over there?" Seth gestured toward the TV. "Or do you want me to go over there?" Seth asked again once he noticed how pale and haggard she looked.

Lillian's dark brown eyes turned away from him. She watched the old man and woman leave the room arm in arm. "Shoes nut pale," she whispered and put her hand on his arm.

"What?" Seth asked turning more fully toward her.

"Shoes nut…" She put her hand to her head but then she glanced over at the TV looking absolutely bewildered.

A few times since her diagnosis, Lilly lost her words. But she didn't know she'd lost them until no one responded, and then she'd freak out on everyone for ignoring her. Once her brain straightened out, she felt awful that she had no memory of it all.

She looked at him, determined to speak. One of her eyes drifted, her iris pointing askew. This had happened before, and if Seth freaked out, it would only scare her. So he said nothing, only put an arm around her and looked away.

His thoughts went back to the old woman and what she had said. Had someone released another virus? There was a board game he loved called PANDEMIC. It always amazed him how quickly things got crazy playing that game, and he'd wondered if viruses really could spread that quickly. Just as the thought of horrid brain eating pathogens left him wanting his mommy, the nurse brought a wheelchair out and called Lillian's name. The look of despair Lilly cast in his direction tore at his heart.

Seth felt his worry build when the nurse—who looked tired and worn out—deposited them in a room and began small talk as she typed on her computer. But Lilly's lapse of words was completely gone, and she did brilliantly.

"Thank you so much for being here and seeing us."

"Of course. It's my job."

"Well, I know, but with everything that's happening…"

"Yes, but what else would I do? Run away and live out in the woods? I'm not prepared for that, and I can't just sit at home and watch the TV. Besides, the President says we are safe. She's going to take care of us, so I can take care of you."

Seth had so many things to say about that speech, but it wasn't the time or place, so he kept it to himself.

"May I scan your microchip to verify your identity?"

"Uhm, we don't have them. Our parents wouldn't allow it."

The nurse looked disapproving.

"How have they gotten away with that for three years?"

"We haven't lived in the States for that long."

"All right, I will have to get you in the hard way. Name and date of birth?" After she got the information she asked, "Are you both minors? Heavens, I thought you were her guardian. I must be stupid today. Where in the world are your parents? They have to be here," the gray-haired lady sputtered.

Seth looked at Lillian, he didn't have to tell her it was time to bring on the water works. On cue, they both broke down in tears. With the lack of sleep and stress it wasn't hard, except for the hit to the pride bit.

"I'm a minor." Seth choked out. "But I am Lillian's guardian, not exactly legally yet. You see, two days ago, our parents were hit by a drunk driver and, uhm, were killed, instantly." It was the best lie Seth ever told. The nurse totally bought it.

"Oh, no," the nurse exclaimed. "How tragic."

Seth went on with his lie, "Lillian already had this appointment, and it's been such a long wait, and it so hard to get appointments in the first place, and then our friend basically gave his left arm to get this one for her, so though we have a funeral to plan, I just...I *can't* lose any more family. So, we're here, hoping for help. Or a miracle."

Miriam was the friend who paid for this. She made this possible. *My betrayal will save Lilly's life,* he thought. A cold sensation crept up his back, and he pushed it aside, focusing again on the nurse.

Fortunately, the distressed nurse didn't question them further. She just awkwardly put her hand on Lilly's knee. "You poor dear, let's get you well. That's the most important thing."

Seth breathed a sigh of relief and they continued the digital paperwork.

FORTY MINUTES LATER, Lillian was having yet another MRI and CT scan which left Seth in the waiting room again. This time, he sat on the children's side smooshed in with fifty other people, watching the news over their heads to catch a glimpse or two.

There was indeed another virus. Gryberstraud virus or GSV they were calling it. It attacked the spinal cord and killed its victims within twenty-four hours. It was airborne in Africa and a single day after the first case was classified, there were hundreds dead and dying. There were reports of it as far as India. Seth cringed as he watched. But it also felt like the graphic scenes in front of him were familiar, possibly from a movie he'd seen.

The worst of the outbreak was in Africa and the Middle East. But according to the scientist, a lab in Chile contained an even worse virus. The news anchor reported signs that it also had been released. However, it moved slower, taking five days to kill its victims, but did so in a much gorier fashion.

The fear tingling up Seth's spine chilled him so much he had to take a walk. He left the children's room and moved back to the other side. He couldn't find a chair, so he paced.

Thinking about the real danger they were in depressed him; how the world was falling apart, wondering if he was right to leave Edenia when it seemed none of this fear and devastation had even touched the people there. He felt his heart long to turn toward that little comforting presence he'd felt while in Edenia.

Itch, itch. Itch.

His head, apparently of its own volition, turned toward that itch, which he knew now was Miriam. There were so many reasons he wished his reality were different, and that she was merely one of them, but this constant reminder—via the itch in his head—irked. It also irked that he was not the only one. Willis all but told him that every last person that Miriam had messed around with felt the same as he did. But his brain held more than just that itch, and when he was away from her, he understood it for what it was. He wanted her. He'd held her even as he was betraying her. All the right parts of his brain lit up with crazy, desperate desire.

He stopped this by putting himself mentally back into those last few moments with her. Those glorious violet eyes, dilated with drugs, lids tight with fear.

Guilt and sorrow washed away all the needs of the moment, and his mind snapped out of the fantasy.

Seth looked around at the sound of the nurse calling his name. She led him back to Doctor Lillehei's office where Lillian sat. The man's dark skin, short black hair and black eyes brightened his straight white smile and made him feel trustworthy. But the moment he spoke, Seth's stomach fell out the bottom of his feet.

"I'm so sorry that you were subject to those tests, Lillian. My DO did not realize I had talked to your parents over the phone. We are a little scattered at present." His eyes narrowed as he examined the two of them. "Forgive me, but I am a little confused as to why you are here." When Seth and Lillian looked at him just as confused, the Doctor held up a file folder. "According to my last phone call with your mother Jenna Johnson, you have been on my DIPG protocol for two months. That you have had wonderful results. You have been able to go about your life. I see you participated in chess club and..."

"Doctor Lillehei, I'm sorry to sound stupid but what is DIPG protocol?"

The man set down the folder and squinted at Lillian. "It is a regimen of vitamins and drugs..." He paused and shook his head. "I'm confused."

"Welcome to the party. Our parents told us that today was Lillian's appointment to get her brain tumors removed."

Doctor Lillehei's eyes widened to enormous circles, his mouth forming an O. "No, Lillian, no. Your cancer diffuse intrinsic pontine gliomas is fatal. It's inoperable, I mean I am working on it, like my life depends on it. But the protocol is the only thing we've come up with in twenty years that helps. How could you not understand this?"

Seth stood. "No, no, no. *No.* Lillian has a brain tumor. She is here to have it removed. We came from Cairo to have it removed. We came here because you are the specialist in removing these things."

"I am a specialist for DIPG. I don't even perform surgeries anymore. Surgery only weakens DIPG patients and offers them no long-term benefits. Please, Mr. Johnson, sit."

Seth sat, but only because he was so stunned he couldn't do anything else.

"I've reviewed all your information from Dr. Pachard's check-up today." He stood and held up two plastic x-rays to a light panel. "This is from two months ago. Dr. Rynhard, your Cairo doctor sent it, and this is from today. Look at your brain stem here." He pointed. "See how the tissue has changed so rapidly? Much more of your tissue is covered in tiny tumors. Typically, when a brain reaches this point, my patient is being kept alive artificially because they are brain dead. Yet here you are, talking, moving, eating. That, my dear, is a miracle of epic proportions and is something I cannot explain with any science I know."

Looking from the doctor to the x-ray, Seth instantly saw the problem. You didn't need to be a doctor to know that the dozens of small white masses spread throughout each picture were bad news.

Still hyped up on whatever excitement he felt from their sad, yet strange circumstances, the doctor remarked, "What you can't see is that each of these tumors have armlike tendrils that wrap around brain tissue. You can see it on this largest mass." He pulled out another slide and held it up. It was an image of one slice of Lilly's brain. The mass looked like a four-year-old's depiction of a sun, with a round center and rays like tendrils extending out of that center. "It is strangling these arteries which bring blood to other parts of your brain which is why we have secondary issues like motor control and speech issues. In a rather morbid way, it is quite fascinating, and Lilli's situation is unique."

In Seth's shocked state, he half wanted to agree with the Doctor and half wanted to just punch the man right in the face for his lack of bedside manner.

For the first time in the last few minutes Seth remembered the hand that held his and how it trembled.

Lilly spoke. "Are you calling the thing that is killing me beautiful?" With tears running down her face, she carefully pushed herself back from his desk and attempted to wheel her chair from the room. It took her a few tries, but she got herself out.

Shocked by this all, Seth didn't call her name, didn't chase after her, or even get up to help.

The doctor apologized and followed Lilly to the door where he called for a nurse to help her. "She shouldn't be alone. Get her an IV with 500 milligrams..."

Seth tuned him out. How could this be? Seth had pinned all his hopes, all his faith on a lie. A lie his parents had told him. The betrayal dropped his stomach to his feet, and he reached for the trash can.

After he finished violently heaving up nothing (his stomach was empty already) and everything (the motion felt like a release of overloaded emotion and worry) he sat back, wiped his mouth, and let his mind calculate the cost of all he'd done this last week.

Every action had been for a lie: his betrayal, his deal with the Joneses, his own lies, losing Miriam. None of it mattered. He'd failed. He'd failed. His sister would die, and from the look on the doctor's face, it would be soon.

He stood and wanted to flee, himself. As he went for the door, the doctor said, "I'm sorry, Seth."

Like that made a difference. Anger raged through him. "How, how can you not fix this? We came all this way…"

"I'm sorry Seth. I get that you are shocked. And if I could fix her, I would. But I can't. I'm just not God, son."

Seth's head whipped up. God. He sniffed and rubbed the tears off his cheeks. The doctor's words gave him a glimmer of hope as a tiny inkling of possibility found its way into his heart. He had no idea where it came from, but he grasped it like a lifeline. In an instant, he was a man of action again. He nodded. "Thank you, doctor." He opened the door, but he paused. "How long do you think she can go on like she is?"

The doctor blinked, "Honestly, I can't believe she has any motor function at all right now. I can't believe she is upright, I can't believe she can talk. As far as what I can see I would say she is way past living on borrowed time. The only thing I can recommend is checking her in. At least here we can give her drugs that will help with the pain. Then get the rest of your family here as soon as possible. They might not have time to say goodbye if they are not here within hours. I've already made arrangements, Jo is probably getting her all hooked up as we speak."

"Why in the world would I check her in here? You obviously can't do anything for her." There was a definite bite to his words.

The doctor looked sadly at him. "You're right, in a way. But I have an obligation to help as much as I can."

"She said she's not in terrible pain. Could she fly?"

"No, Seth, are you crazy? Fly? How could you even… No, I'm not going to discuss your hopes of heroism. She has to be admitted. I cannot let her out of this hospital without a trained professional to take care of her. She needs drugs and fluids and..."

Seth raced out of the room and down the hall, asking every nurse where his sister was. Finally, he found her. She was lying in a hospital bed in a room surrounded by five other people, talking to an older nurse with a clipboard, while another nurse was about to put in an IV.

"Stop!" Seth yelled, and the startled woman dropped the stint to the floor.

"What in the name of heaven..." the nurse with the clipboard exclaimed.

Seth closed the door. "Lilly, we're going back." Lilly and the nurse's jumbled objections didn't matter. He found her clothes. "Put these on." He tossed them on the bed.

"No, Seth." She looked pale and her hands trembled. "You can't save me anymore." Her eyes were haunted, and she looked at him with love and pity. "I am going to die, Seth. You did everything you could. You did more than any other brother would have. You are my hero." She looked down at her hands. "But I am going to die, and soon. I can feel it. I can even taste it. In my mouth there's the sensation of death taking over life." She looked at the nurses, counting on them to tell her the truth. "Is that normal?" Lilly smacked her lips with a pursed face.

"Here, I'll get you some water, Honey..." He only half heard the rest of the nurse's response because, just then, as it had when he held the vial of drugs over Miriam's food, a feeling came over him and culminated into one idea; trust Edenia.

So many times he'd wanted to trust, but his pride, or his need to help, or his disbelief separated his mind from his heart. Right now, in this sterile and surreal moment, his heart was the only thing that knew what he needed.

With one tiny ingredient on his part, trust, every struggle he'd been through in the last seven days could have vanished. He saw that now. With his eyes opened, he saw beyond this revelation, too. He understood he could have all he ever wanted. His sister healthy, his family put back together, relatives as far as the eye could see, and the girl of his dreams.

Sure, the price was big. In fact, it was huge. He saw this for what it was. A test. There was no logical reason he could think of to explain why this fear of being a freak lay inside him. Why his skin crawled and his heart raced with fear. Why nausea and revulsion infected his body and mind at the very thought of changing to become something other than himself. But all that happened to him, and it was real, as real as people who feared sharks or spiders. It was like asking someone to become a spider when they thought spiders to be the most disgusting, most horrifying thing in the world.

So, personally, the price was massive. But as he looked at his dying sister, as he thought of his other sister heartbroken, his parents devastated, and Miriam imprisoned, he understood how this had controlled him and in turn, affected everyone around him. Guilt burned through every cell. Every molecule of his body screamed at him, *is becoming a freak worse than how you feel at this moment?*

To his ever-lasting shame, he took the question and thought it through, hard.

After several disgraceful moments he concluded, no matter how disgusting freakdom could be, it would never be worse than the consequences he now faced. It would never be as horrid as how he felt now. Never. His heart cried inside him, and its sobbing was for Miriam and for Lilly.

What had he done?

His mind processed all this as the nurse found a cup for Lillian and filled it with tap water. As she came to Lillian with the water, something else became clear, warming his soul, and bringing words to his mind. He recalled pieces of conversations, statements made by his parents and others. Finally, it was almost as if he once again heard words in his mind from an outside force; *Get Lillian back to Edenia, no outside food or drink.*

Seth acted; desperately and full of faith. He jumped to the nurse and knocked the cup out of her hand.

As the plastic and water splattered to the floor, spraying several of the other occupants, all eyes turned to him and the room when silent.

"Lillian, do you trust me?" he all but yelled at his sister, his adrenaline sky-high.

Lilly's eyes were wide with alarm, but her answer was instantaneous. "Of course."

That was all he needed. Grabbing the wheelchair that was still in the room, he wheeled it to her side and said, "Get in. We have to get you back to Edenia. They were right, Lilly, I know that now. They were right, and I screwed everything up."

She sat up, full of trust, and Seth reached to help her. However, a nurse grabbed his arm. "You can't take her. She is...if you take her, she will..."

Seth broke her grip and took Lillian's arm.

The other nurse was less gracious. She pushed the emergency button and stared Seth down. "That girl is not going anywhere. You bring her in half dead, and you think you can take her on my watch? Well, I'm sorry son, but you're mistaken."

These words struck fear into Seth's heart. That old nurse was not going to make this easy. So, the minute Lilly's butt touched the seat, he whirled her around and headed for the elevator. But as he rounded a corner, two uniformed security men headed their way.

Seth knew from experience that running and looking guilty was the best way to get caught. The guards didn't know what they were summoned for, so hoping to play it as cool as possible, Seth didn't change course. Smiling, he continued straight for the guards. They looked at him, but sailed right on by, making a beeline for the room.

Just as Seth reached the elevators and pushed the button, the old nurse walked around the corner and yelled to the guards. "There, they're getting away."

The elevator dinged, and Seth pushed his way on through the exiting crowd. He slammed his finger into the lobby button, and then into the close-door button. Taking their own sweet time, the metal doors finally obliged him. Thankfully, it was before the guards made it to them.

His heart pounded and his head throbbed, but he looked down at Lilly. "You okay?"

She didn't respond. He maneuvered around her chair and looked at his sister's face. "Lillian, are you all right?"

She was so pale. She met his eyes and nodded, then whispered, "I just feel so..." Her hands were trembling, and she gripped her head. "I really think it's going to explode."

He covered her hands with his, "It's not. It's not going to. You are strong, Lilly. Just hang on." For some reason, he remembered the dinner rolls he'd put in his backpack from the last time he ate. Dinner with Miriam. At the time, he didn't know how he'd be received at the Joneses, but he knew he couldn't go back to Edenia, so he'd brought a few supplies. Pulling one out, he handed it to Lilly. "Eat this," he commanded as he took a huge bite of his own.

Just as he began chewing the delicious bread, the elevator doors opened, and a loud alarm rang out. Accompanying the annoying weeohhh weeohhh were flashing lights. Before Seth had gone ten steps through the crowded lobby, a set of guards moved to the revolving door exit. Again, he attempted to be nonchalant as he continued for the doors. Biting into his roll he approached the guards.

"Hey, do you know what this is all about?" Seth asked with a full mouth.

The guard looked at his phone and said, "It's about you." He flipped the phone around. Lillian's image looked back at him. "Or specifically, her." And he stuck a beefy finger in Lillian's colorless face.

Out of nowhere came a fierce defensive instinct. It filled Seth and exploded out of him with a force he could not ignore.

Without understanding how it happened, the world slowed and his breathing slowed, and his heart beat out the seconds, which ticked leisurely by. Within a moment that felt like a minute, Seth noticed everything about the guard, and for the briefest beat of time saw, or more felt, the man's intentions.

Instinct told the guard to go for his Taser, but because Seth stood unmoving, staring, and taking no action, the guard ignored his instincts and only touched the weapon. But as the gaze lingered between the two, the guard's cheeks flushed with adrenaline. However, a question crinkled his brow and slowed the buildup to action. Suddenly, there was fear in his face.

Cocking his head and blinking furiously, he asked. "What's wrong with your eyes, kid? The color..." He raised his hand from the Taser and pointed straight into Seth's face. "They're..." he moved his index finger in a small circular motion.

The other guard spoke into the walkie-talkie at his shoulder as he stared into Seth's face, searching. "Yeah, we got 'em. At the front..." Then, looking at Seth's eyes, he stiffened as well.

But the orders to apprehend Lillian came, and the guards came to attention. They moved toward them.

Seth's insides roiled enough he thought they might just rip through his ribs. He had to get Lilly out of here. Desperation beat at his chest. And then, again, the feeling of slowness and precognition filled his mind. It was almost like a vision opening up, and he could see what the man would do in the next few moments.

Time caught up to Seth, but it didn't matter. With a swipe of a hand Seth pushed the man's finger out of Lilly's face and stared him down. He knew what would happen next, so he held still and let it.

It was as easy as stepping to the side and pushing Lilly's chair to the left. Her footrest smacked the first man's shins, and he went down. As he did so, Seth reached over and easily slid the Taser out of its holster, using the man's own momentum against him. Aiming the weapon, Seth ejected its probes at the other guard's chest who then promptly shook himself into a man-sized heap onto the floor.

Seeing his opening for escape, he took it without a second thought. Lillian's chair entered the large revolving door and they exited into the sunlight. Luckily, a cab waited just outside.

"Romani air strip please," Seth directed as he abandoned the wheelchair and lifted Lilly inside the cab. He had no idea where he got the strength to lift her, but it was there, and he used it.

Once the car began to move, Seth pulled out his cell phone and called Tony, the pilot, from eight hours ago. They'd hit it off, and Tony had offered to give them a ride any time, on Mr. Jones' bill, of course. Seth hoped that the man hadn't received other orders.

CHAPTER 27

Miriam

"Now, I sincerely hope you're ready to talk," came the voice again.

Miriam panted. "You know that I will not tell you anything more." Her body trembled in fear, but her mind was instantly rebellious. "What is that saying...about doing something the same way over and over and expecting different results?"

"Crazy we may be, Ms. Miriam, but with that comes persistence. And that is a quality even you have respect for, I am certain," Willis stated.

Of course she understood persistence from a Jones. For three hundred years their goal had been to take the powers of the Tree of Life and bottle it. This was flawed thinking on so many levels. Still, the stratagems to keep the Joneses out filled Miriam and every Edenian's entire existence. It was their way of life. Frankly, the Joneses kept Edenia going and relevant. If there were no Joneses, there would be no need for Edenia. That was an interesting thought.

As it was, this was a battle of wits and will, of good versus evil. For centuries, her family had protected the Joneses from themselves. She would not be the weak link in that chain. Finding that thought gave her strength.

Looking at Willis she gathered up that new strength to say, "Understand me, Willis Jones. My family has protected you from the Garden for centuries and I will not give up on that. I will not tell you what you want to know, for then your suicide would be on my conscience. So, either kill me or let me go. I tire of your egocentric delirium."

Willis stood staring at her in awed silence for a moment, then he burst out laughing.

"You really are a brave little thing, aren't you?" He let the smile linger a little longer before becoming serious. "But here's the problem, Miriam; we are almost out of time. You see, while all of you have been bundled up and distracted with guarding the garden, the world outside you has moved on. To war, Miriam. War and disaster are everywhere. This morning the Iranians set off two atomic bombs in the holy land, blowing it sky-high. By the afternoon, Russia, Iran, Syria, Venezuela and a handful of other nations signed an alliance and declared war on all democratic Christian nations. And you are probably not aware of the GSV virus that is killing millions of people within twenty-four hours of infection. Not to Mother Nature, who is taking her revenge for all the ill abuses heaped on her.

"So, you see, last night this may have been about pride and anger and greed and immortality, but today, well, it's still about all those things, but it's also about timing and about death. My death. True and immediate death. Be it by exploding volcano, micro-nuke, or pathogens. I am not blind or deaf. I've read the Bible. A hundred times, I've read it. I know what is coming and I do not want to be mortal through the Apocalypse. I don't want my children or my grandbabies to be mortal through the Apocalypse." He paused as if to let this marinate. "And so, you understand me now. The only thing standing between me and immortality at this crucial time is you."

Miriam swallowed hard as the information Willis delivered bumbled around in her head. What on earth was he talking about? Were these more of his delusions? Wasn't the apocalypse a good thing for Christians?

"I figure we have a bit of time. One of those tent cities set up camp about two years ago, and from what I see, they are pretty-near out of food. I know they are truly God's people because I have watched and seen the miracles they inspire. In fact, they are a lot like you lot. They have power just as real and just as effective as you do, though in a different vein."

This confused Miriam. First, if he knew the Edenians were on a sacred mission and that God was helping them, how could he possibly be in this fight? He was pitting his will against a creator. It made no sense. And it made her pity him. Second, what was he getting at? What did tent people have to do with the apocalypse?

But she let him talk because his talking stopped her from needing to. Plus, it gave her time to gain more strength.

She saw the determination in Willis' eyes. It was going to take all of her power and some borrowed from the heavens to fight the man. This was a battle of wills, and Miriam intended to win.

CHAPTER 28

Peter

The room was dark. Of course it was; this was his ribbon room. He looked around and was pulled instantly to Miriam's thread, then pulled further so her thread became a pillar. A pillar which to Peter's shock was dimmed. The light inside it somehow less. However, because of this, Peter was able to see something he hadn't seen before.

Miriam's pillar had...micro-wisps of something ethereal and phantom-like sprouting from it. It looked like tentacles—coming in or going out, he couldn't tell which—except the tentacles were, in and of themselves, loosely organized like they were made of spirit, or particles spread wide.

He examined the tentacles closely in the darkened light and saw that they led to other pillars, dark pillars. He found the brightest one and moved to scrutinize it. And again he was surprised when he recognized the pillar as Gerald, the man he was with now.

A loud bang pulled Peter from his dream. A man had just slammed the door right next to Peter, who had been napping in a chair.

He yawned and rubbed at his neck which ached from sleeping in a seated position. "This is taking forever," he complained, his mind mostly forgetting about his dream.

He'd been in the little shed with Gerald for several hours. The others were out and about their regular duties to avoid alerting the other Joneses.

Just then, the smoker man (Peter hadn't caught his name yet), came in and whispered something in Gerald's ear. Gerald's eyebrows rose, and he looked at Peter. "Did you bring anyone else with you?"

"Oh no!" He'd totally forgotten about Abby.

Gerald sighed, "Well, I'll take that as a yes. She is in the sitting room at the big house right now. She claims she left Edenia last night, walked for a ways, and got tired, so she slept in the trees and made her way here this morning."

Peter couldn't believe it was morning already. He'd miscalculated how hard it was to plan a grab and go.

"Jeremiah has ordered me to take care of her." Gerald said.

"What does that mean?" Peter asked instantly on alert.

"He wants me to get rid of her. How I choose to do that is up to me as long as it doesn't come back to bite him in the butt. If it does, then it will be me who gets 'taken care' of."

Peter swallowed. "You guys are barbarians. You know that, right?"

The man shrugged his shoulders nonchalantly.

Peter rolled his eyes. "Okay, so, what are you going to do?"

"I am going to use this as an opportunity to show your little invisible self around and flesh out our plan."

"Okay, will I be able to deal with Abby?"

"I don't know, how do *you* deal with people?" Gerald asked.

"In the exact right way, of course."

The man laughed, and it was a jolly laugh. "You are precocious, Peter Miller."

"I've been told that, except whenever anyone else say's it they mean it as an insult."

The man laughed again. "Well, I will trust you to deal with your friend, but there are cameras in all the rooms of the big house, just as we discussed; and there are about twenty men there that are not on our side, so keep yourself hidden."

"Okay."

"You can talk while you are..." he waved his hand up and down.

"Invisible."

"Yes."

"Not exactly, but I have a few other tricks up my sleeve. Don't worry."

"Okay."

"Great. Let's go then."

Peter pulled his Nature to him, and he saw the moment of shocked amazement pop on to Gerald's face again. "That is beyond amazing."

It was hard that he couldn't make a sound while taken, but it also was awesome. Peter practiced his idea right now. He concentrated on only letting go of his Nature a bit and said, "Yes. I know. Of all the Natures mine is the best."

Gerald heard him. Score. "All the Natures?" the bald man asked.

"Yes, that is what we call our powers." He realized that just because he had made a treaty with these Joneses didn't mean that he should give them any more information, so he shut his mouth and pulled Gerald toward the door.

They exited the little shack and began walking toward the house. Gerald was quiet for a long moment, and then he asked, "What do you think they will do with us once we have Miriam safe and sound?"

Peter performed his trick again. "What do you mean?"

"What I mean is, we will have betrayed the Joneses. We will not be able to stay here. The Joneses will go after my family."

"Gerald, you have a family?"

"Not the way you are thinking. Not many of us really have families like that. When you do the things we do...it's just best. It's one of the reasons we go through so many recruits."

"I'm sure that it doesn't help that this is all so hard to explain."

"Yeah, well, as you probably heard, the Joneses have it down to a science."

"They are tricky little buggers, aren't they?"

"Yes, well my concern is with that. I see what's happening on the news. I know what's going on, and frankly, it freaks me out. I need to know that I have a safe place for me and my men when this all is said and done."

Peter stopped, but realized Gerald couldn't see that, so he caught up with him again. "Are you asking me if you can come live in Edenia?"

Gerald turned intense eyes in his general direction. "Now that I know Miriam, that I've seen her...I can't really imagine being away from her."

Peter gagged a little. "Seriously, that is so sick and twisted."

"Regardless, it is how many of the men and I feel. Also, I know your little secret and I don't want that tortured out of me."

"You are not asking this lightly. I can see that, but I need you to understand that the master calls whom he calls. I have no say-so."

Gerald shook his head, a soldier understanding his lot. Peter felt bad for this Jones even though he wasn't technically a Jones. He wondered what he would call these men from now on.

They mounted the steps to the house, and Gerald led him inside to a room right off the front lobby.

When they opened the door and entered, Peter saw Abby. Her long black hair hung in a tangle down her back. There were leaves in it, and her arms bore scrapes. She stood in a weird way and turned to them almost stiffly. In a marching gait she approached Gerald, and as soon as she was a few feet away Peter saw something that dropped his jaw.

Abby's eyes were no longer a black drop of ebony, they were a light amber-brown, and her irises were swirling.

Then she spoke.

"Gerald Fritz McCall, I give you the Summons." And she touched Gerald right in the middle of the forehead with one finger.

Gerald took a step back, his eyes toward the ceiling, his face blank and still for the span of ten heartbeats. Everyone stood there, still.

Someone must have been watching on the camera because a group of three soldiers entered the room. They were all faces Peter recognized, and he knew that couldn't be a coincidence. This is what had taken Gerald so long in the planning. Two men flanked Abby while one stood next to Gerald, calling his name.

Abby, nonchalantly turned to the man on her right and spoke. "Karl Herbert Dunbar, I give you the Summons." And she touched his forehead. He reacted the same as Gerald.

And turning to her left she said, "Remy Bratsworth, I give you the Summons." But before she could get her finger up Remy stepped away and held up a gun in a smooth, practiced fashion.

That did not stop Abby. She instantly went invisible, and less than a moment later Remy had the same look as the other two. Just like with Uncle Brian when Abby went invisible, Peter could still see her. She looked like a smudge, though. Like she wasn't supposed to be in this realm of existence. The light sort of bent around her, making her unclear. Yet to his eyes, she glowed like a Goddess.

She turned to the last man in the room. Though he couldn't see her, he was wary, pulling out a weapon and stepping behind Gerald. Just then, the big bald man came to, and when he turned and saw that his friend was frightened, he spoke. "Trent, it's okay. This has to happen, or we can't get out of here safely."

That furrowed the man's brow and relaxed his gun arm. Abby slipped past his guard, her hand up already and poised. "Trenton Jay Walker, I give you the Summons." Her voice rang out and her finger wasted no time touching his forehead.

Once the job was done, Abby let go of her Nature and promptly sat on the floor, her trembling hands on her face.

Peter went to her and spoke before touching her. "I'm right here, you can't see me but I'm here, so you don't need to be afraid." Then he added with excitement. "Seriously, like, how could you be afraid right now? That was awesome. I've never seen the Summons before."

"The Summons, what?" She pushed her hair out of her face. "All I know is you left me in the middle of the woods all night long, you big butthead. If I could see you now, I'd hit you."

Peter was not interested in being hit.

Gerald spoke up then. "Sorry, he was with me."

Abby looked up in surprise and scuttled back, across the carpet.

"I'm not going to hurt you."

Peter chimed in. "That sounds like a practiced speech. Give it often, mate?"

Gerald rolled his eye in Peter's direction and held out a hand for Abby. She didn't take it, so Peter said, "Don't worry, he's with us."

"He is?" Abby asked skeptically.

"Yep. You, my dear, just made it a permanent arrangement."

Gerald added, "Thanks for that, by the way."

The other men were coming to. Karl was the first to speak. "Did that really just happen?"

"Like a vision in my head," Trent stuttered.

"More like a map," Remy corrected.

"Mine was just an intense desire to go that way."

"To Edenia." Peter answered, and all three men jumped.

"It's just Peter," Gerald offered.

"Holy crap. I will never get used to that."

"You won't have a choice when it happens to you." Abby spat out with a sneer.

"Abby!" Peter barked. "Shut up."

She held up her hands toward the sound of his voice and shrugged a 'what' gesture, then glared.

The door creaked open again. It was another one of the men Peter recognized. The moment he was in the room, Abby went into summoner mode. Her face went blank, she rose, stiff like, walked over to the man, startling him, and spoke.

"Richard Luke Talcott, I give you the summons." And she touched him.

Peter understood now. He saw what needed to happen. As Richard reeled back in the summons, Peter spoke. "Do you see what I see, Gerald?"

"She's gonna need to do this to everyone, isn't she?"

"Yeppers."

PETER WAS A LITTLE CONFUSED. He did not understand why these men were practically obsessed with Miriam, nor why they were being summoned. But that was what was happening, so he rolled with it.

It took some doing, but Karl led Abby from one soldier to the next while Peter and Gerald finished organizing what needed to happen afterward. Gerald had to arrange for Talbert, effectively the general of the soldiers, to have a digestive problem that would be severe enough to keep him away from Miriam.

The man had been practically dying in the bathroom for the last ten minutes. It was time for Gerald to go in and ask him what he could do to help.

This part of the plan was *so* cliché, but so necessary. Gerald wasn't high enough up the food chain here to order the boss around. Peter waited, and after a bit of muffled talking, Gerald exited and gave a thumbs-up to the wall opposite where Peter stood, cloaked. Peter smiled. Being invisible was the best.

Without speaking, he led Peter down a flight of stairs and through a long concrete hallway.

Gerald took a calming breath before entered a random door. Peter peeked inside. He couldn't see Miriam, but he heard moaning.

"Gerald?" A harsh voice questioned.

"Tally's sick. He's dumping his guts in the toilet. He asked if I would take over for a few. It's gonna be a while. Just wanted to let you know it was me out here."

"Fine, whatever. Don't let anyone down here. Got it?"

"Yes, Sir." He closed the door and took up his station. Then whispered, "Now we just have to wait for your family."

"They will be here any minute, I'm certain," Peter said, and felt a wave of relief.

"Well, you better get out there and wait for them then. I got this. I swear, if I hear her screaming, I will kill Willis and Les both."

Peter nodded to himself, but he also swallowed. That statement was one that he'd never heard before in his life, at least, not said in seriousness. 'I'm gonna kill you, Peter Miller!' or 'You are dead, you pesky flea.' both had a certain, non-committal feel to them. The way Gerald said it did not have that feel.

He cleared his throat. "Uhm, I would suggest not killing them. It is kind of not good to kill."

"Yes, I've heard that."

"Well, good. Also, you're one of us now, so you will have to learn to act like it."

Gerald glared at the wall, his big head probably ticking through the repercussions of his very hasty admittance into the Guardian family. Then he shrugged. "I've been part of worse groups. If you'll have me, and Miriam will be there, I'm in. But I'm also a warrior, it's who I am. It's who we all are."

"Good for you. Still, don't kill them."

"Peter, shut up and get out of here. I can handle this."

"Okay. Geez. Don't kill them though. Pinky promise. If you break it, I get to break your pinky."

Gerald rolled his eyes and took a swipe in Peter's general direction, but he missed. Peter took this as his cue to skedaddle.

After making his way back through the Joneses compound, he as nearing the exit when he ran into Abby and Karl. He whistled softly at them, "Abby?"

"Peter? Where are you?"

"I'm here by this picture of an old guy."

They walked over. Abby reached out for him and found his arm. "It's time to go tell your father. I have summoned everyone that is to be summoned."

"Awesome, can I just say again how cool that was?"

"Stop it! It was totally freaky." She crossed her arms around her waist and looked green.

"No, Abby, you don't get it, and I don't have time to explain it to you. We will talk, but in the meantime just know you are totally cool!"

"What's next?" Karl asked looking around tensely.

"Gerald is in place. I am going to find my father, and you guys will gather up everyone once the distraction starts, and bring them to the North ridge of Edenia. You have to wait there. It shouldn't take too long for me to update everyone on what is going on, so just hang tight. Abby can get your men what they need, but bring supplies if you can."

"Copy."

"Copy? What is that supposed to mean?"

"Nothing. It's a way of saying, 'Okay, I got it'."

"All right, well that's stupid. Just say 'I got it'." Peter rolled his eyes, but he was still mostly invisible, so the gesture was wasted. "Okay, well, I'm off. Good luck! And Karl, keep Abby safe."

"Sure thing," Karl responded, but Peter was already halfway out the door.

CHAPTER 29

Earlier, Seth used the credit card at an ATM to withdraw some cash for their journey and to arrange things with Tony. The pilot had said he was up to the task, though he sounded as freaked out as everyone about the bombings and the viruses. Still, he barely asked any questions. Seth had carried Lillian into the small airplane hangar even though she insisted she was feeling a bit better.

They sat together waiting for Tony to finish his last-minute checklist. Seth couldn't stop his mind from going around in tortuous circles.

What had happened to him at the hospital, he asked himself for the hundredth time. The whole vision thing? But he pushed the question aside. Seth's stomach growled. He'd hardly eaten anything since dinner with Miriam the night before, and he'd insisted Lilly take almost all the food he'd brought with them. He pushed his hunger aside. He'd promised himself he wouldn't eat again until he got back to Edenia.

His knee bounced up and down. This worthless round-trip had cost him dearly.

What would Seth do if his actions were the very thing that killed Lilly?

More, what would he do if Lilly didn't make it back to Edenia, if she couldn't say goodbye to her parents, her sister? He knew that his father would never forgive him, and it would break his mother's heart. His throat clenched as his eyes flooded. How could have been so stupid?

He couldn't do this again. He'd doubted the feelings he had

before he drugged Miriam, and look where his choices got him. He knew what he felt in the hospital, and what needed to happen now. As long as he held to that, Lillian would be safe, and all would work out how it was supposed to. He took a deep breath to clear his mind.

"Stop it," Lilly whispered.

He looked over at her as she slouched in her uncomfortable chair. "Stop what?" he answered, and reached for her.

"You're beating yourself up. Stop it." Her cheeks had some color to them. Her lips weren't so pale.

"I was just pulling myself out of it, thank you very much. I have made this whole thing a crap shoot, if I do say so myself."

It took her a minute to reply. "Seth, you did what you thought was best, and I love you for it."

He smiled, his heart a little more at ease. "You're looking better."

"I'm feeling better. Why do you think that is?"

He reached into his backpack and handed her the last apple from Edenia. "Eat this."

She took the apple and crunched on it. Seth smiled. For one moment, he let himself look at this with hope. They would make it back with Lilly still hanging on. Edenia would save her. It would be amazing. He smiled again and imagined how life would go on in Edenia. Lilly would be whole, and he would be happy to pay his dues and live there.

He would.

He really would.

But then reality crashed the hopeful party he was attempting to throw in his brain; there would be consequences. What could his life possibly look like in Edenia after all of this? After Miriam? Would they let him stay after that betrayal? And Miriam would hate him, he was certain she would, for perhaps the rest of his life. Heck, he would hate himself for the rest of his life for screwing this whole thing up, with his lack of faith, tricking her, drugging her, and all his horrendous actions toward her. What if the Joneses were hurting her? How could she face him again? How could he face her?

All of his thoughts were based on the assumption Miriam would be released back to her people, or she would escape. What if he never saw her again?

Guilt and fear ran up and down his spine and filled his thoughts, tormenting him until he couldn't stand himself. He wrestled back and forth in his hard metal chair, wishing he could just do the last thirty-five hours over. Wishing the stupid doctor could just have saved Lilly. Wishing he'd had faith. He told himself that if Lillian could survive, he could live with the rest.

But it was a lie.

Seth watched Lilly and tried not to let his anger and frustration get the better of him.

"Are we going to talk about what happened in the hospital?" Lilly asked quietly.

"What do you mean?"

"You like, I don't know, defeated those guards like you were Frank Sawyer or something."

"I don't even know who Frank Sawyer is."

"He's that guy in the books...never mind. Stop not answering." She took another bite of her apple. "It just looked like..." She chewed. "...like you knew what they were going to do before they did it."

Seth wanted to close out those thoughts again, but he couldn't with his sister gazing up at him. Seth saw in his mind the look on the hospital guard's face. He'd seen something in Seth's eyes. The man had looked at him like he was scared, like Seth was a mutant. In an instant, Seth had known what the guards were going to do. Like, he'd seen it happened. It was hazy, but it was there. What did it all mean?

She closed her eyes as she said, "Today is the eighth day, you know."

Seth's jaw dropped.

"Wheels up in five, kids," Tony yelled at them. "Let's get your sister settled." He thumbed at them to enter the plane.

Seth stood, picked Lilly up, and once again wondered where his strength came from. He was not by any means muscular, as in big thick cannons or anything. Still, carrying Lilly shouldn't feel like nothing at all. She weighed like a hundred pounds.

Something had happened to him. Finally, he allowed himself to say the words inside his mind. *Do I have a superpower now? Is that what happened to me at the hospital? Am I strong now?* And part of his mind thought that would not suck. It was useful at this moment. And besides the shock, he didn't feel weird or abnormal, just strong.

But what about the guard and what happened in the hospital? How did that fit into his powers from Edenia?

Blinking, he focused on the task at hand.

Lilly.

Ensuring Lilly was comfortably sat in her seat.

He needed a plan.

What in the world was he going to do once they landed?

Yes, he would think on that, remembering his first ride into Edenia one week ago. How would he do this?

With that thought, Seth considered prayer, because if he was being honest, he could use all the help he could get. Closing his eyes, Seth interlocked his fingers and sent his mind into the universe, hoping his thoughts would reach the ears of a greater being than himself.

CHAPTER 30

Peter

Popping out of nowhere, Peter demanded, "I've been waiting hours for you all. What took you so long?"

His father jumped. The man's face went all scrunchy and red with surprise and alarm. This made Peter grin.

"Peter Gabriel Miller, what in the name of all that's good and holy..."

He didn't have time for a good-old tongue lashing, so he got down to business.

"Father, respectfully, be quiet. I only have a few moments." He looked at who was with his father, making sure he had everyone's attention. "I have no idea what your plan is for getting Miriam back, but I need you to forget it and trust my plan instead. I have a ridiculously cliché one and it is chopping along beautifully. We have been waiting for you to get here so you can cause a big enough ruckus to get Willis out here. So that is your job. Do it well. I will take care of extracting Miriam."

His father swallowed his anger and looked bug eyed at Peter. It took him a full ten seconds to nod. "I trust all the sneaking around you've done..."

Peter interrupted him again. "I have to go, Pa. Please trust me. I will get Miriam and we are going to drive her home. I will get word to you as soon as the deed is done. Then come home. I have so much to tell you. Also, the Joneses are not kidding around. They have been torturing Miriam since she got here. They will not hesitate to shoot you all."

He heard Eve and Hannah gasp. He saw his brother Garren's jaw muscle's twitch, and his Uncle Jai approached him and said, "You are amazing, Peter. What a way to start off your Guardianship!"

Peter couldn't help himself. "I know. It's like the Master had this all planned out. Every step has led to the next." They all shared a commiserating look. "Remember, be careful. They are going to be furious once Miriam is gone. They will kill you. But you must go wreak some havoc. Make some noise. Blow crap up!" He smiled and pulled his Nature to him.

Running for all he was worth, Peter headed for the small grey building that secured the entrance to an underground tunnel. Soon, huffing and puffing with a side ache, Peter stood concealed to the left of a large metal door. As soon as the distraction pulled Willis away, smoker guy—Ben—would let him in, and they would race to get Miriam who hopefully would be shackle free, thanks to Gerald.

He hoped this distraction would be enough. He also hoped no one got killed.

PETER WAITED AND WAITED, and when nothing happened, he jogged back up the hill right into the viper's nest. He got there just in time to see the guards posted at the gate get taken down without a problem. It had to be Uncle Brian who did the deed simply because Peter couldn't exactly see what went down. Brian's earth Nature concealed him.

Peter pulled his Nature to him, and sure enough, he saw the shadow of Uncle Brian.

He watched as the guards who stood ready for anything fell to the ground. When Brian was done, two ginger eyed rock Natures took the gates down. It was weird to watch his tall, willowy sister Hannah and Gregory pull down iron and stone gates like they were moving a pile of kindling. He'd never really seen them in action such as that. A little thrill went up his back.

He turned to his father, who was staring up into the trees. Peter looked around and finally saw several security cameras, some on the now demolished gate, but some in the trees around it. He knew they'd recorded the take-down. He wanted to warn his father about the cameras, but he should have known the man would be on top of it.

With the wave of his father's hand and vibration of his irises, Peter knew that the recording had ceased to function. Hopefully his father also thought to find the electrical hub so all the recordings would be toast.

It didn't take long before four more armed men showed up. They hurried right past Peter. When they approached the gate, a fierce wind blew the gravel from the long driveway directly into the men's faces. The pain of it brought all four to their knees.

Garren and his team darted into the open and weaved in and out, taking the men with them. Then it was just a matter of removing their weapons, hog-tying them, and having a ginger pile them up. They were not attempting to be discreet and hide their Natures as they normally would. Peter wondered why.

Probably because Edenians never rescued Jones prisoners as they did now. Peter knew that Willow, Eve, Gregory, Hannah, Wallace, Jeremy, and several others stood watch over the captured Jones because he could see their little circle obscured in the trees not too far away. All the Joneses looked about to pee their pants.

Peter grinned.

The ten or so Guardians in charge of making a ruckus did not waste time. They spread out, jogging through the woods. Peter went with them, fully aware that his duty lay in the opposite direction.

But he just couldn't miss this fight.

The first altercation was Uncle Jai and a Jones with a wicked looking scar on his cheek. The moment the man saw Jai walking through the woods twenty feet away, he aimed his massive gun and fired it.

Fear spiked through Peter. Sure, Uncle Jai was super-fast, but Peter wasn't sure if he was faster than a bullet. The bullets rained and fanned out. Jai blurred. Peter blinked. Then Uncle Jai had the man face first on the ground. Uncle Jai held the gun in a relaxed posture with his boot on the man's neck.

Peter took two delayed, reactionary steps toward Jai, his hand raised, but he stopped when the man on the ground wasn't struggling. Like, at all. He must be unconscious. How in the blink of an eye had Jai done that? A surge of pride welled up in Peter as a sound caused Uncle Jai to blur behind a tree.

Another Jones came running out of the trees, a blur at his heels. When he got to about the same place Uncle Jai's fallen man lay, some part of the blur struck the man in the back. He tumbled and somersaulted on the ground. It looked like a practiced move which ended in the man taking a knee and pulling his gun around toward the blur, which Peter could now see was Garren. He wasn't moving at top speed like Jai had been.

Suddenly, that changed. Garren burst into movement. He was like a hummingbird zipping between flowers. He darted in at super speed and paused for a moment so Peter could see him kick the gun off aim. The weapon went off in a series of shots up and to the left. Then Garren blurred to the other side of the man and put his palm into the kneeling man's temple. Blurring again, he helped the man go down further by sweeping his bent knee from the ground.

The man lay on his back, and Garren blurred over him for the last strike, but this man was tough. When Garren paused his assault, the man pulled a knife and turned to his side to swipe upward.

But Garren just flowed like the river he was, his hand blurring around the man's knifing wrist. Garren used his momentum to do a tuck in the air, landing on the other side of the soldier. The power of the movement not only broke the man's arm, but flipped his body to face the other way. The Jones cried out in pain.

Knowing the man was beaten, Garren walked normally around him to his back and used his boot to push the man over so his chest touched the ground. He pulled some zip ties from his pocket and secured the wrists of both his man and Jai's fallen opponent.

Without looking up, Garren asked, "Jai, will you get Eve? I think I damaged this one a bit more than required."

"You think?" Came Jai's sarcastic reply in his Indian accent. "I don't feel it's safe for Eve out here quite yet."

"Well shoot, I guess he will have to suffer until it is safe."

"I suppose so. With that in mind, do you think we could try to do a little less showing off and a little more getting the job done?" Garren was silent for a moment as he finished his work. Soon enough, he stood and nodded, his eyes still on the ground, until Jai added, "That responsible bit out of the way, I must add how totally brilliant that was. I mean, you should have seen his face. He didn't even know what hit him."

Garren looked up, smiling. "It was really fun. Most of the time all I think about is not being seen, now that we don't care, it's like freedom, man. This is the most fun I've had in ages."

"Agreed, my friend. Agreed." Jai paused and looked at his hands before adding, "Shall we go get some more then?"

"Are you kidding?"

Jai smiled again, "After you then, Master Ninja."

The two men laughed out loud as they blurred off. Despite his emotions running high, and a strong desire to follow them tempting him, Peter realized that it was far past time for him to make it back down the hill.

It didn't take long before Peter heard gunfire again. His ears rang from the loud pounding sound, and he longed to leave his post and watch the fight. It was totally awesome. Surveilling it helped him understand many of the things his father had allowed lately. Things the council was against; like Garren and Gabe forming a group to teach the hand-to-hand combat training they'd received while on sabbatical. This fight was proof of its usefulness.

Even Uncle Brian and Gregory had been practicing a seriously remarkable maneuver at home. Here and now, Peter watched as Gregory threw Uncle Brian toward the enemy, and once the invisible man of stone hit the enemy, he totally went hands-of-rock postal on them. It was pretty radical.

He'd never understood before now, but he had to admit that Papa was led by a power Peter did not know. It made him ache to get out there and get his hands dirty. Smiling longingly, he told himself that his part of this war was to secure Miriam. His role was key. It was the purpose of the mission and the whole point of this distraction.

Peter reached the door he sought, and it instantly opened. The smoker man—Ben—stood there looking this way and that. Peter walked through the door as the man whispered, "Peter?"

Peter tapped him on the shoulder and let go of his Nature.

The man jumped. When he turned around, Peter yelled. "Boo!" and smiled.

"Why you little..." with effort the man bit his tongue.

"Come on, you can't tell me that wasn't classic. You would have done the same thing. How could you help it?"

The man rolled his eyes, and that was when Peter got serious.

"Where's Miriam?"

The door shut, and the smoker man said, "Follow me." His voice was grumpy.

Peter couldn't imagine why.

CHAPTER 31

Miriam woke up to the sound of voices, but the moment the deep tones brought her mind back to her, her body screamed in pain. It was impossible to hold back the sound as waking brought her more torture.

"...too much last time. Let us just make sure not to give her too little. After what she told us she can do...I do not want even a chance of that happening." That was Willis' voice.

"She is quiet cooperative when the dose is right, but even then, she evades us on the tree." Les' voice sounded perplexed, and it made her shiver.

There was a grunt of disgust in response.

Everything felt acute. Her breath, her heart beating, her eyes blinking, and her ears hearing.

"Time to answer my questions." The voice was harsh, impatient, and seriously annoyed. A hand slapped her squarely across the face.

Jolted by the abuse, her eyes bulging in the bright light, she bit her lip in pain. Her eyes found her attacker.

Willis Jones' sculpted jaws and biceps clenched as he looked into her face. "Now that I have your undivided attention, where were we? Oh yes, you were going to tell us how to get past your defenses."

Panic ripped through Miriam's mind. This wasn't the same question. Had she told him things? She raced backward through her memories to hunt for the slightest betrayal, but the memories were so ethereal. She couldn't collect them enough to search.

Not knowing what to say she asked, "What have I told you so far?"

"Oh no. That is not how this works. I ask the questions; you give the answers, or Les gets to have his way with you. How do we do it? How do we surpass your defenses?"

Miriam thought. There was only one right answer to this question, and it was one she knew she could give. "You don't."

She was not expecting the slap, but once it landed across her flaming cheek, she knew she'd been stupid. She needed to go on.

"You don't understand." Her voice cracked and tears fell from her stinging eyes. "You're asking me how to beat the Supreme Power. I have no answer for you. You can't do it. No one can. Not pharaoh with all his riches and slaves, not Jonah with his running feet, not Caesar, not Nebuchadnezzar, not Lucifer himself. Who do you think you are to go against him?" Miriam did not glare back at this man as she defied him. She did not need to.

The fury radiating off of Willis seemed to bend the air in the room. At that moment, her friend, the big bald guy—the one that had saved her from the murderous man attempting to slit her throat—burst into the room, shouting.

"They're here."

He looked different, though. He looked like he had a halo about him. She wasn't sure what it was, probably a result of the drugs she was on. She blinked rapidly at him as Les and Willis pulled firearms off the walls.

Both wore grins. "Wonderful. Just as I'd hoped. They won't be protected from our weapons here. This flushed them out."

Fear flooded Miriam's heart. He was speaking of her family. They were here to rescue her. She felt relief, but Willis' words frightened her. Since they were not in Edenia, under the protection of the wind Natures, could they be shot? She imagined they could. Though it caused her pain, she wriggled in her restraints to no avail.

"Gerald, you stay here with the girl. Do not let anyone get near her." Willis looked pointedly at Gerald, and the man nodded.

Miriam watch Gerald during this exchange, but again she had to blink. He looked blurry like there were two of him. Focusing, she wondered if he would be her salvation. He'd said he wanted to help her, hadn't he?

Willis and Les left, and the moment the door closed, Gerald ran to her side. "Are you all right?" he asked as he began untying her manacles.

"Yes," she said as she shook her head no. "I mean no, I mean what are you doing? They will kill you."

"Better me than you," he said as he looked deeply into her eyes.

She cleared her throat. "Okay. Please. Can we please get out of here?"

Gerald snorted. "I thought that was what I was doing." He grabbed the fetters again and began working some sort of magic with them.

Soon, Miriam was free from the chair, but when she stood, her legs gave out. "It's fine, I'll carry you to the car."

The burly man picked her up. The pain in her chest made her nauseous, but before she passed out, she touched Gerald's face and captured his attention.

"Thank you. Thank you so mu..." darkness.

ALL TOO SOON, the world of darkness began to take on the swaying motion of a swing, and she felt yanked out of the blissful ethereal nothingness. Her stomach felt unsettled. Her chest and head ached, and the ache grew until it was pain. She smelled soap and sweat and chemicals. Her eyes fluttered open with the sound of a familiar voice.

"We might run into some of them on the way out. I let them know it would be us, so they won't blow up the car or anything." A hand gripped her leg. "Oh, thank goodness. She's not dead. Miriam?"

Miriam turned her head toward the voice. "Peter?" she whispered.

"In the flesh, my dear."

"You shouldn't be here, what are, what..." she didn't have the energy to speak.

"Master, did I say thank you for sparing Miriam's life? What I meant was, forget it Master, you can have her."

"Hey, that's no way to talk." An unfamiliar voice commented.

"Yes, but, she's so bossy. Here I am saving her life..." Miriam tuned him out to look at the source of the other voice.

It was at this point that Miriam registered that she was being carried by a huge man. She blinked. He was blurry, but familiar. He panted, and sweat dripped from his brow, but he continued to move with her long, willowy frame in his arms.

She instinctively sat up straighter. "What is..." but her words were cut off by a horrid burning pain that immediately stretched from her neck down her arms and chest.

The big man calmed her, "It's okay Miss Miriam. I'll get you out of here. We're almost to the car."

Miriam leaned back into the man, too weak to care about what was happening around her.

They burst through some doors and onto the most beautiful grass she'd ever seen. A black car waited. Carefully, the big man put Miriam in and moved to sit behind the wheel.

Peter slid in beside her and began looking her over.

"Are you all right?" He tugged her sticky shirt away from her collarbones, and she screamed in pain. His hand shot away from her. "Oh my gosh, Miriam. I... They...they branded you! With their name. Oh, my..." His hand moved toward her shirt again and she glared at him but was too tired to make it really effective.

The car began to move, and her stomach lurched again.

Peter looked away for a moment, but when his eyes returned, they contained horrible, bone deep, make-her-want-to-bawl pity. Ashamed, she focused on his chin.

He also had that hazy look to him. Blinking several times, she attempted to clear her vision, but to no avail. She must have blinked too much because Peter commented on it.

"Did they do something to your eyes? Why do you keep blinking?"

Gerald answered, "It's the drugs."

Something hit the window next to her. Startled, Miriam saw a blur of movement that stabilized into something solid, but still liquid in its movement, and thus unclear to her already compromised eyes. The blur kept pace with the moving car.

Peter leaned over her and made the window float down. How he knew how to perform this task, Miriam would need to find out.

He yelled.

"Garren, it's all right. We've got her. Tell everyone to go home. Gerald's going to drive us." Peter thumbed at the big man.

The blur shifted away from the moving vehicle, and Peter floated the window back up. This time she watched and saw the small button he pushed. Once he sat back, Miriam made a conscious effort to move her hand over to the button. She had to do it carefully because the movement required muscles that were connected to her chest. Her hand made it there just as a door on the far side of the car opened. It made a startling sound, and the driver swerved.

The blurry shape from before flowed into the car and solidified into Garren, her elder brother.

Blood pumped through her body at her startled reaction, and her mind cleared enough for Miriam to realize her thinking was compromised. She hadn't even wondered at the shape, or who Peter was talking to. But now with a moment of clarity, all of these thoughts and questions bombarded her mind. Two of her brothers were here at the Joneses. They came to get her, but how? How did they even know she was here?

Gerald sputtered some nonsense that Miriam ignored to struggle with her own fuzzy thoughts, but he also swerved the car as he prepared to be attacked by Garren, and that made her sick.

"There is no way I am letting you go anywhere with one of them," she heard Garren say. However, all the protestations by

Gerald and attempted attacking by Garren, and crazy driving were interrupted by Peter's voice.

"Stop Garren! Calm down. I have this all taken care of. Gerald here is on our side."

Garren stopped, but Gerald continued to look at him with wide eyes and a raised arm between them.

"What?" Garren asked, still eyeing the man skeptically. However, Peter was silent for a moment and Garren looked back. His eyes found Miriam, and all the anger from before morphed into concern. Turning all the way around in his seat he stated, "I will talk to you about this in a minute." He reached for Miriam, touching her leg. "Thank heaven. Miriam, are you alright?" Garren asked.

Her mind wandered all around the question. How did one answer a query like that?

Her thoughts were interrupted by Peter.

"What is she supposed to say Garren? Come on. Not only is she loopy because of the drugs—that's how they stopped her from using her Nature by the way—but she's in shock. They tortured her. You should see what they did to her chest." He leaned in and whispered, "They branded her." He leaned back, and Miriam attempted another glare, but her heart wasn't in it. He turned away from her and softly said, "I don't think she's going to be all right for a long time."

Miriam watched Garren's eyes dip to her shirt, and he bent his neck to see better. Miriam wanted to move her hand to cover her burns, but that would just hurt, and besides, everyone would find out soon enough. Garren's face went red as his gaze met hers. His irises began to swirl with his Nature. He clenched the fist that draped over the seat, and his eyes moved to Gerald.

Miriam wanted to stop him, but again she was usurped by Peter. "Don't, Garren."

"But he's a Jones." Gritted teeth spat the words.

"Not anymore. He's a follower of Miriam now," Peter said with a distasteful twist to his mouth.

"What?" His anger shattered as he looked back at Peter. "What are you talking about?"

Yes, Miriam wondered, what was he talking about?

"Please, Garren, I don't want to explain it a million times, just trust me. He's taking us to Edenia, and when we get there, and I have Papa in front of me, I will tell you everything."

Garren relaxed after nodding to Peter, but he kept his eyes on the man driving the car.

After a few minutes of silence, Peter commented cantankerously, "I see that none of you were concerned for my safety. I've been gone for over ten hours."

Garren smiled. "The best ten hours I've had in about thirteen years."

Peter laughed, "Touché."

And even through her confused state, her pain, and her blurry vision, Miriam smiled, but only on the inside.

CHAPTER 32

Seth started awake, heart racing, brain swirling, joy overwhelming. He shook his head and tried to recall why he was so excited and relieved. He gazed out the airplane window as his mind tried to grab onto a momentous discovery, and the pieces settled into his conscious. *Talbert Jones is my biological grandfather; his wife was a soldier, not an Edenian. Talbert dropped his father off in Edenia like an orphan. The Miller family had adopted him. They were not his family by blood, only by adoption.*

"Miriam's not my cousin," he whispered out loud into the noise of the plane. "She's not my cousin." His heart leapt into his throat. "We are not related to the Millers, not by blood."

He looked across at Lillian, wanting to share the news with her, but he remained in his seat when he saw her pale form slumped, asleep.

He sat straighter in his seat and placed a hand over his heart. *Miriam.* He focused on the spot in his mind that felt connected to Miriam, and he turned instinctively toward where she was.

He closed his eyes in the moment of bliss, and a different sense began to build inside him. Instantly, his breathing was hard and loud. His hands clenched the arm rests, all while the power of that other force built within him.

Then it exploded.

He opened his eyes. It was if he was no longer on the airplane. He was in a house in Edenia standing before a scared, shaking Miriam who would not look him in the face. He tried to explain himself, why he had done what he had. She covered her ears, unwilling to listen, and began to cry. She clutched at her chest with a protective vigor, and Seth knew she had been hurt. Then her father was there.

The scene before him vanished.

Seth understood, but had no idea what just happened to him. Miriam was hurt. What he had done had hurt her. The road ahead before them would no longer turn out the way he desired. He could accept that, or make it worse.

He shook his head. What was happening to him? It was so real. What did it mean? Was he just hallucinating?

A little tickle at the back of his mind told him he was a freak. And he did not even want to consider what that meant.

Tony's voice came over the speaker system announcing they were fifteen minutes away from landing.

AS THEY EXITED THE PLANE, Seth expressed his gratitude over and over again to their pilot. Tony asked what the doctor had said. Seth explained that they gave her some medicine and that she would be right as rain.

Tony also told them the latest news while they waited for a taxi. A whole bunch of dangerous countries had declared war on America.

"Of course, the President is practically lapping that up. You know how she is; she thinks she has balls that are as big as a bull's. She's cat-calling them," Tony said.

"I'm not surprised. I don't know that much about your president, but she seems obsessed with power."

"Oh, she is."

"How did she get elected twice?"

"Don't ask me."

"I will say something for her. Her confidence has infected this country. Less than three weeks ago I was living in Cairo, and there was no transportation there. There was looting, and martial law, and bad crap. My dad is a diplomat, and that is the only reason we were able to get out."

Tony looked at him in awe. He got that a lot. It usually was about his dad, but today the awe was different. "I wouldn't go telling people that you are new to the country. Have you heard about the viruses?"

He named the one he'd heard about today, GSR or something, but that wasn't the one Tony referred to. It was a virus from South America. It was put into a bomb and dropped with a drone on the city of Bogota Colombia. Millions of people were exposed and would die.

Seth sat in stunned silence. He didn't really know how to process what was happening in the world. He didn't understand it all. Cairo had been volatile the entire time he lived there. He was used to the life of being careful and not going out after dark, staying in his gated neighborhood with its armed guards. But this...this was the whole world.

For the first time in ages, he really wanted the comfort of his father's strong arms around him, the love of his mother, and the camaraderie of his sisters. He was scared.

Once Tony stopped talking, Seth used the money from the ATM at the last air strip to hire one of the men from the hanger to drive them. He carefully placed Lilly inside the man's car.

"I'm Conrad. So, where to?"

Wasn't that the question? He knew he needed to get to Edenia as soon as possible, but he wondered what he should do about Mr. Jones. They would pass right by his compound. A crazy thought crossed his mind. Should he attempt to get Miriam back? The instant it came to him though, he berated himself for its stupidity. If he recalled correctly, everyone in the compound had guns.

However silly, Seth couldn't help wanting to break into the compound himself once he got Lillian safe.

"Hey kid, I gotta get back to work. Where to?"

Seth pulled out his phone, tapped on his maps app, and pulled the map out so that it showed not just his location but the spot he knew held Edenia.

He held it up for the driver. "Sorry, it's not an address, but could you get me as close to here as possible without going by this place?" He pointed the Joneses compound.

"Uh, sure. Let me see your cash. I'm not going all the way out there for nothing."

The driver eyed the wad of bills and then glanced at Lilly. "You guys didn't come from overseas or anything did you?"

"Yes and no, why?"

The drivers hand stopped mid-reach for the gear shift. "What's she got?" A look of panic filled his face.

Seth was surprised when Lillian spoke up. "I have a brain tumor and only hours to live, so could you step on it?"

The man sighed visibly, and the car started moving. "Shouldn't you be in a hospital or something?"

"Yes..." Lilly croaked, and the rest of her words came out in a whisper that not even Seth could recognize.

"Lilly. Please hang on. We are almost there." Seth took her hand and cuddled her into his side.

After about twenty minutes of driving, the driver asked, "You guys aren't some of those crazies living in white tents out here, are you?"

Confused, Seth asked, "What are you talking about? There aren't any white tents."

The guy looked confused. "That tent city isn't where you are headed? Well then, where in the world are you going with that sick girl?"

Seth didn't have any idea what to say to the man, but his mouth spoke anyhow. "We're going home." The words shocked him, and even Lilly turned impressed eyes up at him.

She smiled and whispered, "Home."

"Oh, home, well that makes me feel much better. So, you are going to the tents." He eyed them suspiciously in his rearview mirror and adjusted himself uncomfortably, but pretty soon he couldn't hold it in any longer. "Are they really healing people in those tents?" He raised his eyebrows. "Ya know, calling on the power of God and such to raise the dead and stuff? That's why you're going out there, right?" He paused. "Come on, you can tell me."

Seth was so confused, all he could think of to say was, "I cannot divulge that information at this time. You don't have the proper clearance." It was something he'd seen on a show, and it seemed to cover all the bases.

Lilly laughed. It was weak, but it was still a laugh, and when he looked down at her, her eyes looked alive. They looked brighter and shinier than he'd seen all day.

He smiled at her. "How are you?"

She swallowed dryly and nodded her head a smidgen. "I don't completely suck," she whispered. "I'm thirsty and hungry."

That was awesome. The first thing to go was her appetite, but since arriving in Edenia she'd been eating more regularly.

Once again, Seth felt guilt. The signs were there. The signs that Edenia was good. He just didn't have the right eyes to see them. Literally.

"Okay, we are maybe thirty minutes out, can you hang on?"

She exhaled and nuzzled back into his shoulder.

He took that for a yes.

IT DIDN'T TAKE LONG, but it felt like forever. They were close. He could feel it. Seth saw a guy on horseback. He said, "Hey Conrad, pull up next to that guy. I'll ask him if he can help us." The second he said this, that thing happened again.

Seth was transported to someplace else. He saw himself watching the horse get spooked by a loud noise, rear up, and stumble into the ditch, falling backward onto the cowboy. Seth heard the crunching of bone and the cries of pain. The vision felt familiar, like he'd seen it before.

When he came back to present life, Conrad was already slowing, and waved a hand out the window to hail the cowboy.

Seth rolled down his window. "Hi, sorry to bother you," he began, still a little discombobulated from the weird other world he saw. He shook his head and focused, "But we are in a rush. We are looking for a little town out here. It's called Edenia."

The guy looked to be about twenty-five, thick through the chest, blond, really round symmetric face. He was tall and fit, with large hands and a big cowboy hat. He swished thick lips to the side, thinking about Seth's question. Then he said in a completely emasculatingly low voice. "Nope, sorry."

Seth sighed and looked back up at the intimidating man. Did the Greek gods make cowboys? If they did, this guy would be the poster boy.

Seth got back to business. "Do you know what's over there? Beyond that hill?" He pointed in the direction he felt drawn.

"Um, there's a little abandoned town over there."

Seth brightened. "Does it have wooden houses and a really tall, like, fence thing around it?"

"With sentinel-like structures every so often?"

Seth nodded.

The cowboy nodded back. "Yeah, it's about five minutes down this road and on your right."

"I told you, Conrad," Seth said to the driver.

The man snorted.

Seth turned back. "Thanks." Because he thought maybe it would help, he added, "Be careful. There's a ditch on the side of this road. I wouldn't want your horse to fall."

The cowboy smirked at him. "Buttercup is trained to a T. I think we can handle it." Then he tipped his hat to Seth.

Seth sat back in his seat and nodded to the man and started to roll up his window.

"Wait," the cowboy said in a panic. Seth looked back, and the guy cleared his throat. "What's over there?"

Seth squinted at him. "In Edenia?"

He nodded.

Not knowing what exactly to say about Edenia Seth answered casually, "Oh, nothing, it's just my home." And with a smile, he finished rolling up his window.

Lillian moaned. She was pale. Seth whispered, "We're almost there." And without a second thought for the cowboy, said, "Get a move on, Conrad. We know where to go now, and we don't have much time."

Then time went in slow motion. Conrad's right arm was draped across the back of his seat. Seth watched as they pulled forward. His hand moved as if through jelly toward the stirring wheel, and Seth knew he was going to honk the horn as a 'see ya later'. It took his mind longer than it should have to realize the sound of a honking horn was what Seth had heard in his little vision, second-sight thingy that spooked the horse.

Seth watched Conrad compress the horn. He whipped his head around just in time to see the beast rear up in reaction to the sound, fall backward because of the ditch, and then roll over her rider.

Through the liquid-like moment of slowed time, Seth yelled, "Stop!"

The man slammed on his brakes, turned and yelled "What, what in..."

Seth interrupted him as a tentative thought came. "Didn't you say that there was a tent city out here and that they were doing healings and stuff?"

Conrad looked annoyed.

So, Seth explained. "Turn around. The guy that helped us, when you honked, it spooked his horse and it threw him."

Conrad looked behind him, and so did Seth. Both horse and rider were on the ground. Swearing, the driver yanked off his seat belt and burst from the car, running up to the cowboy.

What would have happened if he had reacted more quickly to the vision thing he had? If that is what they were. This situation confirmed that he really was seeing the future.

He didn't want to think about it. He made sure that Lillian was still settled and then got out to run to Conrad's side. "Are ambulances still running?" Seth asked as soon as he was next to the man.

The horse tried to get up with Seth's approach, but Seth could tell it wouldn't get anywhere. Its back foot was wonky and it couldn't move it, much less stand on it, without a scream of pain. Conrad, who knew nothing about horses, stayed away from the beast. Seth moved to calm the beautiful mare.

Conrad touched the young man's neck feeling for a pulse as he answered Seth's question, "Of course...I think."

Once certain the young man was breathing and had a heartbeat, Conrad pulled out his phone to call 911 as he said, "if they have something available it will take an ambulance an hour, at least, to get out here and an hour to get back to the city, and this guy doesn't have that kind of time."

Seth looked at him even as he continued to stroke the horse. "Seriously? What should we do then? You're not telling me that this guy is going to die? That there is no way around it?" The moment the words were out of Seth's mouth, his second sight came over him again. He saw himself stealing Conrad's car and racing it into Edenia. Next, he saw his father, Lillian, and Miriam's mother, and he knew they could help the cowboy.

The question was, did Edenia have a way of healing people? And if they did, would they help this guy? Their secrets were the most important thing in the world to them.

Conrad was yelling at the cowboy, "Hey, can you hear me?" and the man poked at the younger guy. Seth was sure he had some broken ribs and maybe a broken spine as well because his torso looked disfigured. Horses weigh a lot. Conrad repeated the question, but there wasn't any answer. Seth looked around. There was a large rock to the side. It had blood on it. He had hit his head. This guy could really be about to die.

Conrad pulled out his phone to try 911 again. Then Conrad was talking to the emergency operator. Seth furiously considered what to do. Should he follow his vision? He had in the hospital, and it had worked out. He hadn't with the cowboy, and now this man might die.

Seth nodded to himself.

Heat emanated from the car as if to draw Seth's eye. Conrad had left it running, and he was distracted with his phone conversation as if this whole scenario was just as the gods wanted it to be. Seth knew this would be his only chance.

Stepping casually away from the fallen man, he slid into the open driver side of the car, slammed the door, and locked it. Shoving the gear into drive, he slammed on the gas and took off. Conrad chased after him.

Turning the other way around in his seat, he yelled at Lilly, "Hang on." Her eyes popped open, and she looked around wildly. "Sorry, are you okay?", he asked, while attempting to maneuver the car quickly down the road.

She didn't answer, but when he glanced at her, he saw something both horrible and heartening. Her black irises were not exactly black any longer. they were swirling with green or blue, he couldn't tell which. Blood rushed to her face. She looked vibrant for one second, and then the effect left her. The moment it did, she slumped.

"Lilly, Lillian?" Seth called anxiously.

Knowing he had to get her to Edenia now, he slammed the gas pedal to the floor. The dash GPS said it was about four minutes away. It took him exactly one minute at seventy miles an hour to see the Edenia fence, and about two minutes after that to follow it around and swerve onto the Eden Road.

He floored it, passing the ball field on his right, and thought of Miriam for two seconds. However, the moment he passed into the town, the car wigged out. The electrical system sputtered and sizzled, and the engine completely cut out. With the gas not working and power steering out, Seth just concentrated on manhandling the momentum of the car to get as far into town as he could. It didn't take long for Edenians to file out of their homes and chase after him.

As soon as he saw his father racing up the street, he slammed on the breaks, but they didn't work.

By this time a man he recognized was jogging next to the car. It was Mr. Smith from school. He saw Seth, and instantly his eyes began to swim. He reached out and took hold of the area behind the front wheel, and the car slowed. Seth had to struggle to stop the car from pulling toward Mr. Smith's counter momentum. In a matter of five seconds they were still.

Seth opened his door and moved to the back, when he heard a voice. "Seth Johnson, what is the meaning of this?"

He turned and saw Miriam's mother standing next to him, her eyes so fiery he was surprised he wasn't burnt to a crisp.

His father was there, across the car. "Lu...Lillian."

That was all he had to say before Miriam's mother rushed to the other side of the car next to his father, and the cab door opened. Seth reached for his sister, but so did his father, and he saw the hurt and anger in his father's eyes, so Seth only helped unlatch her seat belt.

Luanne Miller's voice was serious. "Get the doctor, Steven." Mr. Smith was the one who moved, so he assumed that meant him.

"Lilly, baby," his father's calm but strong voice spoke. "Wake up." There was no response, so his father turned to him. "What's happening?"

Seth shook his head. "She was okay, not great, but then she got frightened by my driving. Her eyes did something weird, and then she passed out."

Luanne Miller looked at his father, and the look seemed to speak so many things only they understood. "I'm taking her to the river," his father said, and started moving. "Get the doctor there, will you?"

Luanne nodded and said, "Will, Carl, Joseph, you go with him and gather anyone else you see that might be useful."

Seth went to follow his father, but Luanne caught him by the arm, "No, you will be coming with me to go get your mother."

"But," Seth began to protest.

However, she leveled a gaze at him, and her irises began to move. To swirl. And they looked exactly like fire. The air around him seemed to heat to an uncomfortable temperature as she repeated herself. "You will come with me."

Seth moved, knowing instinctually that he should not fight any longer with this woman if he wanted to remain alive and in one piece. She pulled, and he walked. Then he remembered the guy on the horse.

"Oh, crap." His hand went to his face and up through his hair.

"What now?"

He rolled his eyes. The last person he wanted to admit this to was this woman, despite his vision. "On the way here, we had a bit of an accident. A man was out riding his horse and the animal got spooked by our horn. He is laying in the ditch half dead with the guy I stole this car from."

Luanne stopped and blinked her eyes at him. He was unable to tell what she was thinking. Finally, after a long moment she asked. "Did you speak to this man?"

"Yes, he helped us find Edenia."

"Did he seem like he was a Jones?"

Seth blushed. "No. They were all soldier types. This guy was just out for a ride, and now, because of me, he might never ride again. I'm pretty sure his back is broken."

She nodded and thought. Swallowing and blinking, she seemed to make a decision. "Well, Seth, it seems you find trouble easily enough." She smiled sadly at him, then turned to a woman rushing down the road, "Joni, go find Esther and tell her to bring a horse. Go quickly. She is at the house."

The young girl blurred into action. Literally. One moment she was standing there as normal as can be, and the next she was gone. A smudge in Seth's vision was all that was left of her.

His jaw dropped. "Oh my gosh."

"Yes, you seemed most impressed with the water Natures last time as well."

"Wa...water Natures, last time?" Seth was not able to collect himself.

She grabbed his arm. "Come. We will meet Esther at the barn."

She pulled him the whole way, his mind too freaked out to guide himself.

He'd obviously seen someone blur out of sight before. He would have remem... Oh, suddenly he understood. Miriam took that memory. That was what he saw that compromised him so much she felt she had to reach inside his mind. He slowed, feeling sick. Then he really was sick. He dry heaved because he hadn't eaten anything but two bites of a roll in twenty-four hours. His aunt stopped and patted his back.

"Are you just as upset as your father? He was concerned with becoming a 'freak' again."

"What?" Seth asked when he caught his breath. "What...do you even know...how could you understand how violating this all..." He dry heaved again.

"Come dear, get control of yourself. You have a man on the side of the road who needs you."

Seth swallowed. And swallowed again. He sniffed and wiped at his mouth and nose. Blinking away the tears in his eyes, he stood. "You're right." Swallowing one more time for good measure, he started walking again.

He wanted to ask a million questions, but he was embarrassed and self-conscious, so he walked. They arrived at the barn just as Esther did. She was at a run, and when she saw her mother she asked, "What has happened?"

"There is a stranger with a broken back right outside of Edenia. And Seth has brought Lillian back. Philip is hopefully engaged with her at this very moment, and Eve is, as you know, with your father. So, I was hoping you might be able to gently move him as close to town as possible, and I will leave word for Philip to join us as soon as he's able."

"Of course, mother." Esther's bright green eyes shone. She loved being useful, it was obvious.

They moved into the barn and saddled the horses more quickly and as proficiently as he'd ever seen it done. Luanne mounted hers and put a handout to him. "Come on boy. I count you've been here a total of ten minutes. I don't know how long it took you to get to us, but that man you injured might be beyond our help if we take too much longer."

Seth took her arm and stirrup and swung himself up. The moment his butt was settled, Luanne Miller kicked her horse into a gallop with Seth grasping to stay on the animal.

CHAPTER 33

Peter

Peter had gotten out of Gerald's black car and gathered up Marigold who was still grazing where he and Abby had left her. He also sent Garren back to Papa with word that Miriam was safe. Garren was not happy about it, but Peter convinced him that retreat was best when they were on the Jones' turf. The mission was complete.

Marigold, sensing Peter's urgency, let him gallop her the entire way home and only made it there a little after Gerald. The man knew where to stop to save his car. Peter asked him to carefully gather up Miriam and walk with her from there. Peter decided to ride ahead to fetch Doctor Harrison. He had Marigold at a trot as he passed another vehicle in the middle of the street. This was an awkward time to have outsiders in Edenia, and how did they get the car so far into town?

Confused, he slowed Marigold, looking around at the empty main street. Finally, when he came to the intersection leading to his family's cul-de-sac, he ran across his grandfather, Edmund Miller, who was all in a rush.

"Peter, where in blue blazes have you been? Your mother is worried sick."

"I have been getting Miriam. I sent word to Pa over at the Joneses. He knows what's up."

"Did you get Miriam back, then?"

"Yes. Gerald is carrying her, and they are right behind me. Where is everyone? I need Doctor Harrison. She's bad."

That got the old man's attention. His ginger eyes started swirling. "Where is she? Can I help?"

"I have it covered Grandpa. What I need is the doctor."

"Last I heard, he was at the river with Lillian."

Peter felt his heart hammer in his chest even more than it already was. "Lillian? She's here?" He pulled Marigold around. "Is she okay?"

"I don't know, Peter. That is where I was heading."

"Come to think of it, Grandpa, maybe Gerald could use some help with Miriam. I'll head down to the river to see if I can find the doc." Peter pointed toward the edge of town, and his sprightly old grandpa nodded and hurried off in the right direction.

Peter sat in stunned gratitude. Miriam was home. She was hurt, but she would live. Lillian was home, and she'd only been gone, what, eighteen hours? She might still have a chance. Pulling Marigold around, he headed toward the river.

CHAPTER 34

The situation looked much the same as when he'd left, except the young man's eyes were open. Conrad was super-pissed at him, but that didn't prevent his jaw from dropping when he first saw Aunt Luanne and Esther. By all accounts, they were both knockouts. This conveniently stopped him from cussing Seth out, at least temporarily.

However, the honeymoon was over soon, and Conrad was having an apoplectic fit. "What do you mean my car is ruined? Do you have any effing idea how..."

"Sir," Aunt Luanne interrupted. "Could you please yell at Seth over there?" She pointed in a distant general direction. "We are trying to assess the damage here."

"Don't worry yourself lady, I got an ambulance on the way."

"Wonderful," his aunt said, and looked meaningfully at Seth.

"Let's go over here, and I'll tell you what happened." Seth pulled the man across the street and faced him away from the Millers. The whole time he talked, and Conrad yelled, he kept an eye on what the ladies were doing, though he couldn't see around their skirts very well. Conrad had just about simmered down when Seth saw the most amazing thing he'd ever seen in his entire life.

The guy started moving. Like floating. Seth's face must have drained of color because Conrad began to turn toward the ladies. Seth caught him by the shoulders just in time, and said, "Thanks for all your help today, Conrad. I don't know what I would have done without you. Here..." He reached into his pocket and pulled out the credit card. "This card has no limit. Mr. Jones expects me to buy a car and pay for medical bills with it. Take it. Get yourself whatever you want."

Conrad took the card and looked at it. "Oh my...this is a Kryptonite Unlimited." His eyes bulged out of their sockets.

"Yes, and I was expecting to put hundreds of thousands of dollars on that card. So, go wild. Really." Seth patted the man's shoulder. "Now Conrad, my friends are going to perform a blessing on the cowboy and heal him."

Conrad began to turn to look over to the scene of the accident, but Seth grabbed his chin and stopped him.

"No, you can't look. If you do, it will ruin it all."

The man narrowed his eyes at Seth, and Seth wondered if he had to use his new power to punch the guy in the jaw and knock him out or something. With that thought, Seth felt that thing come over him again.

And Conrad saw it too. "Your eyes. They're..." His voice cracked and his face drained of blood.

"Listen, Conrad. You have my word of honor that we are going to take care of the cowboy. You can't watch, so either you choose to advert your eyes or I will have to make it so those eyes can't see for a while."

The man blinked. "You can do that?"

Seth raised an eyebrow at him in response and composed his face into a serious expression.

"Fine."

"So, go over behind that tree and wait for the ambulance."

To his credit, he did as he was asked. The man must be superstitious.

Seth moved to the women once Conrad was taken care of.

Esther said, "If I take him that way, I will have grass or moss the whole way until the river."

Her impossibly bright green irises were pulsating and swirling. Seth couldn't help but stare. She was so amazingly beautiful. Her short blonde curls fell into her face as she pulled herself onto her horse. Her eyes sparkled as she concentrated on the young man before her. Seth knew his mouth was hanging open.

His aunt spoke up. "I think you are right. Are you certain you have him? He is badly damaged."

"Yes, mother. There is plenty of grass, vines, and moss. We should have no problem whatsoever."

This answer caused Seth to look more closely at what exactly was happening. To his horror and amazement, the plant life underneath the young man was holding him up and moving him. The actual blades of grass worked together to pass his body inch by inch. It was like he was body surfing on an ocean of possessed prairie grass.

"How are you...?" Seth started but couldn't finish.

"Never you mind. Esther has this under control, which cleans up this little mess for you."

"Mother, what of the horse?" Esther interrupted. "I can handle them both. I barely have to do anything; we can't just leave the beautiful animal for dead."

"Of course. I am sure Doc would be happy to teach Eve how to handle animal mending."

Esther smiled and looked over at the horse. Her hand stretched out toward the animal, but she spoke to the plants. "Up, my dears. Oh, I know she's heavy, but you are strong. You can do it."

Right before his eyes, the horse rose only a few inches off the ground. But it was enough, and the animal began moving as well. Like a million tiny ants were under the mare.

"Very good," Luanne praised. Then she turned to Seth. "Well, you have a lot to think on. I hope that you have learned a thing or two, because now you will have to face the consequences of your actions." She swung up into her horse's saddle and looked over at him judiciously, like a queen pronouncing a sentence. "I hope you are as good at explaining yourself as you are at getting into trouble, because it will take a good one to explain all of this away."

Her arm swung toward the half dead, trampled body of the cowboy and the injured horse. But her eyes burned again that hot amber color, swishing and sloshing like lava. It was terrifyingly beautiful.

"Stay with Esther and help her in any way she asks. I will go get a few more Guardians and the doctor."

Seth nodded again.

"Good. Well, I will await your return. And make no mistake, Seth, you owe me some explanations as well."

She turned the horse and galloped away. He followed Esther's horse who walked slowly along the road toward Edenia along with the injured horse and man next to Esther, surfing among the grass. Seth couldn't take his eyes off them. He opened his mouth to ask Esther about it, but she gave him such a glare he knew it was worthless to try. So he followed in silence, hoping if she needed help, she would ask.

CHAPTER 35

Peter

There was a crowd at the river. By now everyone in Edenia probably knew what had happened, and how Seth and Lillian were involved. Atop Marigold, Peter saw past the milling throng. Ezekiel, Lillian, and Doctor Harrison were in the water.

The two men were talking intensely back and forth. Just as Peter was about to dismount, he noticed movement from the corner of his eye. It was Jenna, Lillian's mom. She ran straight into the river Eden. Apparently, she was unaware of how swiftly the river raged, and she was instantly swept away with the current.

With the crowd around, it didn't take long for a water Nature to catch her. Peter couldn't tell who it was, but the current of the river literally dropped the struggling Jenna and parted to move around her as seamlessly as it would for a boulder.

Confused and relieved, a coughing Jenna stood. The water was up to her chest. The current had taken her past Lillian and Ezekiel, so she turned and tentatively began swimming toward her family members. The pocket of stillness kept with her, and she reached Lillian's side in moments. The calm pool the two men stood in was joined by Jenna and the little family huddled together talking.

Peter dismounted and pushed his way into the crowd. They gave way to him easily enough, and before he knew it, he stood on the bank of the river. The water seemed really loud, louder than usual. He couldn't hear what was being said. He turned to the crowd and found several gray Natures concentrating on the little water-logged group. It was easy to find an unoccupied water Nature. Betsy, his great aunt, stood not five paces away.

"Aunt Betsy, can you help me get out there? I need to talk to the doc. It's about Miriam."

She hesitated before nodding and pulling her Nature to her. Peter calmly walked out into the cold water and soon swam because the water was over his head. He made short time of the swim and took doc by the sleeve.

"Give her some more." The doc said as he held out his arm for Peter to hang onto. He needed it to keep afloat.

"I can feel it building, if my own Nature is any indication," Ezekiel said nervously, "Mine is going to arrive any second."

"It is the right day. Yes, I think it will be any moment."

Ezekiel was breathing hard as he held his daughter in the water and cupped some more water for her to drink.

"Is that what this feeling inside of me is?" As these words left Jenna's mouth Ezekiel threw his head backward and his form blurred. Then everything happened at once. Lillian coughed and struggled, and opened her eyes. She looked around frantically. Seeing her mother, she whimpered and put a hand out for her. When Peter looked into Lillian's face, though, he noticed right away her eyes were no longer black, but a vibrant, almost glowing blue-green.

Ezekiel looked at Peter with extremely shiny grey eyes. "What the heck was that?"

Peter smiled, "That, my friend, is the water."

The man took a deep breath, and Peter ascertained things were not as Ezekiel expected by the shock on his face. He was so shocked, in fact, he hadn't even noticed Lillian.

When he finally looked down, he cried, "Oh, thank you, thank you, God!" and pulled Lillian out of the water enough to hug her. "Is she healed, Doc?" Ezekiel asked over Lilly's shoulder.

Doctor Harrison answered, "Yes, I believe she is. That was very close. It was so wise of you to bring her to the river. I don't think it did anything to actually heal her, but it brought her Nature to her more quickly, and that process always burns away any sickness.

From Peter's side, he heard Jenna gasp. He turned to look into now crystalline blue eyes. She looked at her husband and daughter, and the three of them had a moment. A silent moment.

Then Jenna said, "My dear sweet darling. I can't... I am so glad..." Her words left her for happy tears. The three embraced.

Peter didn't mean to ruin the moment, but he had a mission, and he wasn't going to let how incredibly beautiful Lillian looked with her blue-green eyes take that from him.

"Doc, I need you."

Doc wiped a tear from his own cheek and looked over to Peter who was still hanging on to his arm. Peter gestured that they move away from the family. Once they started back, Peter finished.

"Actually, Miriam needs you. I've brought her back, and she's in bad shape."

The doc got more serious. "Well, why in tarnation didn't you say so? Where is she?"

"Grandpa Edmund has her by now, and they should be heading here."

As Peter waded through the freezing water, Lillian asked from behind him, "What color are they?"

Jenna answered, "They are the most stunning blue-green. Oh my, they are like sparkling gems. You are so lovely, my darling. And you are healed, and I think I could burst from happiness." Then she tentatively asked, "What are mine? No, wait. Let me guess." She was silent for a moment. "They are blue, aren't they?"

"Yes." Lillian happily shrieked, "How did you know?"

"It's strange, I can sense the wind all around me. Like I am half in water and half in an ocean of air."

"They are so pretty, mom, especially with your hair. You look so exotic."

Ezekiel piped up. "You both are gorgeous." And then he laughed a loud, victorious laugh.

There was a cry from the bank of the river to his left. Peter looked up to see Abigail. She finally made it to the river.

His Aunt Betsy said, "It's alright Abigail, you can go out to them. I will calm the water for you."

Within moments, the twins were in one another's arms.

That broke the tension on the bank, because the gathered Guardians erupted in applause. Startled, Peter slipped on the rocks, but doc caught him. He looked back at Lillian.

She caught his eye, and gave him a bright smile, her amazing blue-green eyes sparkling and twinkling, and Peter got lost in her gaze.

"Peter." Doc brought him back. "Let's move. You can't moon over a girl when your sister needs healing."

Grandpa Edmund showed up, a despondent Miriam in his arms and Gerald at his back. The crowd made way at Gerald's shout and grandpa rushed to set Peter's sister at Doc's feet.

Peter leaned over and pulled Miriam's shirt open at the collar to expose the injury. The ugly black and red letters oozed puss. "Get her in the water immediately. Olivia, keep the water still, please."

Grandpa pulled his Nature to him again and easily lifted Miriam. He splashed into the water. "Someone help, for heaven's sake. I'm not putting her in here so she can get hypothermia as well."

It was Aunt Sarah who stepped forward with, "I'm a stupid woman. What was I thinking?" Her amber eyes sloshed and swirled and she moved her hands in a dramatic way. "Hold that bit of the pond steady, Olivia, and I'll warm it up." The women worked together, and in not too long, Grandpa hummed with a smile and allowed Miriam in.

He looked lovingly at her and brushed her ample hair away from her wounds.

While grandpa took care of that, Doc worked on something of his own. The bank of the river had several interesting plants blossoming in its grasses. Doc plucked this and scraped that from several, then shouted, "I need a mortar and pestle quickly, Guardians."

Sherman Walker's ginger eyes blazed. He took a large round river rock and scooped the center of the thing out as easily as scooping water. It left a bowl-shaped crater. Obadiah Collins' ginger eyes swirled as he formed a smaller stone into a makeshift pestle. The men handed them to Doc, who then set to work grinding.

Peter felt a cold hand on his arm. Turning, he saw Lillian with her black hair soaked, her lips trembling. She was gorgeous. He thought he could just bask in it forever. "Peter, will she be okay?"

Peter turned back to Miriam who was now getting the salve Doc concocted smeared on her chest. Miriam kicked feebly and cried. At least she was awake.

Confidence sounded in his voice, "Yes, she will be fine."

"G...g...good," she stuttered.

Taking a deep breath, he turned to find his great aunt right behind him. "Aunt Betsy, will you help Lilly? She's frozen."

The round, white haired woman took her worried grey eyes off of Miriam and looked down at Lillian.

"Oh dear, of course."

Peter turned back to his sister. He knew Lillian was in good hands with Aunt Betsy. She would be dry in two seconds flat.

Miriam made a fuss, and the two men had a hard time containing her. Peter stepped forward and heard her say, "I don't want it to go away. I need to keep it. I need to remember."

She'd lost it. Peter's worry ratcheted up a few dozen notches. They'd cracked her.

At that crazy moment of panic, his mother and Esther arrived on horseback. She yelled, "What is going on here? Where is the doctor?"

Esther's voice cried, "Mother, it is Miriam."

Peter watched her dismount so quickly he would have thought she was a water Nature. She ran to the water and plunged toward her daughter. "Miriam. Oh thanks be, Miriam." Soon grandpa was pushed out of the way, and his mother held her daughter. "Shh, my darling, shh, I am here."

Miriam calmed, but she still pushed Doc away.

"What is it?" Luanne's amber orbs blazed at the doctor.

"She doesn't want me to heal her. Not all the way, at least."

"What do you mean?" His mother asked as Doctor Harrison pulled back Miriam's shirt, which got her kicking and fighting again.

His mother almost dropped Miriam in the water as she shrieked. Her hand going to her mouth.

Miriam repeated her mantra, "I need to remember. I need to remember."

With a look of utter horror in her eyes, Luanne Miller covered Miriam back up, and for once in her life didn't fight back. Her eyes met the doctor's, "Is she sound besides this?"

He nodded. "Yes. All the wounds on her wrists and ankles are gone now. Her face was battered like she'd been punched or slapped..."

His mother gasped. "Stop. I, I just cannot know." And then his mother did something he'd never seen her do. She turned to the crowd and asked, "Will you all hold vigil with me? Miriam is in a dark place. She needs our strength."

That was all that needed to be said. Soon, the river was full of Edenians, hands reaching toward Miriam and his mother, eyes closed, heads bowed.

The silence only lasted a few moments, but Peter felt the strength of it to his toes.

When his mother raised her head, she looked to her father-in-law and pushed Miriam toward him. "Papa, please get my daughter out of the water."

All their Guardian friends and family proceeded out of the water as Grandfather did as he was asked.

The moment Miriam was out of the water, Grandpa's sister Betsy pulled the water from her and grandfather and everyone. It shed in a sheet, and his great aunt coaxed it back into the river. It obeyed her, slithering like a baby snake back to its mother.

"Thank you, Betsy dear," Grandpa said, and turned toward town.

"Doctor, we have one other patient for you. Esther has him down the river just outside the wall." Doc turned away ready to move on, but Peter's mother grabbed his arm. "Thank you, Philip." She spoke the words with feeling.

Doc patted her hand. "Of course."

His mother saw him, then gave him a sad smile. "My boy. I assume this is your doing, since I do not see your father."

Peter nodded.

His mother wrapped him in a tight side-hug. "If I did not want to tan your hide so often, I might just kiss you to death for your brave heart."

Peter smiled as his heart warmed.

She let him go and continued. "I see you also found your friend." Her nose went up, and she spoke down at Lillian. "Hum, she will be a fine healer. One who can understand pain and sickness is one who can heal the heart as well as the body." His mother reached and touched Lillian's cheek. "I am glad for you. Do not squander the time others have paid for."

Peter was so amazed at his mother. She was a saint. Peter was practically in love with Lillian and he was still angry about what she and Seth had done. Admiration and love filled his heart at his mother's example.

Taking a deep breath, he realized how tired he was. It had been a full day and a half since he slept. Rubbing his eyes, he turned to follow his mother home, but couldn't help feeling a sinking sensation. Would he dream?

***

PETER FELL into his bed and was asleep before he knew it. He entered into that place where time lay before him in the disguise of a woven ribbon. He knew he would never see anything but this place in his sleep for the rest of his life. It was his Nature.

As he looked at the ribbon, the pattern he'd watched before—beautiful and strange in its lights and darks, its non-repeating, yet exquisite design—seemed to be in an uproar. It was all he could think of as he watched previously stable threads veer haphazardly this way or that. It was chaos. He saw an inordinate number of threads cut off from the pattern, and many of those threads were in the same area of the weave. Death reigned supreme in the ribbon today, and other things moved rapidly as well, fluctuating, shifting, altering the face of the ribbon. Peter watched, and it reminded him of all the things his father had read from the internet. This was the world, and the world was in chaos, churning with war, death, disease. This change, this shift was—or seemed to be—lining up light and darkness. Instead of mixing, the two sides seemed to be separating. Peter could barely comprehend a mass polarization of this magnitude, so much so that the weave started to form strips of darkness and strips of light as those of like mind gathered.

And the death, it winked out hundreds of threads every moment. These deaths were not like some he had seen where the spirit of the future thread remained, so there was a choice involved. These were deaths where the thread disappeared suddenly, and the weave moved on without it.

The ribbon zoomed him close to his own thread, and he saw his current moment and the immediate future that was not yet woven into fact, only existing in spirit. His attention pulled to his father's thread, and how his thread and his father's thread were connected in this near future. They were connected in such a way that Peter's mind knew he had to use his other Nature. He needed to be a rock for his father, to stay by him. He had to.

A bone-deep fear raced down his back. He looked further to the future threads that stretched upward into the great black unknown where they became a shadow of a shadow. And there he saw that his father's thread only existed as a clear cylindrical space, a place holder. He knew what it meant— Death, absolute death.

CHAPTER 36

Miriam

There was a mighty struggle before Miriam. On one side, there was a lake of fire. There was anger. There was hate. There was insanity. On the other there was white light and calm and love.

She couldn't explain why the fire drew her in more than the light. She didn't understand why she wanted with all her soul to bathe—even revel—in the snarling and clawing that consuming anger would bring.

In her mind, she went in that direction, but she did not choose it. It was more like magnetism. Like it was out of her hands. She was pulled. Rather than acting, she was being acted upon by her fear, the fear of letting go and losing her anger at his betrayal. She saw nothing but the faces of those who did this to her. They were the objects of her clawing and snarling.

But she heard something. She heard a small sound. In her lust for the fire, she'd forgotten to look at both sides before choosing, and this small snuffling noise turned her attention.

There was a being under the white light, covered in the calm. On her knees. Her face in her hands. Shoulders shaking. She was crying. Miriam recognized those hands. Now, without thought, without choice, she felt herself pulled to her side.

"Mother?" She whispered, but here in this place she did not make any sound. She was a wisp, a fragment, a ghost. It was what she always knew she would be. Her Nature pulled the light and the color out of her so often, this incorporeal feeling wasn't foreign. But she heard, and now she heard her mother's words.

"Please, please bring Miriam back to us. Please, protect her.

Please, I beg of you. She is so good, so innocent. Please..." Her shoulders quaked. Miriam's heart pulled. "Nevertheless, if it is not your will that she come back to us, please help me to forgive. Please comfort her father and me, for we will be lost without her."

Miriam's heart and soul connected, and she chose. She sucked in a breath, feeling the pain of it. Hearing her own voice moan, the flashbacks began.

CHAPTER 37

Seth

While they were trudging slowly through the wilderness, he'd gotten a little too far in front of Esther. He was antsy. What was happening to Lillian? What if she died while he was out dealing with this mess? He felt wild, like he was going to explode.

And he felt hungry. He hadn't eaten in forever.

Budding panic grew. This was all his fault. All of it. Every bit. Tears welled up in his eyes, and he attempted to force them back. Then he said, "No. I will not do this again," out loud to the trees and continued the one-sided conversation. "I will have faith in the feelings given me."

He moved his mind to a different topic while keeping his feet moving, and checking on Esther behind him occasionally.

Wanting to get out of the sun, he moved off the road and wandered into the trees. He ducked through the thickets and saw the outer wall of Edenia. He ran to it and put a hand on the sturdy timber.

After several minutes of not seeing Esther following him, he decided to keep moving as the cool of the shade invigorated him. He began to wonder if he might be able to climb the wall. His gaze went from the ground to the sky.

His ponderings were interrupted by the sound of talking. He paused and turned toward the sound, but couldn't make it out. The voice was muffled by some other sound, water. The river must be close by. Sure enough, after rounding several large trees and an octopus-like ground-covering vine, he saw two figures, both on horseback, moving quickly toward him.

The doctor arrived on the same horse Luanne Miller had been riding. "Hello, there," Seth said. "Esther is just up the road."

"I'm right behind you, un con," she cursed at him in French. "Move out of the way."

"Esther," the older man chided.

Seth moved and heard a muffled grunt coming from the bush. He stepped back as he saw the young man from earlier cradled in the large vine.

Seth moved to the doctor. "Can you tell me of my sister?"

Esther butted in with narrowed, bright green eyes flashing. "And what of *my* sister?"

The old man chimed in. "Esther!" It was a quiet rebuke. The man spoke to Seth even as he approached the cowboy. "Your sister is fine, lad. You should head back to Edenia." He glanced up at Seth and narrowed his eyes but not in the same way Esther had. It was assessing. "Yes, you must get back, your time has already come. You need to find your father. He can help you, yours once was his." The man turned away.

"My horse," the cowboy croaked.

The old man asked, "What's your name, son?"

"Westley. Can you help my horse? Her name is Buttercup."

Esther went over to the horse. She only looked at the animal briefly before saying, "Her ankle is snapped quite in half. The bone is protruding. And wow, she is a stunning animal."

Seth saw Westley panic.

The old man said, "I am a doctor, and I can help both your animal and you if you will cooperate."

Westley's eyes went big, and he nodded slightly.

"All right. Where are you from, Westley? I mean, do you live around here?"

The cowboy paused and looked around before answering. "I live at the Adam-ondi-Ahman tent city."

"It is as I suspected."

"Fascinating," Esther commented, and came closer to him.

"Will people be looking for you?" the doctor asked.

"Yes, I am surprised they haven't found me already."

"Well then, we have some decisions to make." The doctor looked to Seth and then to Esther and paused for a few long seconds. "Here is what I suggest. I do what I can for you and your horse here, and I send Seth to find your people. If he is successful, then we will let them take care of your rehabilitation."

Seth heard the words and felt a sinking in his gut. This plan was wrong. That strange thing, that power, took him. Time slowed, and he saw in his mind—like he did at the hospital—what needed to happen next, exactly Right-Now-Next.

"No," Seth said to the duo. "No." Seth heard and saw all that was happening around him, but it was if he had two brains, because he simultaneously was in a vision of the immediate future.

The doc smiled at him. "Ah, there it is. What do you know, boy?"

Seth pointed at the river, "Do your healing Doc, then both he and the horse need to go into the river and follow it to Edenia. Esther, you must go get Betsy, Percival and Hannah."

"So it will be done," The doc said, and Esther looked at him as if he were crazy.

"Excuse me, but what just happened?"

Seth shook his head, and the feeling or foresight or vision or understanding left him. He very much wanted to know the same thing.

Doc smiled again. "We will talk of it later." He turned to Westley. "Sorry to tell you son, but your back is fractured."

"I know." Westley grunted. "If you are going to put me down, just do it now. I can't help with the war like this, anyway."

That caused everyone to pause.

Doc spoke first in a quiet reassuring voice. "What war?"

"Armageddon, of course."

"Of course." Doc said as he looked over at Esther. "You'd best get a move on."

Esther nodded. "Yes, I'm going." She mounted and looked down at Seth. "Assist the doctor if you have enough conscience left to help out the people you hurt." She glanced once more at Westley then turned her horse and kicked him to a trot.

Though he deserved it, her words wounded him, and they also foreshadowed how his life in Edenia would be from here on. Defeat began in his mind, and it didn't take long for it to feel as big as a landslide.

He heard the doctor from behind him. "That was beneath her. I am sorry. She is a mama bear, and always has been." There was a pause, and Seth turned around to face the old man to ask him what was happening to him, but what he saw made his jaw drop.

Writhing, wiggling plants were growing, moving, exploding from the earth all around the two men. They snaked under and about Westley, lifting him off the ground and wrapping him tightly in their viny embrace.

He saw a smear of green around Westley's lips and noticed the guy had passed out.

The doctor looked over at him. "That horse could use some comfort. See if you can get her up on her belly instead of lying on her side. She's suffocating. I can hear her."

Shaking his head at the impossible scene he'd just witnessed, Seth quickly went to the horse.

Unstrapping her saddle in a frantic rush, he pulled as much as he could reach off to relieve the pressure. Then he grasped her reins and touched her head. The horses' eyes rolled, and she kicked feebly at him. But he could hear how labored her breathing was.

Soothing her with some shushing sounds and stroking her face and nose, he attempted to pull her head around so that she would move herself up. Miracle of all miracles, and free of the saddle's straps, she did move; like she wanted to move the whole time, but just needed a little help.

Doc said, "Good work, Seth. I think you might have just saved that horse's life."

Still massaging her head and neck, Seth smiled at the beautiful beast. Then he looked over at the doctor and couldn't understand what was going on.

Westley was tightly wrapped in vines and plant life. He looked like a mummy, but he was face down. Doc had his hands intertwined with several kinds of leaves and flowers. They looked like twirling, slithering rings around his fingers. Some of them he seemed to be spitting on and others he chewed. Soon his hands were covered in a sort of multicolored goop.

Doc then lifted his eyes to the sky and Seth heard him whisper, "Master, by thy will and with thy power." And he plunged his hands with the writhing vines into the guy's back. He moved them up and down Westley's back, and it was only then that Seth noticed the young man's shirt on the ground. It was ripped to shreds.

"Can I help?"

The doc didn't answer him right away, but a few minutes later he replied. "Yes, fetch the bowl from my bag, go fifty paces that way," he chinned the direction, "and get some water from the river Eden. Quickly, boy."

Seth ran to the task. He crashed through the woods following the sound of the water. It only took him a few minutes to return, but when he did, Doc had moved on to the horse. Westley was face up once more and returned to the ground.

"Perfect timing, Seth," Doc said, and Seth watched as the man took the water and made some goop with the plants he'd just pulled from the ground. Seth felt his amazement waning and his creep factor ratcheting up.

It didn't matter that the man was saving these creatures, he was using something freaky to do it. The doc smeared one goop on the horse's sides and the other on its ankle. The magnificent animal bore it all with patience.

Seth watched with wonder as the goop seeped into the horse's skin, like it was a drain.

Soon the doctor stood. "Well, that is all that can be done for both."

Doc turned his palms to the ground and Seth noticed for the first time the man's irises. They were shuddering and trembling and swirling. As Doc lowered his hands, Seth watched in utter horror and fascination as the out-of-place plant life slithered back into the dirt. Once he was done, the little clearing looked just as it had before, except Westley was still wrapped in vines.

Seth stared at Doc. The man gathered up his few tools and put them back in his bag. Seth stood and watched him do it. He did not move. He did not take his eyes from the man.

Finally, Doc looked at Seth. The two stared at one another for an uncomfortable minute.

Then, the older man spoke. "I suppose you are freaked out right now."

"That doesn't even cover the half of it."

"Well, all will be answered in time." And somehow Seth knew that was the end of the discussion. "For now, you look like you're half-starved. I have some nuts in my bag. You're welcome to them."

Seth instantly became aware of his stomach, and other things in his life. "Yes please. And my sister. She really is okay? How is that even...?" He looked at Westley then back at Doc. "Did you save her?"

Doc shook his head. "Her Nature did." He handed Seth the small container with nuts. "It took her fully while I was assisting the river Eden in slowing her death. Truly, you got her back in the nick of time. Her Nature and the river Eden burned all the sickness out of her. I suspect this miracle was the entire reason your parents came to Edenia, despite the personal trauma such a return has wrought on them."

Seth was overwhelmed with gratitude, and just dying to say his apologies to the whole Miller family, not to mention his own family.

He saw Esther, an elderly woman called Betsy, Hannah, and a large man he knew was Percival as they arrived. Two of these people were strangers to him, except he knew exactly who they were. He knew the truth of them before he saw their faces. How, he did not know.

Betsy would use the water to carry Westley and the horse to Edenia, and because the way to the river was filled with rocks and dirt, they would need to be carried physically, and not by the plants as Esther had done. Seth knew Esther could do it, but she did not like to make things grow where they should not and where they would be killed. So that was why they needed Percival and Hannah, both with strength Natures.

"What can we do, Doc?" the large man asked.

Doc turned to Seth. "This one will tell you."

Seth blinked at him.

"Go on, son. It is your calling."

Seth nodded and started uncertainly. "These two need to go into the water," he pointed at the horse and rider, "and float against the current into Edenia."

There was an exchange of hesitant glances. "I do not know this boy," said the old lady who dismounted off Esther's mount.

"He is Seth, Ezekiel's son."

The old woman regarded him carefully. "I see," she answered. "Well, all right. And who is this sad, damaged creature?"

"Do not fear, Betsy, he is a friend."

"He is an outsider," Percival stated strongly.

"He is from the tent city."

The two older ones acted like this information changed everything, and they instantly went to work.

Hannah asked, "I am meant to take the boy?"

"Yes," Seth said.

Seth watched as his foresight came to pass. Hannah's ginger irises began to swim. She went to the boy and lifted him as if he were a pillow.

"His back is broken a hands pace from the neck. I have set it and soothed the nerves, but try not to jostle him," Doc added.

Hannah nodded and headed toward the river.

"Doc?" Percival asked.

"I knocked the horse out so just drag her the best you can. Seth, get that saddle."

Seth didn't need to be told to do this because he had already seen himself doing it. He swallowed hard and watched the big man size up the horse. He already knew this man could move a thousand-pound horse because he'd seen it done in his mind.

Percival bent and inched his chest against the horse's chest, managing to get the front legs over his shoulders and neck flopped to one side. Then giving it a bear hug, he heaved mightily and took the horses' weight onto himself. Stepping to one side of the legs and rump which still touched the ground, he dragged the animal.

Reaching for the saddle, Seth gaped stupidly as Betsy led Esther's mount toward him. "Fancy a ride with an old lady?"

"Uhm, sure," Seth mumbled, knowing the exact words of their conversation.

He secured himself on the back of the horse, and Doc handed the saddle up to him, which was totally awkward. Then they headed toward the water. He watched as the big man plopped the mare into the river as soon as he saw Betsy.

The older woman spoke. "Doc, you going in with them?"

"Yes. I have to. I need to get some of this water down both their throats."

"So be it." She moved her hands in an odd way and both Westley, who was already in the water with Hannah and Doc, and the horse began to move upstream towards Edenia.

Betsy walked the horse alongside the bank keeping her eyes on those floating in her slip stream. Esther was the only other one not in the water. She and her mount walked behind Seth.

He turned around to look at her, but she was staring up at the sky as she rode, her face twisted with worry. Wondering at the look, Seth followed her example, and through the trees he saw thick columns of dense white clouds gliding heavily by.

Seth looked back at Esther just as she stopped and placed a hand on the trunk of a tall tree. Closing her eyes, she held her mount oddly still, then her voice broke out in a warning. "There is a huge storm coming." Her eyes shot open, and she kicked her horse into a canter. "We need to move."

The moment the words were out of her mouth, Seth felt that thing again—like a quick build up and then an explosion outward. But when the thing inside of him burst from his body, he saw it like a bubble exiting all around him, and with it a new vision of the world around him. A foresight. But this world was in slightly darker colors, deeper purples, darker browns and blacks. He saw them getting to Edenia, and he saw a tornado. And he saw Hirum Miller being the most bad-A Guardian in this place, but he also felt very strongly that Peter had to be with Hirum as he acted as a tornado wrangler.

"Holy crap!" He exclaimed as his real mind snapped back in to focus. He still felt the other mind, but he ignored it to say, "There's a tornado coming. It is going to hit Edenia like right on. So, we need to get back ASAP. But hey, don't worry, Hirum is like the world's most amazing Guardian, so we will all be okay."

Betsy glanced over her shoulder at him and then looked at the people in the water before saying, "Hold on, y'all," as she both kicked the horse in the ribs and pushed those in the river along. Once the horse moved at a good pace, she glanced behind her again and said, "Seth, be a dear and hold on to the reins. My mind is a little occupied."

"I can't with this saddle."

"Toss it back to Esther."

"Do what now?"

As soon as he asked, a foresight of him tossing the saddle back toward Esther, her green eyes swirling, came before him.

So he did it. "Esther," he yelled behind him. "Catch this, will you?"

He caught sight of her eyes and then threw the saddle, which weighed much less than a saddle should, now that he thought about it.

As he saw in his foresight, a tree branch of willow whipped out, caught the saddle, and dropped it into Esther's lap all while she was cantering.

Awed by the exchange, but still in a hurry, Seth did as he was told. He took the reins, and Betsy clucked at the horse. Once that job was off her plate, Betsy turned more toward the water and focused on the five humans and one beast she floated—rather quickly—upstream.

This all felt surreal. Everything was like a fantasy, or at least totally not reality. And in the back of his mind, he recognized that this was his life, a life he chose, and a life he accepted for his sisters. He was freaked out by the people surrounding him, but as he watched the sky and the water, he also felt a small bud of genuine awe develop in his chest.

By the time they returned to Edenia, the sky was black, the wind howled, and the rain began. It was the first weather other than *nice* Seth had experienced in Edenia.

Right at the beginning of Edenia—at the mill—they slowed their flight. Frantic for his family, Seth jumped off the horse and hurried to help the ginger eyed muscle people get the animal and the young man out of the water. But they had it in hand. Once both were settled into the mill, Seth ran for his home even though he knew he wouldn't make it there. He had that foresight, that premonition, that vision. He knew what would happen.

There were few people on the streets. The sky pelted him with hail and rain, and it really was creepy how dark it was with the sun blotted out.

Many Edenians, running faster than a normal person should be able to run, crossed his path. He recognized one of them right away.

"Seth, is that you?" Miriam's father and his Uncle Hirum, or his 'not Uncle' Hirum, asked.

"Yes."

Seth turned and looked into the man's eyes. His crystal blue orbs swirled as Seth heard a terrible screeching sound. It vibrated his bones, ratcheted his heart rate, and deafened his ears. He looked around for the source and saw in the distance to the south of Edenia the most terrifyingly gigantic cloud formation, a black cyclone. The fully formed tornado rapidly headed their way.

Hirum tried to yell at him, but he just couldn't hear what was happening. A strange sensation took over him. He felt something, some sort of strength, a kind of power. A bit of protective spark overtook him. It popped out of his center and outward toward his limbs. And for the space of a breath, the blink of an eye, the beat of a heart, time stopped around him.

Life stopped around him.

The wind no longer blew his hair. Peace, silence, and stillness enveloped him.

Seth saw with clarity what would happen next. Hirum would run towards the tornado, not away, and Seth had to go with him.

He was slammed back into the tumultuous weather. Hirum's mouth was formed for words, but his lips stopped as his swirling blue eyes examined Seth. When Seth blinked back at him and pushed his hair out of his eyes, Hirum came closer and took Seth's chin in his hand, staring intensely into Seth's eyes.

Then he yelled in Seth's face, "You have your Nature, boy?" and the words made it to his ears, like the air around his head was still.

Seth didn't know what to say. He'd thought it but he would not accept it. Except now, Hirum's words made it a reality. His Nature. He could not believe it. He didn't feel any different. In fact, the foresight felt natural and exactly right for him. It was not an *out in the open* thing. It happened inside him. And even there, it was shocking, yes, but not anything freaky, like he thought a Nature would be.

He focused back on Hirum's face and he nodded, knowing it was true.

Hirum nodded back, a hard, accepting nod. Then without another word he took off toward the cyclone, just as Seth knew he would.

Without thinking, without considering, Seth turned and did what he knew he had to, and followed the man.

CHAPTER 38

Peter

It was a black spiral of wind, debris, and destructive Godlike fury. It raced toward him as if the sky had ripped, and all the firmaments from all the worlds poured through the gash in a tsunami of air and cloud and hellish energy. Trees bent as if they were frightened street urchins awaiting the beating they knew was their lot. Plants clung to what kept them in the ground and alive. But they were betrayed, for the earth had to sacrifice them to the wind gods. He watched the extreme power take its prize. The poor vegetation ripped with a horrid noise that only added to the already calamitous ruckus, and were flung into the air, then beaten into shredded leaves and splinters.

Peter stood speechless, yet poetic in his thoughts, as the beastly torrent threatened all he knew and loved. The Master would not stop this. He could not interfere. Not here and now. Still, in a way, the Master had interfered long ago by bringing Hirum Miller and his son into existence.

So now he stood on the hill unafraid, though the monstrous storm whirled in front of him like a prophesy fulfilled.

Chilled to the bone, Peter turned just as his father's icy hand grasped his shoulder. His father came to him strong, wise, and full of the power of his Nature. His swirling irises questioning Peter, emboldening him with the question, *'Are you ready, son?'*.

Gathering his faculties around him he blinked into the face of his father—and his destiny—and nodded.

As a duo they moved toward the twister.

Peter pulled his Nature to him, feeling the rock, the stone, the water, the earth. He was one with it all, a boulder anchored to the very continental plate under his feet. He pushed his father down so the man was of a height with Peter and put arms, as heavy and as strong as steel around Hirum's middle.

Hirum raised his hands toward the cyclone as it raced up the riverbed toward them and pushed at the sky, his attention completely dedicated to his work. It felt like nothing and like everything with a whole ocean of gasses hitting him in the face, and then nothing.

Peter opened his eyes and saw, of all things, Seth, below him in the town. He had Charity Bartlet in his arms. The little toddler was always getting away from her family. Seth pulled her through the Mason's cellar door and looked around and above as if he were seeing something Peter could not see. Seth raced her to a house across the dirt road.

Wondering at what the traitor was doing, Peter's eyes lifted to look above him. The swift moving cyclone still twirled in full force, but its tail no longer extended all the way to the ground. His father had seen to that. He saw up through the mess of debris and dirt.

Looking back at Seth's movements, Peter saw him climb into another house across the way. No sooner had he shut the door than a finger of a second twister touched the road and blew the Mason's home into oblivion.

Somehow, Seth had saved himself and Charity.

Peter yelled. "Pa, to the north. A second one."

Peter saw his papa's hand reach out toward the new spiral of destruction as it took another home. Instantly, it was cut off in the middle as if it had been sliced with a gigantic invisible finger. All the boards and mess of the destroyed house paused in midair and then fell like rain to the earth.

"Keep your Nature, and let's move, Peter."

Peter did not let go of his father—though his father turned around, so Peter carried him chest to chest—and he did not let go of his connection to the earth. Walking was awkward but Peter knew this was the dangerous part. Debris fell from the sky, trees were flung in the air, rocks cannonballed everywhere.

He kept his eyes alert, too, so that if anything flew toward them, he wouldn't miss shielding his father. Several times in their flight, Peter turned his back protectively and allowed all manner of rubble to slam against his back of stone, saving his pa from it. He didn't feel a thing. It was a thrill to be his father's armor.

Peter felt awe as he looked into the raging center of the two tornados spinning above them. Then glancing at his Papa, who was keeping his eyes on the twisters, Peter felt awed again. The vicious fingers of these miraculous storms could not touch Edenia, because his pa faced them bravely and did what he had to.

Within thirty seconds of the tornadoes traveling through town, the huge, twin spirals had moved out of range. The wind was already calming down, and the rain had begun again.

Peter let go of his father, feeling the job was at an end, though he could see Hirum Miller was still concentrating hard.

"What are you doing, Papa? It feels like we are done protecting Edenia now, aren't we?"

"I want to control the path of the storm as long as possible."

"You don't normally do that, do you?"

"No, but we don't normally have a huge group of tent dwellers in the path of a tornado in these parts."

"Oh, yeah." The tent people.

"I need to be taller." He rose to tip-toe. "The trees, I can't see past them."

Instantly, Peter pulled the part of his Nature that made him hard as stone and went to one knee. "Stand on me, I will hold you balanced."

"What a smart idea, Peter," his father commented as he carefully stepped on Peter's thigh and then up to his shoulders. Peter used his earth power to steady his father and himself. Then he rose to both feet. "That is perfect. Exactly what I needed. Thank you, son."

Peter felt the strength of his father's Nature stir the air, and when the rain came back, he knew that it was over. His heart swelled at the idea that his father battled a tornado, and with *his* help, won.

CHAPTER 39

Seth

Seth's breath came rapidly. It was still loud as a freight train outside, but the basement of this house had strong brick walls and a large colonial fireplace where they huddled. He'd never been in this house before, but with his Nature, he knew that it was the safest place for them. They were supposed to be here. He'd seen it.

Pinching his eyelids shut, he told himself he couldn't think about that right now. When he opened his eyes, the lights were flickering.

"Don't be scared," he yelled to the child.

"I'm not," she yelled back.

"Really?"

She shook her head. "Your eyes are black," the little girl yelled over the wind at him.

Seth looked down at her impatiently. "What?" he yelled back, but he'd heard her. Once she repeated herself, he replied, "I know."

"I've never seen black eyes before," She persisted.

He huffed a great breath out and turned to her. "Sure, you have. Everyone in my family has them, and I know you couldn't have missed seeing at least one of us."

"I did meet your family today, but they don't have black eyes." Her little voice sang excitedly. She was not nervous at all, even though a tornado raged outside.

"What do you mean?" Seth's own body felt uptight, hands bracing against the bricks of the fireplace, eyes looking up toward the chimney.

His mind felt calm, and the girl was calm. Strangely calm.

"I saw your mama and papa and sister get their Nature today, in the river. I've never seen it when it happens, so it was awesome."

That got his attention.

"When I got there, your pa and ma were in the water with your sister. She looked real sick. Then everyone's Nature took them all at once, and like a miracle, the sick girl was better, and she has her Nature, too, and it's healing. Isn't that cool?"

Seth understood what was bothering the little girl. "You think it's weird that I have my Nature now too, but my eyes are the same?"

"Yes, I do. Unless you don't have your Nature yet?" She asked with a raised voice.

He didn't know what to say. If he said the words out loud, that would be it. It would be an acceptance of this all. Of what had happened to him. He waited for the emotional recoil, but nothing happened. And before he realized it, he said, "I do have my Nature. I guess it just didn't change my eye color." And he was still calm.

"You're like Peter and Miriam...except not...because they both had blue eyes and brown eyes before."

Seth balked. Miriam with blue eyes. Never. "What do you mean?"

"I guess it happens, sometimes. Like, someone with blue eyes may still have blue eyes after they get their Natures because blue is wind Nature. But if you did get your Nature and your eyes are still black, that means you have a Nature I've never seen before, just like Miriam and Peter do."

Seth adjusted himself nervously in the little space as he sorted out what the little girl was saying. "Okay..."

The little girl blinked her own perfectly normal blue eyes up at him.

"So, you don't know what the whole black eyes means, as a Nature."

She paused still looking into his face intently. "I don't have the foggiest," she said super serious-like.

And that was when it happened again. A vision of Hirum and Peter and lightning.

"I've got to go, Charity. You stay here, and I will be right back."

He ran.

Out in the street, he saw them. In his mind, he knew the distance was too far for him to make. But then his body propelled him faster than any human should go.

He got there just in the nick of time. Without preamble he grabbed Hirum by the shirt-tails and pulled him down toward the ground. The man was not expecting this and toppled forward at the waist, his hands shooting out to brace for the fall. But Peter still had his father's calves in hand and was too strong, too firmly planted in the earth magic to allow his father to tumble.

Seth yelled, "Let go!" in Peter's face. Time seemed to slow. Peter, not really sure what was happening, clung to his father who was trying to right himself.

Seth yelled again, "Let..." and some realization happened in Peter's face. "GO!!"

Lightning struck Peter. At the last possible micro-second, Peter's fingers released their hold and his father fell away. The man would have blasted away in the wind, except Seth was there, Nature upon him. Seth held Hirum Miller to the earth with a power so grounded and strong he might as well have been a tree with roots all the way to the core of the earth.

Seth watched as if in slow-motion as the energy flashed from the sky; down, down, down and into Peters body. It descended Peter's spine and shot out of hands and feet, barreling its way into the ground, all without singeing a single hair on Peter's rock-hard, Nature-filled body.

ON THE WALK to his house after dropping off Charity with her grateful yet strangely unworried and almost smug parents, Seth pondered what in the crap had happened to him.

He had power now.

In all instances, with the security guards at the hospital, at the river, and with the tornado, Seth saw the future in a blink. He didn't feel like it took time away from his actions. Like he didn't have to pause to have a foretelling. It just happened. In an instant, the images of the future filled his existence. Then, within the space of a blink, he was back to reality.

Seth explored his emotions in a way he'd rarely done before and found that he was not repulsed by himself. He actually felt relieved.

Now, what to do with the other messes he'd made? His mind instantly went into defense mode. He'd been kept in the dark about all of this, and he'd chosen the wrong path. It was a mistake. Yes, Lillian almost died because of him. But how could he have known that this place contained the only power to save her?

The back of his mind told him he could have trusted his parents. He could have believed, but he recalled with perfect clarity the moment he'd chosen to be the hero, to trust in his own plan, his own ability. He looked back and saw each step he'd taken along that terrible path. Still, he was forced down it by the lies of his father, neither of his parents communicating Edenia's role.

As he walked toward his house, he knew that he had to put it that way if his father would listen to his side at all.

He took a deep breath and hoped it would be all right.

Now, to his other problem. The problem that was entirely his fault, Miriam. What had become of her? As his mind pictured her, as he allowed himself to really breathe her name in his thoughts, he cringed. His body reacted viscerally to her memory.

A review of their time together, sans the emotion of a dying sister, revealed that she'd tried to pull him back from his choice. She'd done all she could. A sudden shame and anguish engulfed his soul.

He remembered the moment he touched her face. He

remembered how angry he was about her messing around in his head. Even then, he recalled how he couldn't stop himself from being affected by having her so close. Her skin so pale and soft and innocent. Her eyes so confused. Tears stung his eyes, and he sniffed, his fists clenching at his sides.

"Why? Why did I screw this up?" he growled at himself.

He knew he couldn't take any of it back. But he considered what he'd give in exchange to go back to that moment—the fateful moment when he dumped the vial of drugs into Miriam's soup. That moment of struggle was real. And he'd felt the weight of it then. But now, now it was a boulder around his ankle. He would drag it with him for the rest of his life.

He pushed his knuckles into his eyes. A great sob rumbled in the back of his throat and shuddered through his mouth, and that was when he noticed the people. Edenians were out of their houses looking up at the sky, peeking out of windows and doors, and standing on porches.

His sound of agony drew their attention, and bright Edenian eyes watched. More ashamed than he could handle, Seth decided to run. He ran and ran, and when he finally got to his parent's porch, instead of going in, he sat on the steps and let his emotions take him.

It was a bright blue-green eyed Lillian that came out to him ten minutes later. He pulled back from her as she sat next to him. She paid him no mind and wrapped her arms around him, only pulling away after several minutes.

The first thing he had to say was, "Holy crap, Lillian. Your eyes." He sounded all stuffy from the crying.

"I know. They totally rock, right?" She smiled so brightly, so happily, so healthily, that he couldn't help but blink back the terror of emotions from before, and smile at her.

"Yes, they totally rock." He wiped at his nose and eyes and then added, "Lilly, you look so healthy, so beautiful..." He felt the stupid water works coming back. "I...I am so glad you're all right. I don't know how I could have lived with myself if anything had happened to you." He felt the sobs that contorted his back shake the small body of his sister as she clung to him.

"I know, Seth. I know you only thought of me. Everything you did, you thought you had to do. I was one hundred percent on your side, remember? It was my choice, too. I didn't believe Mom and Dad, either. I believed you would be the one to save me." She squeezed him tighter. "No other brother would have risked everything for me the way you did. I will always have that, you know. The knowledge that everyone in my family risked everything to make sure I could live. Mom and Dad left everything and brought us here. You and Abby did too. And then you double risked by making a deal with the Joneses to save me again. Seth, you are the best brother in the world. Thank you."

Seth let the words ooze into his mind. He sat there as his sister's arms did their work on his heart. After what felt like a long time, he sniffed.

"Mom and Dad? Do they hate me?"

Lillian shook her head as Seth heard the screen door behind him creak. Looking behind him, he saw his mother and father standing there, arms around each other, tears in their vivid, oddly colored eyes. Together they came to him. They sat next to him.

His mother whispered, "We could never hate you, my love." She pushed back his hair and touched his face.

Seth glanced at his father. The man's grey eyes penetrated Seth to the core. "I'm sorry, Dad. I just didn't..."

"You didn't trust me."

Seth shook his head.

His father bowed his head and bit his lips, breathing deeply.

It was his mother that answered, "We lied to you. We had a very good reason. I mean, how do you explain this place in a way you would have believed?"

His father butted in. "But still, we lied. And we are sorry."

Seth stared into his father's miraculous grey eyes and saw that he had been on his own journey of pain, yet he still wanted to make things right.

Tears tumbled down Seth's cheeks, and he bit his lip before saying, with complete honesty, "I forgive you."

Then there was the creak of the door and Abby said, "Can we all just kiss and make up?"

Seth smiled, but his eyes stayed with his father who said nothing, but the set of his brow and softness to his face told Seth that the man was over it.

That was all the feeling Seth needed. Abby plopped herself into the middle of their little family circle, pulling everyone around her. Then everyone was hugging everyone. They were one big mush, and then they were laughing and falling over sideways.

For the first time since Jeremiah Jones contacted him in Cairo about the watch and broke the trust he had in his father, he felt like things might be mending. The dynamics were back in the right place, and a little stitch was sewn into the wound that was Seth's heart.

It was Abby who brought it up. "What are we going to do about Miriam?"

Seth's mother and father exchanged a look, and Seth felt his heart speed up.

When no one said anything, Abby spoke again. "Seth, Lilly and I practically sacrificed her life for Lilly's."

He heard his breathing before he understood that it was him, hyperventilating. He grabbed his mom's arm. "She's..." He swallowed. "They killed her?" It came out in a choked whisper.

His mother reached for him, concern in her bright blue eyes. She looked so beautiful with blue eyes, he thought as his vision went a little blurry. He'd killed Miriam.

"No, no." His mother said. "She's not dead, but I'm afraid they did hurt her, badly. The poor girl."

Abby added, "Thanks to Peter and me and a few other people, she was only with them for like, twelve hours."

"That's plenty of time to cause a lifetime of damage," his father added, unhelpfully. "We will face them together to make things right. Apologize."

"What good is that going to do?" Seth whispered. "I betrayed everyone here, and most of all, Miriam. How could she ever forgive me?"

"They need to forgive us," Lillian offered. "We live here now."

"Actually, no, they do not have to forgive. And we don't know what is going to happen with living here. Between the apocalypse and the Joneses..."

"What's the big deal with these Jones characters, anyway? I talked to a few of them, and they seem really normal to me. Well, except that they are obsessed with Edenia," Abby offered.

"They want immortality," Seth inserted.

"So, let them have it," Abby offered.

Their father cleared his throat and said, "You don't understand. Free agency only goes so far. Immortality is a gift with a price, and only the Master gets to say when it is time for that gift to be given."

"You're speaking crazy again, Dad. What do you mean?" Abby countered.

"It's a deep, religious conversation, covered in rich historical contexts. Are you sure you want the answer?"

Abby sighed. "Are there Cliffs Notes?"

Their father and mother laughed. "Not really. But if you start at the creation story, you might understand a bit better."

"Can you give me the Cliffs Notes of that?" she asked brightly.

He shook his head. "No, but if you recall, we did promise to tell you about this place if you stuck it out for a week."

Seth shook his head as Abby sighed.

His father laughed. "A week ago, you were so confused you would have given anything for me to tell you all. But now it's not that interesting to you?"

"It's not that, Daddy," Lilly said. "Abby just wants to go back to the bathroom and stare at herself and her new brown eyes some more."

"They are not brown, they are amber." Their father said. "And I have no idea why He always gives the power of fire to hotheads."

Abby smiled, "It's called a Nature for a reason," she added. "And they are way better than black any day of the week."

"Okay, we all need to walk on eggshells around Abby, or she'll burn our hair off. What's new?" Lillian said.

Abby stuck her tongue out at Lillian, and then they fell on each other on the porch, hugging.

"I'm so glad you're back," Abby said sincerely.

"I'm so glad I'm back, too."

They snuggled up.

Seth smiled at their antics, full of happiness that all was well, and grateful to the power that made it happen.

"Excuse me," his mother interrupted the revelry, "...but your father has something important to tell us all. I had to wait, too. So, let's listen."

"Yes, I will give you the history, but also, since we have committed to being honest with you all, I have some other things I need to tell you first. Things about the Joneses."

His father's tone got Seth's attention. Everyone quieted.

The huge man turned sparkling grey eyes on his children and said, "Talbert Jones is my biological father. Your biological grandfather."

There was complete silence in which Seth decided to not let his family know he was aware of this history. Besides, he wanted to hear if from his father's perspective.

Nobody spoke for ten long seconds.

And then his father spoke again. "Talbert is Willis' brother. He is also the leader of the Jones'...militia, I guess you could call it. They call him General Tally."

There was one family member that was able to use her head. Abby. And she was pissed. She yelled, "So you lie about not having family, then you lie about coming to Edenia, then you lie about why we are here so badly that Seth feels like he has to take Lillian's life in his own hands..." she took a huge breath then adds "...then you lie about how this is your family. I played nice with those old, smelly Millers for two hours because I thought they were my grandparents."

Seth looked at his sister and saw her eyes were glowing like twin flames.

"Abby, calm down."

And that was the wrong thing to say, because two seconds later, his dad's shirt was on fire.

Luckily, his father's Nature was water, and he was a trained military man. He fell on to the ground and blurred. Classic stop, drop, and roll, but on crack.

When he stood, his shirt was barely singed. He moved back toward them in a fumbling stagger. "That was a bit of an overreaction, Abigail."

Jenna stepped off the porch, reaching for him and asked, "Are you okay?"

"I'm a bit motion sick."

Lilly chimed in, "Well, you deserve it. I can't believe this."

Seth pursed his lips and raised his eyebrows in agreement.

"All right, so maybe I did deserve it, but you can't just go lighting things on fire, Abby."

"I've been walking around with this ability all day, and you're the first thing I've lit on fire. So, justice is a biatch, Pops. Deal." She glared down at him, her arms folded, her back straight as a warrior princess.

His mother huffed, "Abigail Elaine Johnson, language."

More amused than mad, his father wiped his face, shook his head, and then he gave in and started to chuckle.

His mother rolled her eyes. "Oh my goodness, you think this behavior is funny."

Seth chimed in, "It's kinda funny, mom, and totally on point, if you ask me."

"Okay, okay, we'll consider justice served," Seth's father said, still diverted.

The Johnson family all eyed one another, and Seth wondered who was going to start the questions first, so he did. "Well, how about you start from the beginning?"

"There isn't much to tell. My mother died in childbirth, and Talbert didn't want me. So he and Willis came up with a plan to abandon me in Edenia in hopes that I would grow up to be the spy they have always wanted. Edmond found me the next day, and when no one knew where I'd come from, he kept me. I was raised by those smelly Millers you spent two hours with. They are my parents in all the ways that count."

"So why does it matter? Who are the Joneses to us, then?" Lillian added. "Marth and Edmond are your parents; they are my grandparents."

"They are, and I love them very much."

Abby asked, "Well, I don't get it, then. If you love them, why did you leave them?"

Their dad sighed. "That, my dear, is a whole other story. One that—if done correctly—could fill an entire novel."

"Is there a Cliffs Notes version of that one?" Abby asked, her manner gentler now.

"Hum." He sighed heavily and was silent for a good ten seconds. "Well, Abby, in honor of my commitment to be more truthful and open, I will tell you one thing from when I was your age that—and I am ashamed to say it—contributed to my leaving Edenia.

He paused for a long moment. "When I was a boy, I didn't have a perspective on life, and it made things hard. You see, I was prideful and entitled and I would get obsessed with things. When I was thirteen and about to get my Nature, I was just positive I would have water Nature. I wanted it so badly. It was a new Nature, and only a few people had it. I watched them move so quickly, and swirl water into whirlpools, and I felt jealous. Which, looking back, was a sign to me that I *did* know—at least on some level—that I was not meant for water.

"But you are water, right?"

He sighed, "Yes. I am water now." Those grey eyes fell on Seth, "But I was born with black eyes. Black eyes that stayed black when my Nature took me." He let that marinate for a few seconds, and Seth felt a horrible sense of premonition. His father's gaze found his. "Seth, I assume that you were taken by your Nature today the same as the rest of us?"

Seth covered his mouth with his hand and nodded.

"Well son, I'm sorry. I am the reason you are cur...you have that Nature."

He was about to say *cursed*; Seth just knew it.

"You see, before I left, I was you. Son, it is because of my weakness, my inability to do as I should..." his father was on the verge of crying "...it was taken from me, and now it has fallen upon you."

Seth felt for the man, but he didn't understand why it was so terrible. "Dad, Dad, calm down. I've already used my Nature, like four times, and I like it. I mean, I'm super happy about it. It's not some weird, move plants, or water, or fire--sorry to anyone offended. It's completely inside me, and I didn't even have to change my eye color. Of all the Natures I've seen, this is the only one that feels exactly right. I feel normal. I'm surprisingly grateful," he explained.

Lillian went to him. "And look, Dad, you got what you always wanted. You're a water Nature now. I mean, how perfect is that, almost like it was meant to be."

Ezekiel Miller pulled himself together in a hurry, sniffed, and added, "I don't know if you fully understand what will happen to you, Seth, but I will say I am greatly relieved at how you are handling it."

Abby added, "Me, too. You should have seen him a few nights ago raving about how he didn't want to be a freak."

His father patted him on the back. "Well, Seth and I will have to speak more about it later. I get the feeling he will walk a mile in my nineteen-year-old shoes at seventeen."

Seth looked around at his other family members, confused. "What do you think he means?"

"I don't know. All I heard is he doesn't want to tell *me* his life saga, he only wants to tell *you*," Abby said with annoyance, glaring at their father.

"So, going back to the elephant in the room. Do we have a relationship with the Joneses or not?" Lillian asked. "Considering they gave Dad up when he was a baby, talked a desperate teenager into spying on his own adopted family, and just tortured the girl Seth is in love with, I vote no."

"Considering they torture people in general and they are weirdly obsessed with the garden of Eden, I vote double no," Abby added.

"I agree with the children. No Joneses. And speaking of the Garden of Eden, I've been waiting almost thirty years to hear this bit of history, so could you all just keep your smart remarks to yourself for a minute and let your father talk?"

Seth looked at his mother with incredulity. "You told us you knew."

"No, Seth. I told you to trust us."

"But how can 'us' mean only Dad?" Seth asked.

"He's gotcha there, Madre." Abby said.

"No, it is the 'royal' us. Meaning both of us. Meaning your father can speak for me because I allow him to, he has my blessing."

"How, how could you trust him that much?"

Abby said, "Yes, that is far too much power for one husband to have, Mother."

His mother sighed and pulled Seth closer. "Because I know him." She looked deeply into his eyes. "That is what marriage is. It's trust and choices."

"And love." Lillian added quietly.

"Movies and novels want you to believe that, but it's not true. Attraction is a bit out of your hands, yes, but even that can grow. Love, though...love is a choice. It's the choice to sacrifice self, for someone else, for an 'us'."

Seth let those words roll around in his head. He didn't really understand what that could mean.

"I have a lovely story about love. It also happens to be about Edenia's history if you would like to hear it."

Seth turned to his father ready to listen, ready to accept whatever it was that brought them all to this point and place and time.

After no one objected, his father began. "About five hundred years ago, a strange tale began floating between Native American tribes...

His father continued , "Before volatile irises and Natures, miracles had, in one way or another, stopped invasion. The Edenians did their part by laying traps and being tricky, but that only could help so much. And as time and the modernization of man progressed, those means became moot.

"Then, about sixty years ago, the Joneses stopped attempting to be gentlemen and implemented guerilla tactics, and the frequency of their attacks skyrocketed. That was when it happened.

"Those in Edenia began to adapt, to evolve. They became enhanced. A full-on ability or Nature—that's what they call them because they seem to derive from a natural tendency or knack already held—emerged.

"As the Joneses used their worldly tools to break into the town, the Edenians used their Natures to keep them out. Metal of any sort could easily be warmed to blistering temperatures with a fire Nature focused on it. Knives or bullets cannot harm stone. Night goggles cannot see the wind. Natures were the perfect way to fight back without fighting at all.

"The Joneses tried to be clever, and they did a good job too. But, still, wooden weapons could not be kept in holsters or hands when an earth Nature was about. Enemy communications could be listened to and relayed when a wind Nature chose it. And who could fight with the speed and agility of a water Nature?

"Through all this, they never really let the Joneses get a good grip on what was happening. Stories of ghosts and supernatural occurrences spread.

"The Natures adapted, and here we are today, adapting still. Look at Miriam, and Peter, and Seth."

Abby snorted. "That story had nothing to do with love."

His mother's head moved back in surprise. "Yes, Abby, it did. It had everything to do with love. Love for other humans was the reason this place was started. Love of human life to the point of sacrificing one's own was the whole historical lesson here. I could point to ten acts of supernal love in that one story. Don't you see? The Edenians love the Joneses. They are saving the Joneses from themselves. They are stopping the Joneses from suicide every day as they seek a false immortality."

Lillian understood first with awe in her tone. "And they don't even know it."

"I don't know about you guys, but I could get behind a mission like that. It feels like, extra magnanimous," Abby said.

"Well, we all know how you like to be magnanimous, Abby," Seth quipped, and everyone laughed.

"I like the idea of it," she answered defensively. "I guess we will see how I like it in action."

"Yes, I guess we will." Their father cleared his throat. "I need to say something." He took a deep breath. "I'm sorry to you all. This whole debacle is a result of me lying about who I am and keeping my truth a secret. I know my silence has frightened you and caused you to distrust me. I ask your forgiveness, and I promise to be more open."

Seth's family remained silent, and it was good, because his mind fluttered around the words his father spoke, tasting them, feeling them, allowing them to heal him.

Finally, Abby broke the silence. "Well, I guess I can forgive you, Dad, but I'm pretty sure your promise is useless. What other secrets could you possibly have?"

CHAPTER 40

Peter

The fireflies would be out any minute. The crickets were already chirping, which was a welcome sign after the storm. Peter leaned up against a tree, his mind whirling with all that had happened in the last day. At the top of his list, his father hadn't died today. He should have. Peter saw on the ribbon of time that he had. But he didn't.

Because of Seth.

Seth was the thing that changed the future. Was that his Nature? Peter wanted to know, but he had something else more pressing.

Though there was so much work to do after the tornado, and so many questions he needed answered, Peter intentionally sat down tried to relax in order to enter into his ribbon room. He badly needed to know what his father's thread looked like now.

He closed his eyes nervously—he had never chased the ribbon room before, it had always come to him unbidden—but he relaxed, giving himself permission to fall asleep. It didn't take much.

In fact, it felt almost instant.

The ribbon room was before him. It was still chaos, perhaps even more so than before. Threads veering at crazy angles, many getting lopped off, the weave looking strange and monochromatic in the striped sections of the weave. Peter moved toward the part of the weave he knew was Edenia and quickly found his father.

He looked down at the point where his father should have been snipped from the weave. There was nothing. It was normal. He looked into the future of his father's weave, no breaks. Peter gave the mental equivalent of a sigh.

Whatever Seth had done, it was done perfectly.

Peter went over to Seth's thread and pulled his focus tight so the thread became a pillar. He examined it closely. As he did so, he focused his mind and quieted himself. And without understanding how, Peter saw Seth; like SAW him. Not just a face, he saw what Seth REALLY was. It was a jumble of a million different sensations. It was so catastrophically clear who Seth was at his core, in his essence, that Peter understood him inside and out. He felt all the things, he knew all the substance. It was simultaneously so vast and minute, that as Peter tried to think about It, all he could form in his mind was the image of the full ribbon. Trying to grab something about Seth and think it over was like trying to explain the details in the pattern of the full ribbon. It was impossible.

Still, somehow Seth was known to him so fully it hurt whatever brain Peter had inside this place of time.

Pulling back from Seth's pillar, he circled around it and saw something that confused him. Seth had a tentacle, just like the ones Miriam had. The armlike appendage to his pillar lit up the same way a flashlight beam lit up dust in the air. It was just a grainy tube of matter. Peter did not understand it, so he decided to follow it. Moving through pillars, Peter kept the tentacle right before him, eyes never blinking. Before long, he ran headlong into another pillar. Looking up, he saw it was Miriam's. Seth and Miriam were connected. He must have concentrated too hard on Miriam, for he felt that huge knowing sensation pulling him in, and saw her face on the surface of the pillar. Not wanting to get sucked into knowing his sister completely, he pulled away quickly to examine the other tentacles coming off her pillar. He picked one and followed it. Gerald was on the other end. He moved to another, this one was Karl; another, this one was Josie; another, Ben.

He thought of what Josie had told him, what Gerald had said about his connection with Miriam. That was all it took for Peter's suspicions to be confirmed. Miriam was connected in a tangible way to all those who she'd taken memories from. They were aware of her and she was connected to them. What could this mean?

He pulled away and set to working on the problem when he felt something shake him.

"Peter. Peter, wake up."

Peter opened his eyes and felt an acute pain in his temples. He cried out and grasp his head.

"Peter, what is it?" He heard his father's voice ask him. "Peter, should I fetch the doc?"

Peter couldn't speak as he passed out.

⚬

He had well and truly passed out, not going into the ribbon room. That, and he had no idea how he'd come to be in a bed. He felt the softness under him and wanted to snuggle down and go to sleep.

"Peter." His father tapped him on the cheek. "Peter, wake up."

He blinked his eyes open and saw the doc and his father both leaning over him.

"Sleep." He moaned and tried to roll over.

"Peter," The doc said in his business voice, "Your father said you had an episode. He said you were holding your head like it was going to explode."

Oh yeah, Peter thought.

He opened his eyes again and looked at the men before him. His mind went back to what had happened. He was woken from his ribbon room and had a massive headache.

He thought about what he learned there, about Miriam and about Seth. The moment he thought about Seth and all he learned, his head began to hurt again. And his instincts told him he was not allowed to understand someone so well in his physical form.

He stopped thinking about the Seth he knew from his room and started thinking about the Seth he knew here, on earth. Seth had saved both Charity and his father. Seth loved Miriam.

A deep part of him knew these facts with such intimate detail that Seth's being was clear, but he did not think about that part of himself. He continued to list things. Seth betrayed Edenia to the Joneses in order to save Lillian. Seth had a strange Nature.

"Papa, what is Seth's Nature?" he asked, surprising both men. "He has a new Nature, right? Something that has to do with the future. That's why he was able to do what he did, save you, I mean."

"Peter, you want to talk about Seth, right now?"

The doc added. "Before anything else can be done, I need to know that you are okay, Peter."

"I'm okay, Doc. I just think I did something I wasn't supposed to."

Doc and Pa looked at him questioningly, but he wasn't about to let them know what had just happened. How could he possibly explain it? "Do you know what Seth's Nature is?" he repeated instead.

The men looked uncertain, "We think that might be Seth's story to tell."

"In other words, you *don't* know." Peter shook his head at them and let his mind work over the facts he knew, and tried to connect the dots himself.

Though Peter saw time, he didn't really see the future clear enough to change its course. Like this afternoon with the tornado; Peter had needed to be with his father. He also knew beyond doubt his father would die that day. There was nothing to change. He just knew what would happen.

Yes, his being there had stopped his father from being sucked up by the cyclones; but it was also clear as day that with only Peter there, his father would have been fried to death when Peter got struck by lightning.

Somehow, both he and Seth had worked together to save his father using their own special Natures. He thought of the tingle of the lightning as it coursed through his body of rock and earth and barreled into the ground with tremendous force. It had almost tickled.

But there was no doubt in his mind that it would have killed his father. Seth changed that death, somehow.

He looked at the silent men and said, "I just want to know. Seth really has turned this place upside down."

"He certainly has." Peter's father grimaced. "He reminds me of his father. Barreling through life and people and circumstances and ending up leaving a mess behind him, but somehow that mess turns out better than it ever could have been, once it's all put back together."

"That he does," Was Doc's only response.

"Peter, I'm uncertain of *all* Seth can do, I saw him become...well, that's not my story to tell, but what I do know is that he is what we named a Revelator in the past. He can see a short way into the future."

Peter's eyes bulged. "Really?"

"Yes. And I am worried about what it foretells about our future," his father stated ungenerously.

"No," Doc said, "He is far more stable than his father was at seventeen. Seth is going to do very well. I have a feeling." The doc turned to him. "I would like you to get a few hours of sleep, young man. And let's see how that helps your head."

Peter didn't argue, but he added, "Papa, will you wake me in an hour or so? I want to help with the cleanup. Plus, we have another problem heading our way that I will need to be a part of."

His father's eyebrows knotted at him. "What's that, pray tell?"

Peter smiled. "The rest of Miriam's Joneses should be here tonight."

CHAPTER 41

SATURDAY
Peter

His father did not wake him up until early morning. And the Joneses hadn't come. Perhaps the tornado had gotten in their way. Perhaps Willis was keeping them captive. Peter wasn't sure. Still, when he got up, he immediately began working with his father and several other Guardians cleaning up the mess from the tornado.

"That was one heck of a night," Peter's father stated conversationally. His father had stuck by him all morning chatting about this or that.

Peter smiled. "The work feels amazing, though. I feel like a man. Like a Guardian."

His pa chuckled and slapped him on the back, "As you should son, as you should. You had a grand adventure yesterday, I couldn't have had a better Guardian at my back, and you're working your tail off this morning."

Peter basked a little in these words. His father proud of him? Who would have guessed?

The quiet only lasted a moment before Peter interrupted it. "Papa, are you the only one who can do that?"

"What?"

"You know, stop tornados?"

"No. Any wind Nature can."

"Why don't they?"

"Well, I think they just expect me to do it."

"You don't think it's because they are scared?"

"Sure, that might be part of it. They just happen so rarely that it's never seemed like a big deal to do it. We always have plenty of warning from the greens. Plus, I don't go anywhere. I'm always around."

"Except yesterday."

"Well, I got back in time, didn't I?"

"What happened at the Joneses?"

"After you got Miriam out?"

Peter nodded.

"Well, we tried to leave. But they pinned us down and wouldn't stop shooting at us. So, we had to wait around until we came up with a plan."

"Yes," Peter said excitedly. "What was the plan?"

"Let's just say I might have started this weather hiccup myself."

Peter's eyes widened in surprise. "You did what?"

"I might have gotten a little carried away and pushed the wind around a bit too much. Maybe that's another reason I always take care of the tornados. It's probably more often than not my fault they come in the first place." His father laughed.

Peter grimaced. His father's laugh had the feel of a man used to being the reason a natural wonder coalesced and spun throughout the land.

"I have never once thought of any Nature having an effect on the outside." Peter said seriously.

"That's because none of the others do."

Stunned by this revelation he walked in silence for a minute. Soon their house came into view.

His father slowed. "Peter, what am I going to see when I go in there?" he paused and eyed his home warily. "With Miriam, I mean." He kicked at the dirt road. "Am I going to want to take my belt to Seth Johnson's backside? Or did she get out of there okay?"

There was so much hope in his voice that Peter didn't know how to answer. Then he thought of his mama. "If Mama can talk to Seth and not burn him to a crisp, I think you can handle yourself."

His father's hands clenched. "So, it's bad."

Miriam—as far as he could see—was not only physically damaged, but she was crazier than a nut farm. After careful consideration, he added. "You will have to see for yourself." They were in front of their house now. Peter stopped, not wanting this special time with Pa to be over. "Did you know that the river could heal?"

His father blinked at him, "Of course. Didn't you?"

"No, I mean I had my suspicions, but I didn't know."

"Goodness, Peter, how do you think we stay so healthy? Out in the world, people get sick regularly. What in the world are they teaching you over at the school? That was basic curriculum in my day."

"Well, I've got news for you. They don't teach us anything useful. So, does that mean I can stop going?"

"Nice try." His father swatted his bottom lightly and mounted the porch. After pulling Butch the maniac screen door open, he held it wide for Peter.

CHAPTER 42

Miriam

A single sound drowned out everything. It raged through her brain like a torrent of audible chaos. She wanted to raise her hands and cover her ears. She wanted to cry and hide. But she knew she couldn't do any of those things.

She couldn't move. She was strapped to a chair. She was being tortured, held in the clutches of the enemy. But then there was Peter. He'd come. He'd rescued her.

Someone touched her, then spoke to her.

"Miriam, my darling girl. Wake up. Talk to me." The voice was quiet and tender, and the loud racket was gone. The hand smoothed her hair back and brushed her arm lovingly, and Miriam felt her heart break loose from the prison she'd protected it in while being tortured.

"Mother?" she heard her own voice croak.

"Yes." The voice was excited. "Yes, my darling, it is me."

"Mother." She said again and moved her hand to reach out.

"Fight, Miriam. Fight. You are strong and good. Fight the battle you are having inside you. You are braver and more dedicated than you know. Fight, my darling. I am here."

She felt the power in the words, and they did buoy her up. She opened her eyes. "Mama? I saw you."

"There you are, you brave girl."

Miriam reached up to touch her chest. It did not hurt anymore. In fact, it did not hurt at all. A sense of panic overwhelmed her. She had to have the scars. She would show Seth what he did to her. She scrambled at her shirt and saw it. The red, angry marks were there, just not sore and not burnt.

"We left them, just as you asked," her mother said, her voice tight and tired, but not unapproving. Their eyes met, and her mothers were full of wisdom. "You want him to know what he did, what his choices wrought. I do not blame you. In fact," she sighed and leaned back in her chair, "I understand the sentiment more than you could know."

They stared at each other for a long moment, then her mother reached for her hand. She took it. Squeezed it. Then leaned down and kissed it. "I am sorry, Miriam." She looked up. "Can you forgive me for shutting you out? Can you forgive me for not *seeing* you? For not understanding?" She paused and looked at the floor. "I...I did something when I was younger. I fell under the spell of someone with an internal power such as you have. It scared me. It is not an excuse, I promise. No matter what happened to me, I had no right to treat you the way I have. But I have. I did it. And I am sorry. Can you forgive me? Can you let me be here for you now, and from now on?"

Miriam felt all the millions of cuts on her heart, the ones that had her mother's name on them, heal instantly with these words. And it wasn't the words, it was the fact that she knew her mother. She had seen her mother repent many times. These were not hollow or empty words. They were an expression of fact. She knew that if her mother said she would be different, that she needed forgiveness, it was because her mother had already done the hard work of changing inside, and that this was a promise that things would be different.

The light and love that entered Miriam's heart pulled all the pain out of her. She felt it clean her of her anger and hurt. This one moment of forgiveness healed her soul, wraithlike as it was. She pulled on her mother's hand as tears dropped down her cheeks. They hugged tightly as Miriam said, "Thank you, Mother. You do not know how long I have needed to be close to you. I love you."

"I love you too, my darling."

No sooner had the hug ended than Peter and her father came into her room. He took one look at Miriam, and huge tears formed in his eyes. Her father's jaw clenched, and his breath exploded out his nostrils in great huffs.

Peter's mother went to him. "Calm yourself, Hirum. What is done is done, and we cannot undo it." She touched his face. "We have her. She is safe. She will pull through this."

He did not listen, but backed away. "My strong, darling girl, how did this happen?"

But Miriam could not be upset with her father's reaction after the moment she'd just had with her mother. "Do I truly look that awful, father?" she asked with humor behind her words.

He bit his lips together.

But Peter wasn't afraid to speak up. "You look like a two-day-old bowl of cornmeal mush."

"Peter!" their mother chided.

Miriam ignored him. Peter could no longer bother her; they had a truce. And he was next on her list of loved ones that needed gratitude. She held her hands out to Papa. "Come Papa, give me a hug. I do not feel bad. I feel rather wonderful." She glanced quickly in her mother's direction. They shared a small smile.

Her father sat on the side of her bed and embraced her, kissing her hair and whispering his love for her. Instantly, she felt safe. Peter jumped to the other side of the bed and squeezed into the hug, giggling and elbowing everyone, and Mama joined in. She felt loved, and whole, and everything good.

When the hugs loosened, Miriam said, "Thank you, Papa and Peter, for coming after me, for saving me."

Peter interjected. "That was all me. If it were only up to Papa, they would have had way more time to torture you."

Peter's mother instantly corrected him through clenched teeth, "Peter Christopher Miller."

"What? It's true. Papa was dillydallying, and I was not going to wait. I knew what was happening to Miriam and no one would listen, so..."

Both of her parents turned toward Peter. Her father was the first to speak, and he did so as if he were treading toward a deer in the forest. "Peter, I know you have figured something out about your Nature. Do you feel comfortable talking about it yet? We would all love to know."

Peter sniffed and tongued his teeth as he sighed. "Yeah, okay. So, not long after my Nature took me, I started having dreams."

"What kind..." her mother began, but without taking his eyes off Peter, her father put a hand up. This silenced Luanne immediately. "Yes," he said, coaxingly.

"I've been having dreams. That's all." Peter looked at the floor and then away.

This was his tell.

Her father knew it, so he waited patiently, his eyes remaining on his son.

Peter couldn't take it for long, and began to squirm, and then he buckled. "And I can sort of see...time?"

Their mother took a step forward, her face pale. Father's hand went up again, and she stilled.

"Time?" Miriam's father asked softly.

"I have dreams, and can see a big ribbon of time in my head, okay? Geez, it's not as if I have the plague." His tone was defensive, which made clear to Miriam that he was feeling uncomfortable. Miriam felt a little vindictive smile form on her face and she settled down deeper into her covers, interested to see where this story went.

"What does it mean to see time?" Papa asked. "I don't understand how Miriam being in trouble and seeing time are connected."

"No, they aren't." He grunted with frustration. "You see, this is why I need to keep my mouth shut. Just never mind about how it looks or works. I barely know myself. Regardless, I knew we needed to help Miriam at once. So, I did."

Her father nodded at Peter's declaration that there would be silence on this matter. "That will do, Peter, for now." And they all understood what her father was saying.

Mama adopted the soft, calm voice of their papa and said, "That was you being the bravest and most loyal brother ever."

Her father smiled as well and added, "Not to mention a kick-butt Guardian." He turned to his wife. "If you will pardon my language."

"I will allow it," Luanne Miller added, "When it is the truth."

Miriam smiled and felt her heart bulge with love for her brave little brother.

With everyone smiling at him, Peter blushed and got up from the bed. "It seems that now might be the best time to tell you something you are not going to like."

Instantly everyone was on their guard. With Peter, one had to be.

"What?" Their fathers voice asked.

"Miriam, you know how you took memories from a whole bunch of Joneses?"

"Yes?" She said warily, not knowing where he was going.

"Well it seems the process had consequences."

Their mother jumped in, "Consequences? What consequences?"

Peter began pacing, "Uhm, well you see. It sort of gave those Joneses an inner sense about Miriam."

"Inner sense?" Miriam asked, curious about how this tied to her experience with the Joneses.

"Yes." He stopped pacing. "Basically, they know where you are, all the time."

"What?" Her parents yelled, all pretense of calm gone.

"They thought it was just Edenia." Peter rushed out. "But when Miriam went to the compound, they realized it was her. These guys are not dumb. They knew something was happening to them and they put two and two together.

"What does this mean?" Miriam asked after a loaded silence.

"I don't know, except they have all left the Jones compound. Well, they were supposed to, but then there was a tornado. I was expecting them last night..."

"Leave the Jones compound for where?" Luanne Miller asked in her business voice.

"For here," Peter said slowly and with a winning smile.

Miriam watched her Papa's forehead wrinkle quite thoroughly.

"Meaning?" Miriam's mother asked.

"Every one of the Joneses that Miriam used her Nature on, well, they are coming to Edenia, tonight. I invited them." Peter held his breath.

Miriam couldn't feel anything but shock.

"No," her mother said. "No, what are we going to do with them? They cannot stay here. They are our enemy."

"Not really," Peter contradicted. "They are, like, obsessed with Miriam. They would never hurt her. You've seen Gerald. He's like a tame Rottweiler."

Peter gestured as if he was about to say more about the men, but Miriam interrupted, stunned at the news. "Gerald? Where is Gerald? Is he here?" The memories were still jumbled, but he had helped save her.

"Yes." Her mother's hand went to her forehead like her head was going to explode. "He's sitting outside your door with Garren. That huge lummox has been there all afternoon. He won't leave."

"He is waiting for answers," Peter advised.

"What answers?"

"Uh, the kind that will explain why he is now obsessed with a sixteen-year-old girl and willing to give up life and limb for her, as well as betraying his friends and employer for her."

"I don't know the answer to that," Miriam screeched.

"Well you best figure it out Miri, because pretty soon there are going to be thirty other Joneses here, wanting the same answer."

This news sent a chill up Miriam's back. Then she looked at her brother, "What have you seen about it? Have you had any dreams that might help me figure this out?"

"Nope."

Her parents look at one another and simultaneously took in a deep breath.

"What?" She asked as she looked at them. "What was that?"

Her mother sat down next to her and took her hand. Then looked at her papa.

"Miriam, baby. Seth came back."

Miriam felt as if electricity zipped through her. "What?" she exhaled out.

Her mother answered. "He brought Lillian back in the nick of time to save her life. The whole family is together, they have their Natures, and Lillian has been healed."

Her father continued, "She had a fatal brain tumor. Seth didn't know. His parents led him to believe her condition was operable."

"To keep the hope alive in their house," her mother added directly after. It sounded like she was defending the Johnsons choice to lie to their children, which confused Miriam.

Her father jumped back in. "Because he'd already received the summons, and he knew that Eden could heal Lillian."

Her parents tag-team explanation was making her dizzy. She looked away from them and felt tears on her cheeks. Her mind raced over this news. The pain of their last moments together, the rejection, betrayal, death-bed confession rolled around in her mind. What did this mean? Would she have to see him every day? How could she look at him? How could she not fall in love with him again, if she could look at him? How could she not hate him and want to hurt him? Then the full words she'd just heard repeated. *Lillian had a fatal brain tumor. But Seth did not know. He thought there was hope she could be saved.* No wonder he betrayed her.

Her mother must have read her mind. "Because Seth did not know what was happening here in Edenia, he thought his parents had just come here to let Lillian die. He did not understand because he thought they were coming to the States to meet with a special doctor that would cut the tumors out. He took Lillian all the way to Baltimore by himself to the doctor."

Miriam looked up at that.

Both her parents were shaking their heads. "And *that* is when he found out that surgery was never an option. Death was all that was left for his sister."

Miriam felt the compassion they were hoping for. She did not understand why they wanted her to feel compassion for Seth, but… but she got stuck on this last bit. "So he just ran back here. It sounds exactly in character for Seth Johnson. Mother, you were right. He is a faithless creature." Her eyes narrowed, and she turned away from them, her mind and heart aching at the anger behind her own words.

The room remained silent as she worked through her heartache and wiped her tears.

Her mother squeezed her hand, and Miriam turned back to her with, no doubt, a red, puffy face.

"What?" She said and sniffed.

"There is more."

Her brain caught up with her emotions. "Why are you telling me this?"

Her parents nodded, appreciating that she knew them well enough to discern that they would not bring up such a painful subject without reason.

Her father answered. "Well, my darling. Because Seth got his Nature."

He stopped there.

Her stomach lurched. "Yes?"

He took in a big breath and said, "He is a Revelator, Miriam."

Her eyes searched their eyes, and then the quilt. "Which means…"

Peter butted in. "Which means, he is probably going to be the one to tell you what to do about the Joneses you've collected. Oh, and it means he can see the future, which just so happened to save our fathers life during the tornado. Yeah, without Seth being here, Papa would be dead." Her mama's eyes went big as saucers, and her papa glared at Peter. He held up his hands and went on quickly, "Or maybe it just means the Master will tell *me*, the *other* sort-of future seer, what people need and what we do with the 'Miriam Joneses'."

He put finger quotes around this, just like the Johnson twins did all the time. "I mean he probably does not want Miriam to be tortured any more than necessary, right? She's been through enough."

Her parents shook their heads at him and breathed deeply before her father continued. "Which means, he is here to stay, Miriam. He's not going anywhere. He very well may take my place as the leader of the Guardians. Those who get called to see the future are who we all count on."

Why? Why would the Master choose him? She voiced this concern.

Both of her parents shook their heads at the question. "It was Ezekiel's responsibility at first, but he left it."

"It was not that simple, Hirum."

"How is it not simple?"

"I will not fight with you about this in front of the children." The look her mother gave her father, irises blazing, shut him up.

He turned back to Miriam, "Which means..."

"Which means I should just get over what he did to me."

"No!" her mother said fiercely, and Miriam watched as her amber irises started sloshing. "It means you take as much time as you need, and you punish him if that helps." Those amber eyes of hers glanced toward Miriam's chest. "But then, you allow yourself to let go of the pain and move on. Not because that is best for him or the community, but because forgiveness is what is best for you, for your happiness."

Her papa put a hand on her mother's shoulder. "It means that we will all send you strength and energy and love for your trial. I will never agree with Seth's choices, of course, and if I could rip the skin off his bottom with my belt, I would. But that does not change that he was acting out of love for a sister, and many of us are responsible by not communicating the truth when we had the chance."

Miriam thought of Peter's Nature, and how it came when it did. The Master had given them chances to avoid this, if only they'd spoken to one another.

Peter held up his hands. "Not me. I am not responsible, and I am more than happy to exact a poo-venge." He sat on the end of Miriam's bed as a slow, devious smile curled his lips. "Do you want me to make sure he gets random dung filled clothing items for the rest of his natural life? Just say the word."

Miriam rolled both of her lips between her teeth, in an attempt not to laugh but it all went to the pits when her mother chimed in. "Peter, I have never been fond of your proclivity toward dung, but now I understand. And if fifty years from now, Seth is not occasionally cleaning out his boots because they are filled with manure, I will be deeply disappointed in you."

The comment hung in the air like a bubble everyone was waiting to burst. When it did, it was with laughter. It hurt to laugh so hard, but it also felt good.

There was a knock at the door.

Her father answered it. "Hello, Gerald. What is it?"

Miriam saw the big bald-headed man that had, by her count, saved her life twice, maneuver his gaze past her father to meet her eyes. As soon as he saw her, he smiled and said, "Seth is in the living room for Peter."

Peter stood, confusion on his face as Miriam's stomach sunk to her feet. The last time Seth was in her living room it was date night. Tears sprang to her eyes as she recalled the best and worst night of her life.

Gerald barged into the room past her father and leaned over her. "What is it?" His eyes searched her face, and she saw his utter concern. She felt the connection they shared. It was true. But she knew this already, didn't she? The part of his soul floated to the surface of her consciousness. "Is it that Seth kid? He's the idiot that brought you to The Compound, isn't he? You want me to hurt him?"

Her father was on Gerald in a moment. "Gerald, that won't be necessary, but, thank you."

Miriam surprised everyone in the room when she reached out to Gerald. She took his arm and whispered through her emotions and her tears. "Thank you, Gerald. Thank you for saving me. Thank you for helping me. You are my hero. And if I ever need Seth Johnson *hurt*, you will be the first person I call for."

The big man sunk to a squat beside Miriam's bed, his face melted of all anger. "All right. I am so glad you are feeling better. I'm sure all the guys are as concerned as I am."

A look crossed her father's face. "Speaking of the other guys, I wonder if that is why Seth has come. Maybe they have finally made it through the wreckage of the tornados." He took Gerald by the shoulder. "We better go check."

Gerald nodded and rose. He patted Miriam's hand before leaving with her father.

When they were gone, Miriam's mother turned to her with gigantic eyes. "Well, that was interesting."

"Yes, it was."

Luanne bit her cheek and then whispered, "I cannot help it. He did remind me of a trusty hound, did he not?" She covered her mouth and laughed behind her hand.

Miriam smiled. "He did indeed. What in the world am I going to do with thirty of them?"

"Only the Master knows."

"Yes, well I hope he tells one of us soon. And preferably Peter."

Her mother nodded. "That is not the way it works, my love." She gave Miriam a sympathetic glance and patted her hand.

And it did not matter that their subject was a hard one. The sympathy her mother just gave her proved she was keeping her word, and that felt better than any fear of Seth, or of her future, or her past.

CHAPTER 43

I *should not be here. I should not be here. I should not be here.* His brain was a constant stream of doubt and fear.

Then Peter was there. His yellow eyes blazing, glaring, questioning. Seth decided to just say his piece and get out.

"Hey, uhm, I had one of those vision thingies, and I needed to let you know that within about ten minutes, those Joneses—the ones that are somehow your friends now—will be on the north hill."

Peter's expression changed completely. "Really?"

"Yeah, and if you don't get Gerald down there to take care of them, they might cause some problems with the people living in the tents. PS, I'm really confused right now, about Gerald and the Joneses in Edenia. It's the only reason I didn't run and hide from this vision."

Garren and Jai blew in the front door. Garren demanded as soon as he'd settled onto two feet, "Where's papa?"

Their father's voice came from the hall. "I'm here." They heard his step move quickly, and then he was in the front room, Gerald at his heels. "What is it?"

"Joneses, a couple dozen of them, walking our eastern border."

Hirum Miller looked at Seth, "What did you see?"

Seth did not hesitate, "If Gerald is not there when they arrive, they will cause trouble with the tent people."

Hirum narrowed his eyes, "How much time?"

"Eighteen minutes." Seth answered.

"You can do that?" Peter asked wowed.

Seth shook his head. "Nope, I saw of vision of this conversation and that's just what I said then, so I'm saying it now."

Garren and Jai looked at their father, confused. "He is a Revelator. Get used to it," was the man's short answer. They glanced at him, took a deep breath, then nodded in acquiescence.

Hirum turned to Gerald. "Will you be freaked out if one of these men gives you a ride to the hilltop? We cannot walk there in eighteen minutes."

"By ride, you mean..."

"You ride on my back, Jones, while I run faster than a cheetah."

Gerald smoothed a hand over his bald head, but Seth had to hand it to the man as he agreed to the trip.

"Jai?" Hirum asked.

"It would be my pleasure, dearest brother-in-law."

Quickly, the four of them left Peter and himself alone in the living room. Seth stood there awkwardly for five seconds, then said, "Well, I'll be going, then," and he moved toward the door.

"Seth," Peter called.

Seth turned, "Yah?"

"I totally hate you for stealing my sister and almost killing my new friend, and you probably will find horse poop in your boots for as long as I'm alive because of it, but...thanks for saving my papa yesterday."

Seth bit his cheek to hold back a smile or sob, he wasn't sure which. But he nodded to Peter as he opened the front door. As he left the Millers house, the screen door—almost as if it knew he deserved it —thwacked his elbow so hard as it closed, it brought tears to his eyes.

He heard Peter say from behind the door, "Don't let Butch hit you on the way out." But Seth heard the smile in that little craphead's tone. He rubbed his arm, then wiped his eyes and knew he would be paying dearly for his mistakes. Who needs the devil when there is a Peter Miller in the world?

The minute he exited the Miller's house, his other sight pulled him into a vision. It was of the guy from the horse accident. Westley.

He was in a house Seth did not recognize, but Seth saw himself and the doctor in a panic over the man. Seth knew that if he did not go to that house as soon as possible, Westley would die, and for some reason, he knew that was a bad thing.

Looking around himself frantically, he realized he was in no way capable of helping this situation. He turned back toward the Miller's screen door and gritted his teeth. Pulling it open and twisting the handle of the front door, he stuck his head inside. His vision must have only taken an instant, for Peter had not left the living room yet.

The brown haired, mischievous faced boy turned back around, and when he saw Seth, he was puzzled.

"I need to know where the doctor lives, and I need to know fast."

Peter, a credit to his calling, did not hesitate. "Well, let's go." And he moved to yank the door out of Seth's hand.

Seth, with his other sight, saw himself pulling Peter on to his back and moving as fast as the wind.

He blinked. "Uhm Peter, we have to move fast, I am supposed to..." He motioned giving Peter a piggyback.

The boy's expression changed from confused to surprised to impressed in a flash. And again, a credit to his calling, he mounted Seth's back as if he did this sort of thing every day. Which maybe he did.

When Seth stood there, uncertain of what to do, Peter said, "I'm not up here for my health, man. Run that way." He pointed to Seth's left.

Not knowing exactly what to expect, but also feeling the now-familiar superhuman-ness that happened when he was about to do something superhuman-like, he obeyed Peter and began to run.

Before Seth understood fully what was happening, he was being pulled, or pushed maybe, over the ground faster than mortally possible.

"Left," Peter yelled in his ear. "Right." They ran. "Right." Peter pulled back on his shoulders as if he were a horse. "Stop. It's here." The boy hopped off his back and raced up a walkway to a larger one-story house. He pulled open the screen door, and Seth moved behind Peter. They burst through as one. The doctor was sitting on an uncomfortable looking sofa, a book in his lap. Peter looked at Seth with the expression of *spit it out*. And for a split-second Seth wished with all his heart he could have the courage and moxie of this fourteen-year-old.

"Westley is in danger," Seth spat out to answer the doctor's wide, questioning eyes.

The older man was up out of his seat faster than Seth believed possible for a man his age.

Seth and Peter followed him down a wide hall to the last door. They burst in and threw on the light, only to see Westley foaming at the mouth, his head spastically trembling, his eyes rolling.

The doctor quickly touched Westley's blanket covered foot, his irises swirling. "He is bleeding in his brain."

Seth watched as the doctor stepped to the side of the bed. There, he stuck his fingers into the nightstand. No, it wasn't a nightstand, it was where the nightstand should be, but it was a planter box full of dirt.

Instantly, live and growing things began to burst from the dirt. The doctor directed, somehow, the vines as they exploded outward toward Westley. They touched his face, and to Seth's utter disgust and fascination, entered his ear. Then, the doctor touched Westley's skull, probing it gently. "Ah, it is at the hematoma. It cracked the skull."

Seth watched as the man did that same creepy thing he'd done before. He reached inside Westley's skin.

"Yes. I will just move these bones back into place. Peter, water, please."

Peter fetched a pitcher from a table on the same side of the bed as the nightstand of dirt. He moved quickly to the dirt and poured it over the plant that was growing up Westley's ear hole. Then he moved to the other side of the bed and asked, "Where?"

"Over my hands, slowly."

Peter did as instructed. Westley stopped shaking, and the mood of the room calmed measurably. As Peter poured the water on the place where Doc's fingers entered Westley's skin, Seth asked, "What are the vines doing?", his face scrunched up.

The doctor was concentrating, but his fiercely twirling irises turned toward Seth. "It is Shepherd's Purse. The leaves work as a coagulation. They will stop the bleeding." He grunted. "They are also offering me help with these pieces of skull from the other side." The man met Seth's eyes. "I will need Comfrey soon to knit the bones together. Why don't you give it a try?" His head jerked toward the planter.

Seth stepped back, "Me? Uhm, no. I don't do that."

Peter looked over at Seth and then back to the doctor. "That's what black is? It's everything?" His eyes looked back at Seth. "You lucky dog."

Seth's eyes were going back and forth between the two Guardians in the room. "What are you talking about?"

Peter answered, "You have all the Natures."

"Plus, revelation," added Doc. "Peter, more water, please."

Seth's brain felt like pudding.

"Don't believe me? Stick your fingers into that dirt and ask the Master for some Comfrey and let's just see what happens. I'm going to need it in about two ticks."

Seth wanted to know who this Master person was and what the heck it meant to ask him for something.

Peter interrupted his thoughts. "It's like the running, Seth. Don't think about it. Just walk over there and do it."

So he did. He refused to let his brain get in the way as he plunged his fingers into the dirt and mentally said, *I need some Comfrey... please.* That same otherworldly feeling tugged on his mind. He pulled his fingers out. As he did, a plant with long, narrow leaves of a furry variety followed.

He looked at Peter, amazed, and the boy gasped. "Your eyes. The black of them is swirled with turquoise. I can see that your Nature has taken you."

Seth blinked his eyes and looked back down at the plant. It was still blooming out of the dirt.

"Now, Seth, pluck those leaves and dehydrate them by pulling water Nature to you and telling the water to leave the leaves. Then use fire Nature to heat them, but only a bit. It will cause them to go nice and crackly dry."

"What?"

Peter snapped at him as if he were an annoying dog. "Seth, just do it."

Seth did. He plucked several leaves and looked at them, and when he felt that sense of power inside him, he mentally thought, *I need you to be dry...please.* And before his eyes the handful of leaves shriveled and dried.

"That is so cool. That time the blacks of your eyes were swirled with grey and then amber," Peter exalted, as if Seth were the most interesting person on the planet.

"Thank you!" Doc said and took the leaves from Seth. He crushed them in his palm and with a cupped hand covered the place where he'd been digging in Westley's head. He pressed the green into the scalp. It went inside.

The stems of the narrow vine retreated from Westley's ear, and the man opened his eyes, but only to look around before he closed them again. It startled Seth, and he stumbled back from the bed. At that point, he knew that Westley would be all right.

Half mumbling, he said, "If you don't need me anymore..." and he stumbled out toward the living room, where he fell into a chair, his mind a fog of disbelief at what he had just done.

Furthermore, what he had just done felt completely natural, normal, fulfilling, amazing. He looked down at his own hands. "I was afraid of this," he whispered to himself, mystified. "I was so scared, I ruined everything." He recalled how absolutely freaked out he was thinking that Miriam had used her power on him, but he'd just seen

Doc use his power on Westley, and he had saved him. This was not freaky, it was remarkable, incredible.

What if he had Miriam's power, too? What if he could take memories? What if he could take away the memory of the Joneses torturing her?

Peter came back into the room. "That was awesome, Seth. You are like the coolest Guardian ever. When your Nature took you like that, and your eyes went all crazy, it was...wow!" Peter sat down next to him, and it was if they were buddies, all things forgotten and forgiven.

"Nature, took?" Seth asked.

Peter crossed his leg. "Yes, the power you just used is called a Nature. And when it fills you so that you can use it, that is called *taking*. It takes you and makes you a Guardian."

"Okay. Thanks." Seth nodded.

"No problem. It's important to know the vernacular."

They sat in companionable silence, then Seth asked, "Peter, do you think I have all the powers?"

"Natures," he corrected.

"Natures."

Peter palmed his chin. "Well, I saw you use water, which was the speed we got here with. Fire, you used to dry the leaves. Healing, you used to make that plant. What else have you done?"

Seth cleared his throat, "I was freakishly strong. Is that something?"

"Yes. Power, that is hazel eyes, like uhm, who would you know? My sister Hannah, or Gregory, Eve's boyfriend, Grandpa Miller."

"Okay, I gotcha."

"Anything else?"

"I can..." Seth moves around in his seat and licks his lips, "I see, like, visions of future things."

"That sounds..." The boy stopped talking and scratched at his cheek. "Uhm...what does it look like, when it happens?"

"Look like? That's a strange thing to ask." Seth took a deep breath and answered the best he could. "It looks exactly like our world but like with less color and sort of foggy and sometimes I'm like in a bubble..."

Peter cut him off. "Oh," he said almost relieved like. "So it's like a vision."

Seth squinted at him, "Yes."

"And you see, like, a picture of what will happen in the future."

"I guess."

"Okay, well no one has that Nature. So that one must be your actual Nature and the rest you just are able to sort of hijack when you want. My Nature has two abilities, too, and so does Miriam's."

Seth jumped on the opening Peter had given him. "Do you think I have Miriam's Nature as well?"

"How should I know?" Peter rolled his eyes at Seth. "Why would you want to?"

Seth paused over this. He wasn't sure what Miriam's Nature exactly was, only what he'd been told it was. "So, Peter, I have to confess something to you."

He rolled his eyes again, "I already know. You're obsessed with Miriam and you know where she is at every waking moment. You're not special, Seth. She has a host of Joneses who feel the same way." Then he smiled to himself. "I guess you'll have to fight them all to get to her. That oughta be fun to watch." He flashed Seth the naughtiest grin a teenage boy could give. Seth knew this parley had nothing to do with lasting peace. He was in for it when it came to Peter Miller.

As shocked as Seth was by this revelation of the Joneses and Miriam, he didn't want to let Peter see his surprise, so he asked his original question instead of probing the boy for information. "Really? Okay. Well, I was sort of wondering if I had Miriam's Nature, too, if I could, ya know, take away the memories of her being tortured."

Seth could tell he had surprised the boy, because his eyes widened with intrigue. "That is a real interesting thought, Seth. And I admire the sentiment, but I don't think Miriam would let you take the memories away even if you could."

"She wouldn't, why?"

"Let's just say she kept another memento, one she could have had taken away as easy as you please, but she said she needed to remember."

Seth barely had time to breathe today, much less ask people about how Miriam was doing. He wondered what it all meant, and what Peter was talking about. He didn't feel right about asking, though, so he didn't.

They sat there quietly for a few minutes before Seth said, "So, your dad, he can like, stop tornados. That is totally righteous."

Peter's eyes lit up. "It is, right? I know. He is a total bad-A."

Seth laughed. "Totally." He held out his knuckles for Peter to bump.

"Hey, let's go see what the Joneses are saying to Papa."

Seth nodded and rose from his chair.

CHAPTER 44

Peter

They crested the hill, and Peter immediately heard talking. He and Seth slowly made their way toward the large group of men. Papa had not taken any chances; he had at least ten Guardians with him, and they all looked ready to defend.

"I'm not sure what you mean by that."

"What I mean is your men can't stay inside of Edenia, except you, Gerald. I trust you, I think. But I don't know the rest of you from Adam. And just because you have some strange connection to my daughter doesn't mean I'm going to invite you into my home. Twenty-four hours ago you would have just as soon killed me as spit on me," Papa was saying, and Peter was really glad he'd shown up at this point because he'd forgotten to tell his father something important.

He moved faster as he closed the gap between them. "Papa," Peter said, "With all that has been happening I didn't get a chance to tell you something."

His papa turned around to face him and instantly took a defensive stance.

"Peter, what are you doing here?"

"Papa, I spent all day alone with these men. They are not going to hurt me." He glanced at the men and gave them a cocky smile. "Even if they *could* hurt me."

Gerald winked at him, and he saw several other men smirk. They knew what he was.

"Pa, you know that Abby came with me to the Joneses compound, don't you?"

His papa fully faced him now, his eyebrows knotted. "Yes."

"Well, she went all Guardian while she was there and gave every single one of these men the summons."

It was gratifying for some reason to see his father's jaw drop. "What?"

Gerald harrumphed. "I was trying to tell you that, Hirum, I just didn't have the right word for it."

There was shuffling and murmuring from the other Guardians.

His father turned to them and held a hand up.

Peter added, "For some reason, the Master has chosen to connect these specific men to us. I don't understand what he means by it all, but it's fact."

Hirum Miller was totally freaking out. Peter saw it, and it was a little funny. How would this all work? How could all the Joneses find a place for themselves here in Edenia? It was not going to be pretty. Probably.

"Okay, okay. Well, those who have been summoned can always refuse." His papa looked to the Joneses with hope in his eyes.

Gerald spoke up. "None of us want to be away from Miriam. I know, as a father myself, that sounds strange, but please believe me that it is not weird. We want to protect her." He turned and looked at the men behind him. They were nodding in agreement.

His father looked deeply into the men's faces as he considered this. His words were those that Peter would not have come up with. "Yes, but what, pray tell, do you think she needs protection from that we could not handle?"

The question rippled through the crowd like a pronouncement.

"What, indeed?" was Seth's response. They all looked at him, and he shook his head at Peter's papa indicating that he didn't know the answer to the question either, even as the Revelator.

Peter stepped between the two groups. "Well, it's settled. We have no idea what the Master has in mind for these men, but they are our responsibility now. They have been summoned. They agree to the summons. Correct?" He turned and looked at the Jones men.

Many nodded right away but Karl asked, "What exactly does a summons mean?"

Hirum stepped up in his official duty. "Well, it means that you agree to live here by our rules and traditions."

"Does that mean we are going to become like you all?" a guy from the back asked.

Peter smiled. "You wish!" he called to the man. It was smoker dude, Ben, and he was one of Peter's favorites.

Gerald answered him. "From what I gather, it will take about a week, and then we will be transformed into whatever these people are and we will be given a power that is meant to protect the garden and one another."

His father sighed and pulled a hand down his face, "Why do I even try?" he muttered under his breath.

Peter smiled at Gerald. The huge man was pretty darn effective as a spy. In one day of being in Edenia he had things figured out.

Peter suggested, "Well, I think for now we should make a camp with bunks in the middle of the hay fields, and tomorrow, consolidate homes for the men to live in."

His papa slapped a hand against his leg the way he did when he knew things were out of his control. "I think that sounds like a great plan, Peter. Boys?" he questioned the men behind him, "Who will get supplies and canvas for these men?"

Several people peeled off to go take care of the chore.

"So, we need to get some things straight. We have children and innocent women here. I don't know what sort of lifestyle you were used to before, but we will not tolerate any immorality. No cussing, drinking, smoking, carousing, pornography, filthy speech, drugs, violence, etc. If you can't abide, then you might as well make camp up here on this hill."

Gerald shifted and rubbed his bald head, "That's a pretty thorough list. Let me talk things over with the boys and see what we think." He got serious. "We have a request."

"Yes?"

"The boys and I would all like to get to the bottom of this connection we have to Miriam, which means we would like to talk to her. And we, in general, are more comfortable when we know she is being watched over. I mean, you don't know Willis the way I do. Now that he knows who she is..." he let that hang menacingly in the air.

His papa considered this for a long, hard minute. "I see your point. I will talk to Miriam about it."

"Fair enough."

"Well. I am the leader of my people, as you know, but I don't know you all, and so I feel that perhaps we should leave you in the hands of Gerald for chores and organization. He will coordinate with me for now. Agreed?"

The group nodded as one.

"Okay, well, let's get you settled," Peter's pa said, and turned toward Edenia.

Seth spoke up. "Hirum, I need to talk to you."

His pa paused then looked at Garren. "You deal with this?" And he chinned in the direction of the Joneses.

"Yes, Papa."

His father turned to Seth, "What is it?"

"Uhm, you need to go down there." He pointed to the tents, hundreds of them that Peter had not even noticed in all the tension. "And tell Noah about Westley. You also need to tell them about the Travelers."

Peter laughed, "The what?"

Seth blushed, "Sorry, the Joneses. I just have been calling them the Travelers in my head, I'm not sure exactly why, but that way I don't call them the Joneses. That name...makes me really uncomfortable."

Hirum turned to look after the Joneses. "Travelers? That is a strange name for them. I would think Warriors or something akin would be more apt."

Seth nodded. "Perhaps you are right. I don't really care, I guess. Shall we go down?"

"Yes, let's do."

"Can I come?" Peter asked.

"Peter, go home and tell your mother what we are doing."

Peter huffed. He was sleepy and hungry. And he hadn't done his chores in like two days. So, regretfully, he turned to find his mother.

CHAPTER 45

Seth

It didn't take long to trundle down the hill. However, the tent city was a good thirty-minute walk after that, and Seth was not looking forward to the time alone with the large man.

Hirum set a fast pace, but five minutes into the walk he spoke. "You know that it was me who directed Miriam to take your memories. She never would have done it because she trusted you too much and knew you would come around. I..." He sighed heavily, "I on the other hand, judged you to be like your father."

Seth did not know what to say to this. But he knew what his heart felt. It melted, completely. Miriam was following orders. She didn't want to do what she did. She wanted to trust him.

"I guess we were both right." Hirum added, nailing the insult home.

Seth's forehead wrinkled, anger stirring in his gut.

"Though I must say, I am sorry for the judgment. None of us understood the strain you endured or the pressure you were under. I ask you to forgive me."

Seth stopped in his tracks. The man only took a step before he stopped, too. Seth looked at the ground, blinking rapidly as his brain tried to catch up with his situation.

When he looked back up at Hirum, he said, "You are apologizing to *me?*"

Hirum took one step toward him and cocked his head to the side. "Well, yes. I've thought it over, and talked to my daughter and wife, and I get the feeling that my judgment of you was wrong. That judgment started a chain reaction that ended with you being backed into a corner, a corner you couldn't get out of without making a terrible mistake."

Seth took a step toward the man, surprised by the emotion that rose up in him, and the tears that were forming in his eyes. "Sir, I made the ultimate choices, though. I had many opportunities to get out of the mess I found myself in. I could have talked to your daughter more frankly, for one. I could have trusted my parents, for two. I could have listened to the voice that lives inside me." He pounded on his chest and there were real tears leaking from his eyes now, "for three. But I did none of those things. I was faithless, ungracious, and deceitful. And I betrayed a girl I truly care about. A girl who has helped me and believed in me, and she..." he sniffed and wiped his nose with the back of his hand and then took his shirt sleeve to his eyes. "...and she was very hurt as a result." He turned back toward Hirum and yelled. "She was tortured. Because of me." He pounded his chest. "Because of me!"

Hirum closed the distance between them and took Seth in a rough embrace. "I know. I know," the big man said as he squeezed Seth.

Seth did not hug him back, but he did not pull away either, but he did weep bitterly.

"It's amazing how we all have had a role in this terrifying drama. But I want you to know I am sorry for my role in it and I forgive you yours."

The balm those words were to his soul was incalculable, and they inspired Seth to be something other than what he had been. He couldn't help but desire to be just like this man; humble, forgiving, loving, strong and tender. He released a cleansing sigh, raised his arms, and hugged his uncle.

CHAPTER 46

Miriam

Though she wanted to be out and about, her mother insisted that she not leave the house, so Miriam sat on the couch with a book. She rarely had time to read—and books were not in abundance in Edenia. This one was a retelling of a true story about a man named Moses; he was a man with a stutter, a man raised separate from his people, a man who belonged to no group and every group. She understood him and felt his pain. Especially when his God, the Christian god, 'I AM', asked him to do some difficult things he did not feel he could do. She really understood that.

When there was a knock at the door, Miriam rose without thinking and opened it as if everything in her life was in order.

"Josie." Miriam gasped and took a step back, her hand moving to her chest to make sure the brand was fully covered.

From behind her, Josie's brother Todd said, "Can we come in, Miriam?"

Miriam's eyes glanced past the grey of Josie's and went to the turquoise of Todd's. She nodded at him and took another step back. Todd reached around Josie. These two siblings were not the only kids on her porch. She stepped back deeper into the living room and the kids kept coming in. Soon she was completely surrounded by people who should have been her best of friends.

Foster, with his handsome face of grey eyes, a smattering of freckles, and strawberry blond hair, spoke up first. "Miriam, we all came here today to apologize. We were really impressed with how you stood up to the whole town about your Nature."

Suzanne stepped up. "We didn't understand what you were

dealing with. We're sorry." Then she reached out and gave Miriam the biggest hug.

Todd pulled her shoulder, essentially pulling her out of Suz's arms and into his own. "You were always the funniest, but when you changed, it felt like everything changed. I guess that was part us and part you. Regardless, I'm sorry for my part in it. Do you forgive me?"

Miriam nodded thoughtlessly against his chest. How in the world was she in Todd's arms? It felt like her nine-year-old fantasy come to life.

But then she was passed around from person to person, all the words of apology becoming one big blur as happy tears and healing bathed her heart. And once the crying stopped, all of her friends sat on her living room floor and had the conversation they should have had three years ago. One that was full of compassion for Miriam's strange Nature and interest in what she could do and what it all meant for Edenia.

CHAPTER 47

Seth

The camp was nothing like he expected. It was like a third-world country, except way more organized, like organized to the teeth. Tents laid out in square formations, walkways in between, everyone bustling and engaged in work. It reminded Seth of Edenia, except made of canvas instead of wood.

The most impressive part was how, without walls or guards really, these people remained outside of the world, yet fully in.

Only one person stopped them as they entered the rows of tents. It was a big man with a gun over his shoulder, "Hey y'all," He said in a deep southern accented voice. "Can I help you find someone?"

"Yes, I'm Hirum Miller from just over the hill, I need to speak with Noah."

The blond burly man nodded and said, "Sure enough, follow me."

The rumor mill must have gone faster than they walked, because only a few minutes later as the trio moved to a wider, more central, dirt road, Noah—or the man Seth had seen in his vision and assumed was Noah—exited a tent and strode toward them. Noah looked like a Greek God-man. He was six and a half feet tall with a mess of blond hair, startlingly blue eyes, a bold nose, and a smile of perfectly white veneers. His biceps were probably sixteen inches, and his chest was like a bull's.

He made Uncle Hirum, a big, impressive man himself, look average.

His smile formed into words as they neared one another. "Hirum Miller, I am so very glad to see you again."

The two men shook hands.

"Thank you. I am happy to be here. You have a well-organized camp here. I am impressed."

"It displeases God if His shepherd can't keep His sheep in order," he said without batting an eye.

Seth felt his stomach lurch. Was Noah one of those zealous crazies? Seth didn't have to answer that question, even mentally. He'd seen what these people were doing, how they were living. Then again...Edenia. Who was he to judge?

Hirum was diplomatic, as always. "I know what you mean. Listen, Noah, I just needed to let you know that one of your men, Westley, was involved in a serious accident."

Noah's eyebrows knitted together, but he remained silent, waiting.

"He's okay. We have him in Edenia. We are using all the skill we have to help him, and he is recovering. I just wanted you to know, and when he gets well enough, we will bring him back to you."

Seth felt the pull of his vision and was in it before he could exhale. Westley in bed, a girl at his side nursing him, and something overwhelming happening between them. Something that had to happen. Something that would ensure Westley never would come back to this tent city for keeps. And something that would cement him as an important member of Edenia.

Seth's hand shot out to grip Hirum's arm before the reverberations of his last word, *"you"* had completely died in the air.

He moved to Hirum's ear and whispered, "No, Hirum. Westley is going to join us. It is essential that he stay with us." He spoke this last sentence gingerly.

Hirum's eyes were wide as Seth pulled away. The man cleared his throat and looked up to Noah using that assessing gaze of his. He spoke, "I'm sorry, I didn't know this, but Seth here has just brought it to my attention that Westley has a mission with us to fulfill before he comes back here." He said the last slowly.

"That must be some vision you've had. How can you know? He's only been with you one day."

Seth stepped forward. "It hasn't quite happened yet. But it will." The minute the words were out of Seth's mouth he wanted to suck them back in. What the freaking heck...

Noah looked at him, amused, and when he spoke, Seth felt his jaw drop. "I know Seth, you are the appointed one. The Revelator. You and I will see much of one another in the coming days. I suppose now is my first opportunity to show you that I trust you." He sighed and blinked. "Westley is a great friend of mine. A very wise and loyal man. I knew that he had something coming for him, and that he would be taken from us. I did not know how, though. This is much better a situation than my imagination had come up with."

Hirum moved forward again. "Now, wait a minute here. This is the second time you have acted like you know things you shouldn't know. Tell me how this is happening."

As many wise men before him had done, Noah answered a question with a question. "First, Hirum, explain to me how your boy here knows that Westley will be attaching himself to your people before it has happened."

That shut Hirum up, Seth was absolutely certain Hirum Miller was not accustomed to being put off in this manner.

Noah turned to Seth. "We all have our role to play here."

"Hirum, did you do as I asked yesterday?"

Again his uncle was on the defensive, "You mean read that you have 30,000 plus migrants walking across the country to join you here?"

Noah smiled without showing his teeth this time. His eyes danced though with joy. "Yes. That's it."

"Yes, we are preparing to be inundated."

"Do not worry. They will not bother you. I am in contact with the leaders, and have instructed them to go around your village." He moved closer to Hirum and put a hand on the man's shoulder. "But you need to understand that these are not the only ones coming.

Soon, this valley will be filled to the rim with God's people. But first comes the trial of our faith. For that, I want to work with you all as much as I can. We will have need of one another before this is all said and done. I'm sure of it. So, until Westley is ready, let's have this young man, Seth is it?" The man's eyes clouded, his attention far off for a moment, "Yes, let's have this young man be Westley's companion. They can keep our two camps in contact when need be." He smiled his mega-watt smile toward them both and placed his other hand on Seth's shoulder. "Seth, your name means *replacement*. Did you know that?" Seth shook his head and Noah went on. "In the Bible, Seth was God's replacement for Able after his brother Cain murdered him. He was anointed as the eldest son, gained the birthright, and became God's High Priest. Then, he remained a High Priest for almost one thousand years and did many wonders and miracles in God's name. He also prophesied. You have a grand namesake to live up to, and I have the feeling you will do so with honor." After a probing gaze, he nodded, squeezed their shoulders, and shook his head as if sealing an agreement with them. Then he turned and walked away. "Keep in touch," he said over his shoulder and moved into his tent.

The man who led them in stepped up. "All righty then, this way, boys."

CHAPTER 48

Sleep was not going to find her this night. It was almost time for the cock to crow. She touched her chest for the thousandth time. It didn't hurt physically anymore, but she couldn't help but touch it. When she did, she felt the darkness, the anger, the revenge that felt like life. She hated Willis Jones. She hated Les. They were evil just to be evil. They drugged her and tortured her.

Seth's face came to mind, and to stop herself from thinking about him, she got up out of bed and walked to her door. When she pulled it open, she saw to her left the huge form of Gerald sleeping in a chair. His head resting back against the wall, arms crossed, legs spread all the way across the hallway.

His head came up with her exit. He touched her. "Are you all right?" he whispered.

She smiled. "Yes and no. I am running away from my demons."

He nodded. "That can make your feet rather tired."

"Yes, yes it can. And your heart and mind as well."

"How can I help?"

"How can you help? You have been the one to help the most. You got me out of there. I can never repay you for that."

"This is not about repayment. This is about what's right." He paused, his lips pursing with words that he needed to say. Miriam waited. "Ya know, me thinking about what is *right*...considering that there is a right and wrong in life, now that is something *I* can never repay *you* for. Needless to say, it has been a long time since I even cared about that."

Miriam smiled again and patted his shoulder. She stood there with him in silence for a few moments before Gerald spoke up again.

"Why? Why do you think that is, Miriam?"

She looked down at him. "Why do you desire to do the right thing? I have no idea."

"No, why any of it." He shifted in his seat. "I've been thinking about it. Why do I know where you are? It's like there is a homing beacon in my head for you. Why? Why would that be? Your father explained to me tonight what this place is all about, and about you. It blew my mind, but it also made me wonder why in the world you, of all people, would need thirty trained military men to have your six. Where you gonna go where I need to follow?"

Miriam had not thought of this for even one second. Gerald was astoundingly right. What did all of this mean?

Gerald shifted again, and it pulled Miriam's mind back to him. "Miriam, can I ask you something?"

She licked her lips, nervous of this question. She knew what he wanted, and she didn't know if she could say it out loud yet. After finally telling herself that he deserved to know, she nodded.

"What happened? When you did your thing that made me this way? What happened?"

Clearing her throat, she leaned against the wall of the hall and closed her eyes. "It starts with you seeing something you shouldn't. I pull my Nature to me, that's our powers that we have, and then I just—I don't know—breathe in, and when I do, I pull the connection you have to the electrical and hormonal matter that makes up your memories. I pull them, and then I cut them from you."

He thought for a while. "You don't really know what you do, do you?"

"Nope. I've gathered those words from my science books but I don't even know if I am partially correct."

He thought some more. "The thing I'm concerned with is the words you used to describe it. *Cut it.* Miriam, does that mean it is a physical thing? And if it is, what happens to it? I mean, I think I know because I feel like you are a part of me, so..."

Miriam blinked at the tears that filled her eyes at his words. Her throat closed up. Her heart beat in her ears. She did not know why she felt so ashamed, so desperate to not let anyone know that inside her lived a whole bunch of soul slivers. But she knew as she wept that she had to tell someone.

"Gerald, they are inside me." She almost exploded the whispered words. "I have them in here." She poked herself in the head. "I can't look at them, or re-feel them, but they are there floating around, making me feel like a thief and a wraith of a human all at the same time. I hate that I even have them, and how it makes me feel like I am a vessel instead of a person. I'm carrying a stolen, literal part of you around with me, inside me. It's...it is wrong. I'm sorry. I am so sorry." She put her face in her hands.

And before she knew what was happening, Gerald had gathered her into his arms and was stroking her hair. "Shh. Shh. It's okay." Miriam shocked herself by having a hard cry into Gerald's ultra-hard chest. "I know now. I am certain of it, that this happened for a reason. And frankly, I am glad it did."

She felt such warmth from him. How could this kind and wonderful man be a Jones? Her tear-filled eyes looked up at him, "Really?"

He nodded and took a thumb to a few of those tears, wiping them away. He sat down again and sighed. "I used to be an altar boy." He smiled up at her. "Yeah, I know. But I did. And I loved it. In church, I felt whole. I felt loved and understood by God. I had a relationship with Him, a good one."

Miriam calmed. "What happened?"

"What always happens when men get too much power. I was huge for my age, and not just that, I was strong and smart, my momma said I was a born leader; my country said I was a born killer. I let it go to my head."

Miriam didn't exactly understand, but she nodded.

"But here," he went on. "Here in this strange place, I can't explain it, I've only been here, what, thirty hours? But I feel like I can be both, and that it's necessary for me to be both. The church boy and the killer."

A shiver went up Miriam's back. "I don't think you will be needed for killing any longer, Gerald."

The big man got a serious look on his face. "I'm not trying to argue with you, Miriam, but I know Willis Jones. Intimately. Now that Mr. Jones has passed and Willis is running the show, I have a feeling there is going to be a whole lot of killing before this thing between the two of you is well and truly done."

Chilled, Miriam moved back into her room as she said, "I hope you are wrong, Gerald, but if you are not, I am glad you are by my side."

CHAPTER 49

Seth

He was getting used to the way his Nature pulled him into another reality and then popped him back into his own.

However, this vision was the strangest one yet, and it left him a sweaty mess. He saw the Travelers, or the Joneses men that were connected to Miriam, all lined up in the river Eden. He saw Edenian's standing with them pushing them into the water, and he did not see them come back up.

His heart raced with the image. Were they going to kill the Travelers?

Seth stood. He had to tell Hirum. Now. He pulled on some pants and looked out the small window of his room. It was dawn, about seven a.m. He pulled a shirt over his head and tied his hair back in a short ponytail, the sides of which immediately fell out and hung in his face as he slipped on his socks and boots. He

pulled open his door quietly and slipped through the house and out into the yard.

The fear of seeing Miriam clenched his guts. How could he talk to Hirum as much as he needed to when Miriam could be the casualty?

He sighed and thought about his conversation with Hirum. He thought of what his father had told him. *"The only control you have in this circumstance, Seth, is your own response to it. You can't make her forgive and forget, but you can forgive yourself and move forward choosing better for yourself, and when possible, for her."*

He had to forgive himself for choosing to help Lillian in his own misguided way. He had to forgive himself for losing the only girl he'd truly connected with. Then he had to get over the betrayal and lies and the heartbreak that defined his life over the last year.

His heart ached for self-forgiveness. Looking down at the ground, he pled with whatever power was in this place to help him in the same way he asked for the plant in Westley's room or the way he asked for the leaves to dry.

His sorrow was so real, his willingness to change and be better, to try to trust and be worthy of it. All the parts were there, and just like a miracle, a feeling of peace, of true and full understanding washed over him, and more than anything, an idea of a way to move forward and make things right.

The feeling was so soft, yet so overwhelming, that Seth stopped walking and turned his face to the rising rays of the sun. The warmth of it instantly soaked into him, its light a symbol for his own personal new beginning. This truly was a new day, and he planned to make the very best of it.

EPILOGUE

Westley

The sun was on his face. He felt like a waking cat, warm and comfy. Something smelled delicious, sweet rolls or pie or cookies, he couldn't really tell, but his mouth watered, and a moan escaped his lips.

Something tickled at his ear. Eyelids fluttering, he made a moved to swipe at whatever was interrupting his dream, but instant pain came instead. He sucked in a breath and groaned.

"Don't move. For heaven's sake, how many times must I tell you!" A high, rather grouchy voice bit at him. Then that same voice changed, taking on a musical quality. "I can say it in six other languages. Perhaps you have a hard time with English."

Startled, he blinked.

"Here, you have to drink. You might have damaged yourself further. Really, Westley, what were you thinking? Were you dreaming again?"

The girl above him—he was laying down, she standing over him—had the most incredibly huge, bright green eyes he'd ever seen in his life. One look into those eyes had his brain wholly muddled, yet his soul more entirely awake than it'd ever been.

The bed folded up, and he was in a sitting position. He looked around amazed, but didn't see how she'd managed it. Her small cold hands pushed a straw in his mouth and her high, melodic voice commanded, "Drink."

He obeyed, completely mesmerized.

The delicious water was cool and fresh, and Westley appreciated every ounce. It revitalized his mind, and as he continued to drink, he blinked carefully at the exquisite girl before him.

She had short, curly blonde hair and a long face with sculpted cheek bones. Her delicate nose helped draw attention to her full rosebud mouth. As he took in her entire face, Westley felt completely, overwhelmingly smitten, as if with just a look at her face he recognized her from another time, another place and in that time and place, he knew her better than he'd known anyone.

Something inside him sang.

Pulling the straw from his mouth she asked, "Feeling better?"

He nodded.

"Good, just don't move, and you will keep on getting better."

He watched her lips move as she gave him the instructions and couldn't help himself, the moment she finished talking he blurted, "You are the most beautiful person I've ever seen. Who are you?"

Her face went scarlet and her hands stopped straightening his sheets. Green eyes flashed to his and narrowed. "Are you..." but as soon as she saw his expression, she quieted and stood up.

"I'm sorry," he hurried on. "I just, I am just, I don't know, confused. The doc says I hit my head. All my inside thoughts might be escaping."

She turned her angelic face back to him and the sun from the window hit her right in the eyes, making the green color sparkle like emeralds.

He sighed, "Lord have mercy. Your eyes. They are so amazingly green, the most gorgeous green I've ever seen, my exact favorite shade of green. I seriously think I'm concussed," he blubbered. "I also think I'm overheating here." He looked down at the intricate homemade quilt draped over his body. He needed to toss it aside, but knew he could not move.

She leaned over him and pinned his arms to his sides firmly, but gently. "Don't you move a muscle, cowboy. That is a good sign. You, feeling heated. It means you are healing." Her face was now just a foot away as she pulled the blanket back and the jade irises captured his attention once more.

He didn't move. She stopped moving.

They stayed there examining one another for a very long, very intense moment.

Finally, Westley whispered, "What's your name?"

The girl did not look away. She did not blush again. She just held herself steady and looked into him like no one ever had before. "Esther," she softly said, and her gaze dipped to his lips, but only for a millisecond before they locked back onto his eyes.

He smiled. "Pleasure to meet you. I'm Westley."

"I know." She relaxed and looked down at his arms, then back up to him and raised an eyebrow.

"I swear I won't move."

She pursed her lips at him and then slowly sat down, letting go of him.

For the first time, Westley noticed her clothes. They were strange. They looked unquestionably homespun—the weave thick and imperfect like a horse blanket—but cut and sewn in a futuristic fashion. The room was rustic. All the furnishings were nice, but most definitely not factory made. The quilt he'd already noticed was intricate and most assuredly handmade. No pictures or paintings adorned the walls which were all off-white. A small dresser and desk were on one side of the bed, but that was all that the room contained.

"Esther, I am confused. I have no idea where I am or why you want me to hold so still."

She looked down at her dress and smoothed it. Her green eyes flashed up to him and she said in a tight voice, "A very stupid boy caused you to have an accident on your horse. You broke your back. We brought you here to help you."

Then Westley remembered what happened. He remembered lying in the grass, knowing he was going to die. And more. "Buttercup?"

She was up again. Her hands holding him down. "She's fine. She's perfect. Shush. We took care of her. She's just fine."

Westley blinked, and that was when he realized he couldn't feel her holding his arms down. He felt vague pressure, and nothing more.

Panic again rose in his body and he reacted with heavy breathing and wide glances around. "I can't feel you. I can't feel you!"

Esther took his face in her hands and brought her face close to his. "Westley, look at me. Look at me. Stop! Look at me."

He did.

"You are all right. You are healing, and Doc is positive you will be good as new soon."

Westley stared into her lovely eyes, and he slowed his breathing. She just stood there, perfectly content to let him contemplate. Finally, he used her own words to ask a question he hoped she'd answer. "Good as new?" He whispered.

"You will be perfect. I promise," she answered, her hands sliding off his arms as she stood.

"But how, how is that possible? If I broke my back and I can't feel you touching me. That means..." he swallowed hard, "That I am paralyzed." His heartbeat ticked up again.

"Yes, for now. But you are also in Edenia."

"Edenia?" He narrowed his eyes at her.

"Yes. And I'm happy to tell you this is the one and only place where your broken back can and will be healed." She smiled at him and her eyes sparkled.

If he didn't think she was so lovely, he might just think she was completely insane. "So, what happens now?" Westley wondered out loud.

"Now we wait for you to be healed. We could..." She sat carefully on the edge of his bed and bit her bottom lip in the most provocative way Westley had ever seen a lip bitten. Her teeth let go of the pink lip and she finished her comment, "...get to know one another," she said with a tiny bit of hesitation in her voice. "You could tell me if there is a wife or a girlfriend or a really protective parent I need to know about. Anyone who might come charging into Edenia like a crazy person looking for you."

Westley blinked at her. He wasn't sure he should answer that question, because this girl looked like she was about to eat him.

"I only ask because..." she paused and looked at him through down-turned lashes, blood rushing to her cheeks, and she bit her lip yet again before going on, "because, Westley of the tent people, I think you are the most handsome, well put together man I have ever beheld. Sorry if that is too blunt, but you started it," she said, and raised an eyebrow at him and gave him a dazzling half smile.

Holy mackerel, he just lost his heart to a girl named Esther. He'd heard of love at first sight, the whole world had, but this was...how could he explain this...

It was like chemistry, alchemy, and magic combined. He knew, *knew* that if he had every beautiful girl he'd ever cared about lined up in front of him, he would know that only one of them was his exact right match, fit, equal. It was this one. Esther of Edenia. Even her name felt ethereal. He blinked wildly. Feeling caught up in something so powerful and strange and otherworldly, it overwhelmed him.

Westley smiled. "Even if there was someone out there crazy enough about me to rip in here, guns a blazin', there is not a soul on earth that could take me away from you."

Her half smile broadened. Her cheeks blossomed into the most beautiful blush, and her eyes sparkled like two emeralds. "All right then, I think we understand one another." She settled herself on the edge of the bed and said, "Now, Westley, tell me everything about yourself."

ACKNOWLEDGMENTS

Thank you Holli, John, Penelope, Melanie, Shelia, and all the staff at Immortal Works for your edits and your time making this book great. Thank you to my fans and family members for your support. Thank you God for giving me the strength and the creativity to pull this together.

ABOUT THE AUTHOR

 Theresa has been writing for fifteen years and has more story ideas than she could possibly write and still have a life. She is an avid audible 'reader', boardgame lover, Zelda player, book collector, adventure chaser, and history 'studier', besides being a mother of three, a musician and a homeschooler. Also in her life are, a white schmorkie named Percy Jackson, a hot husband named Andy and many many supportive and amazing friends. She lives on the Olympic Peninsula but is an Idaho girl at heart.

This has been an
Immortal Production